PRETTY LITTLE LIES

JESSICA HUNTLEY

INKUBATOR
BOOKS

Published by Inkubator Books
www.inkubatorbooks.com

ISBN (eBook): 978-1-83756-655-6
ISBN (Paperback): 978-1-83756-656-3
ISBN (Hardback): 978-1-83756-657-0

Dedicated to my identical twin sister, Alice, who is a beauty therapist herself and gave me the idea to write this book.

PROLOGUE

It happens in a flash.

She falls, teetering on the edge of the stairs, but before I can react and grab her, she tumbles backwards, her body contorting into unnatural positions as she bounces down the hard staircase to the corner landing below.

She lands awkwardly, after a sickening thud. Her left leg is horribly bent at a forty-five-degree angle.

Shit.

Oh God...

What have I done?

Everything happened so fast, and now I'm standing at the top of the short flight of stairs over a body lying below me. I lost control only for a minute. No, not even a minute. A second. Less than a second. But it's all over now.

I can't take it back even if I wanted to.

Someone I love has suffered unimaginable torment at the hands of this evil person.

And now she's dead. Very dead.

From the odd angle of her neck, it probably snapped as

she flipped and tumbled down the stairs. I didn't realise I'd pushed her that hard. I reacted out of instinct, running through the smoke like a woman possessed, then chasing her down the stairs. She'd been laughing as she ran away, thought it was hilarious, that she was going to get away with it.

She's not laughing now, is she?

Over the past few weeks, she's pushed me to my breaking point, and this is the fallout. She pushed me and now I've pushed her. A split-second decision that will change my life forever. There's no coming back from this.

It was an accident.

That's what I'll tell the police, but will they believe me after everything that's happened, after everything she's done to me and Noah? I had motive to end her life, and they'll see that as clear as day. Yes, it may have been an accident that happened in the heat of the moment.

But there are no accidents, are there?

Not when it comes to murder.

PART 1

CHAPTER ONE

In my line of work, I torture people daily, but I also make them feel and look good, pamper them while I'm at it. They pay me good money to hurt them, make them squirm and screw up their faces in agony. Some beg me to take a break, to give them a moment to catch their breath. Those are usually the first-timers or the men. They don't know what to expect. But then, once they've finished groaning and sweating, they hand over the money at the end with a smile on their faces, and say, 'Thank you so much. I needed that! Same time next month?' and I book them in again. Some of the wealthier ones even hand me a generous tip.

I'm halfway through torturing my latest victim – *I mean, client* – and she's a bit of a screamer. She always has been, bless her, but she does have super-coarse hair on her legs, which doesn't do her any favours. Luckily, I had the good sense to do the Brazilian bikini wax first, otherwise, I'm not sure she would have made it through the treatment. She almost kicked me in the face when I tore off the first wax strip from between her legs, but I've honed my reflexes over the years and expertly dodged it.

A sheen of sweat sparkles across her forehead and top lip as she puffs and pants, preparing for the next bout of pain.

'Okay, last strip going on now,' I say with a smile as I smear on a thick layer of hot wax across the last of the hair on her left leg.

'Thank God!' says Emma, then rests her head against the back of the couch and closes her eyes. She's attending her daughter's wedding in two days' time, flying to Crete tomorrow, so I've also given her a manicure and a pedicure today, plus an eyebrow wax. She passed on getting a spray tan because she's already gorgeously tanned and will be able to top it up when she's out there, while sunbathing with a cocktail in her hand by her hotel pool.

I expertly whip the wax strip off in one brisk motion, bringing with it all her hair, leaving behind super-smooth, slightly pink skin. All done.

Emma's eyes water. I hand her a clean tissue, and she dabs at the corners.

'Thank fuck that's over,' she says. 'Same time next month?'

'Perfect. I'll book you in now.'

Five minutes later, I leave one-hundred and thirty-five pounds richer.

Ten minutes later, after a quick natter and wishing her a lovely time in Crete, I've packed up my treatment couch, the wax pot, which is still hot, and my mobile box of products, and am on my way to my next client. This one hasn't booked any waxing, but a soothing hot stone massage instead. She's all the way on the other side of town, which is why I've booked her as my last client of the day. I have forty-five minutes to get there, but it's still going to be close, especially at this time of day in central Cambridge.

There are certainly pros and cons to being a self-employed mobile beauty therapist. I spent the first fourteen years of my career working for other people, in hotel chains, spas, beauty salons, but finally decided to quit putting it off, bite the bullet and, a year ago, I plunged into the scary world of self-employment. No boss to answer to. No working over Christmas or New Year. Just me, running the whole show. I haven't looked back since. It's the best decision I've ever made, even though the added stress of ensuring I have a constant revenue stream sometimes makes things a little difficult financially, but the freedom it allows me outweighs any of the downsides.

The late summer heat wave is on its way out but still warrants me turning on the air conditioning in the car as I turn out of the street, signalling left. It's muggy. The air feels too close. I take a couple of gulps of lukewarm water from the bottle I leave in the centre console. A headache is coming on, most likely due to not drinking enough water. I always forget to fill up the bottle after I've finished it. It's hot, hard work being a mobile beauty therapist.

As the four o'clock news finishes, the dashboard lights up via the Bluetooth connection with my phone, signalling an incoming call from my soon-to-be husband, Noah. He's lucky he caught me now, as I'm not far away from my next stop. He knows my job is fast and furious, often with barely any breaks in between. Same as his, I suppose.

'Hey,' I say, signalling right, checking my mirrors.

'Hey. Having a good day?'

'Yep, all good. Are you okay? You don't often call me in the day. What's up?'

'Yeah, sorry. I wasn't even sure I'd catch you, but I wanted to tell you straight away.'

My heart rate leaps, and I'm unsure whether I need to brace myself for bad or good news. 'Tell me what?'

There's a short pause. He clears his throat. 'I've got some good news. I'm eligible for promotion! Rob's put me forward for it, but it's looking like a done deal.'

'Oh! Wow, that's great!'

'Yeah, so it means I'll obviously have a better salary and more options. Rob even said I could end up getting his job when he leaves in a few months, but it also might mean...'

I quickly dislodge the lump that forms in my throat by swallowing. I have a feeling I know what he's about to say.

'It means we may have to move again, and I realise you've only just settled into your mobile business, and it means you may have to start all over again somewhere else, but...'

I pull over on the side of the road, stopping in front of the driveway of the house, blocking off the BMW that's parked there. It's fine. Wilma doesn't mind. She's the one who tells me to park here when I visit.

'Oh, right...' I rethink my tone of voice. 'Obviously, it wouldn't be ideal for me to move again so soon, but that's amazing news about your promotion, Noah. It really is. You deserve it. You've been working so hard lately.' I attempt to summon the enthusiasm I know my fiancé needs right now, but it's an effort, especially at the thought of his success derailing my business. I'm aware I'm being selfish by even thinking it, but moving locations for me is a huge upheaval in my line of work. I take my voice up an octave, and it comes out all squeaky, like a mouse's. 'Congratulations again.' I switch off the engine.

'Thanks. That was it. That's all I called for, but like I said, if I end up getting Rob's job, then we won't have to move, and hey, I might not even get the promotion.'

'Of course you will. You're amazing at your job.'

'Apparently, there's some course I need to attend soon.'

'A course?'

'Yeah, to learn how to manage other officers and run a prison, but to be honest, I know how most of it goes, so it's basically a box-ticking exercise for me.'

I stifle a small chuckle. Noah's always been very career- and goal-oriented. He lives for bettering himself and progressing in life, whether it be in his work life or personal life, so it doesn't surprise me that he's well ahead of where he needs to be already.

'We should celebrate tonight when I'm back,' I say. 'I'll grab a bottle of bubbly on the way home from seeing the girls.'

'You're seeing the girls tonight?'

'Yes, just for a quick catch-up. I did tell you about it.'

'Oh shit, sorry. Yeah, you did tell me. It slipped my mind.'

'I'll be back before ten though. I won't be drinking much as I'll need to drive home.'

'Okay, see you later.'

'Bye. Congratulations again.'

'Thanks. Bye.'

'Love you,' I say.

'Love you, too.'

Noah's been doing everything he can over the past year to earn his promotion, including taking the dreaded night shifts and all the boring duties that most prison officers hate doing, to prove that he is dedicated and hard-working.

I have ten minutes till my next appointment is due to start; the traffic gods were good to me today, so I spend several minutes with my eyes shut, practicing the breathing techniques my yoga instructor teaches during my weekly class. Sometimes, I like to take a moment to breathe. It's easy to forget while I'm rushing here, there and everywhere to pamper and treat other people. It's why I like to attend a yoga session on a Sunday most weeks, to reset my mind and body after a busy few days.

Noah pops into my head again as I think about how excited he was about his promotion, and then I went and said I was going out with the girls instead of rushing home to celebrate with him.

Should I still go out with my friends? It's so hard to get all the girls together at the same time. It's taken us weeks to arrange. Maybe I should have said I'd blow off my friends to celebrate with him instead. Damn it. Now I feel like the worst future wife in the world. I'll call it a night early instead and head home to celebrate with Noah. He deserves it.

He's my Noah.

Always has been and always will be.

He's the man who promised he'd never leave me the way my mother did, who'd never break my heart the way my childhood best friend did, and who practically interrogated my friends for weeks to find out the perfect way in which to propose. He's my one and only.

I can't imagine being a prison officer. Not only does he work in a highly stressful environment, but it's also long hours, includes shift work and takes an emotional toll, not to mention the constant threat of violence against him.

At least my job is relatively stress-free when it comes to dealing with people. Well, apart from one instance five years ago, when a client got physically aggressive with me after a treatment. She refused to pay the spa prices and said I was ripping her off, that her treatment wasn't worth the price, despite the cost being clearly marked on the website when she signed up. I wasn't hurt or anything, but she did shove me against a wall, then ran out of the spa without paying. It shook me up for months. Hell, even now I get a little jittery when meeting a new client in case they turn out to be a raging psychopath.

The police were called. I gave them the details, including her name and phone number, but they did nothing about it. She was never caught, and the spa manager at the time took it on the nose and said to move on. Thankfully, instances like that are very rare in my line of work. Most of my clients are lovely, hospitable people who will talk my ear off for hours on end if I let them.

I open my eyes to see that eight minutes have passed. I pick up my phone and see a new text has appeared from an unknown number. I click it open casually, but when I read the five words on the screen, my blood turns to ice in my veins and a ripple of goosebumps makes me visibly shudder.

You're going to die, Bitch.

CHAPTER TWO

My heart rate shoots up, ruining the last eight minutes of my relaxation breathing. Holy crap. I was not expecting that. It was an unknown number, so I assumed it would be from a new client or one of those random spam messages

My finger hovers over the reply button, but what the hell am I supposed to say to that? There's nothing else to the thread. I'm completely thrown by this random message. Time is ticking by, and if I don't get out of the car now, I'm going to start running behind.

I decide to take the abrupt, yet direct approach and type out a quick reply and press send.

> Sorry. Wrong number.

I pocket my phone, get all the bits and pieces I need from the boot of my car, and knock on the door of my client's house, deciding to put the text message out of my mind for the next couple of hours, but I am still slightly trembling when Wilma opens the door and invites me in with a beaming smile.

Wilma is exceptionally wealthy and spends most of her time preening herself, travelling abroad and spending her husband's money. I don't know what he does for work, but he's never home. Maybe that's the secret to a happy marriage. Who knows?

'Amelia! Right on time, as always,' she coos, planting two air kisses on each of my cheeks. Her dark skin and afro hair are super-striking. Not to mention her slim physique, which I'd kill for. Not that I have a bad-looking body. I work hard, I run regularly, attend spin and yoga classes and a few weights sessions at the gym when I can fit it in, but I'm not sure I've ever heard Wilma say she works out.

She walks in front of me into the spacious living area that's basically the size of my whole flat, which I share with Noah on the second-to-top floor of a block of flats, roughly in the centre of the city.

'Can I get you a drink, Amelia?' she asks, her voice high-pitched.

'Just water, thanks.' Maybe if I start accepting drinks at clients' houses, I'll be able to stave off headaches and possible dehydration.

I set up the massage couch, oils and candles, and plug in the towel warmer. Wilma always has a full body hot stone massage, but she's also got a facial booked in today; two hours' work in total. I'm going to start with the massage. I generally leave ten minutes to set up at a client's house. There are so many products and things to remember. Not to mention a heavy couch to lug about.

Wilma walks in holding a glass of water. She's even

added a slice of lemon and ice. Not just tap water either, I'll bet.

'Thanks,' I say. 'How are you?'

'Me? Oh, peachy! My goodness, your skin is flawless today.'

I smile. The truth is, I'm betting she's just being polite. I often break out in spots on my chin because my own skincare routine leaves a lot to be desired. I should be better at it, considering my profession, but most of the time I forget, or can't be bothered. My dark skin tone hides a lot of flaws, but sometimes even makeup can't cover everything.

I begin her treatment, starting with warming her back muscles, moving my hands in slow, concentric circles, then repeating the movements before working through any tight areas and knots. Wilma doesn't stop talking the entire time. I don't mind a bit of chat, but when a client pays almost a hundred pounds for a deep-tissue massage designed to relax them, I'm confused as to why they spend the whole time talking. Although, having known Wilma a while, I know she loves the sound of her own voice. Sometimes, I wish she'd just be quiet and enjoy the massage.

I'm struggling to focus on the treatment or what she's saying. Not even the soft melody of the music calms my racing brain, which is still going over the text message I received earlier.

'Oh my God, did I tell you about my next-door neighbour, Susanne? She came round for cocktails the other night, and you'll never guess what she told me. She got so drunk, bless her. You know her kids are all at uni now, studying medicine or what have you. They're in their early twenties. She's been with her husband for over thirty years, but apparently, one of her children isn't even his!'

My hands pause mid-way up her back. 'Really? She told you that?'

'Oh, yes. Wouldn't you want to be a fly on the wall when that story's revealed over the family dinner table at Christmas? I wonder which one of her kids isn't his? I reckon it's the boy. He's very blond, not like Mark at all.'

I know Susanne. She's another of my clients. What am I supposed to say to her when I see her next? *Goddamn Wilma and her big mouth.* This is the thing about being a beauty therapist. There are times when I may as well remove the "beauty" part of my job title because my clients often treat our time together like a personal therapy session. They spill their innermost secrets and thoughts to me as if I'm supposed to know the right way to answer them. I do my best and offer them a sympathetic ear. I'm not always sure I give them the correct advice, but they appreciate it all the same. Sometimes, they just need someone to listen to them. That's me.

It's fine. I don't mind it, but over the course of my fifteen-year career, I've heard my fair share of gossip, secrets and shocking stories, some that would destroy lives and marriages should they ever be revealed. My clients grow to trust me, especially if I get to know them over several sessions.

Previously, when I lived by myself in Portsmouth, before I met Noah, I'd built up a vast network of clients. I lived and worked for most of my adult life in Portsmouth, and because of that, I got to know all my clients very well through working in various spas and hotels for big companies. Even when I changed salons or spas, they followed and stayed with me. That's the great thing about the beauty therapist/client relationship. Once you've earned their trust, there's nothing they won't tell you while you pamper and treat them. I've known some of my previous clients back in Portsmouth longer than I've known Noah, watched them get married, have kids, watched their kids grow up. One client of mine even lost her life to cancer a couple of years ago, and it tore me up for months. I attended her funeral as if I was a part of her extended family.

I never reveal their secrets. Not ever. Or, at least, I don't release their names. Noah and I used to have a giggle over some stories. All beauty therapists know other beauty therapists, and we swap stories to see who can share the most shocking one.

When I moved out of Portsmouth to live with Noah in Cambridge a year ago, I had to start my client base from scratch. It was a massive risk, but I decided to choose my future with Noah over my clients and business. It was the right decision because, after a bit of marketing, I'm happy to say I've met lots of lovely new clients and managed to build my business from the ground up.

My old clients in Portsmouth miss me, and I them, but I'm happy here with Noah. It's just that the thought of moving again for his career is enough to send my nerves jingling. We're getting married in less than a year. A move right now would be quite catastrophic to my future career and our wedding plans.

I wave goodbye to Wilma and, as I'm getting into my car, a woman runs up to me from across the street. She makes me jump, appearing out of nowhere.

It must be the text. I'm still on edge. Distracted.

She's in tight jogging gear, her long, dark hair tied back in a tight ponytail that bounces up and down as she moves.

'Oh! Hi... Susanne.' My face warms as my brain repeats

what Wilma told me earlier. I whack on a polite smile, but I can't seem to look her in the eyes. *Dammit, Wilma!*

'Amelia, I thought that was you! You look wonderful.'

'Oh. Thanks. How are you?'

'Good, thank you. Were you just at Wilma's?'

'Uh... Yeah.'

Susanne nods. 'I was just at hers the other night for cock-tails. Oh, I got so drunk.' She laughs, her face colouring slightly.

'Right...' I close my eyes, silently begging her not to bring up the topic of her children or her husband.

'Well, I won't keep you. I just wanted to say hi. I'll text you soon about booking in a mani/pedi.'

'Great. Perfect. Bye, Susanne.' She waves as she continues jogging up the road. Only then do I let out a long sigh before getting into my car.

I check my phone again, even though it's only been a couple of minutes since I checked last. I always keep an eye on new messages in between clients, just in case there's a new booking or a cancellation for the day.

There's another message from a number I don't recog-nise. I open it, quickly realising it's not the same number as before because it's a brand-new message.

> Hello.

I frown, my heart rate climbing. While I'm staring at the text, another one pops up in the same thread. Then another, several seconds later, followed by the others, all roughly five seconds apart.

> My name is Charlotte Whitmoore.

Is this Amelia Jenkins?

You were recommended to me.

Do you have space to fit me in for a manicure tomorrow morning at 9?

I can come to you.

I live nearby.

Thanks.

Charlotte Whitmoore.

xx.

My eyebrows raise. Finally, the texts stop. Why couldn't she have sent all of that in one text? It's a bit unorthodox, I'll admit, but it makes me crack a smile. It's been a while since a new client has approached me. I wonder who recommended her. I always mean to leave more business cards in local hair salons or pin flyers up on noticeboards, like I did at the start of building my business here. Promoting myself and my business gives me the ick, but luckily, I have enough clients to keep me busy and my bank account ticking over nicely.

I send off a text in response.

Hi, Charlotte. Yes, this is Amelia Jenkins. Thank you for your message. You'll have to tell me who recommended me to you so I can thank them. You're in luck! I do have space tomorrow at 9. Amelia xx

I wait for her response. I did plan on getting in an early morning gym session, but I never turn a new client down. Again, the messages spring up one after the other. My phone is on silent, otherwise there'd be an annoying ping or vibration every few seconds.

Yay!

Thank you!

Where do you live?

Susan recommended you.

Or Susanne.

Can't remember.

See you tomorrow!

Bye!

Oh... How much is it, please?

Do you take cash?

Thanks!

Bye!

Charlotte Whitmoore.

xx.

I can already tell this woman is going to be hard work,

exhausting. It's like her brain is working at a hundred miles an hour, and her fingers are busy trying to keep up as she types.

I reply to Charlotte with the answers to her questions, then add her name into my business diary, which is just a simple black book. Noah is always on at me to use the calendar on my phone, but I've always preferred having everything on paper. I don't go anywhere without my business diary. I'm a little old-school in that respect. I even keep all my passwords and logins written down in a book back at home, but that never leaves the flat.

I pull out onto the road just as another long string of messages comes through, but I can't check them while I'm driving, so Charlotte will have to wait. A part of me is itching to check them, not because the messages might be from Charlotte, but because they might be a response to the reply I sent after the text I received earlier.

There hasn't been a response, and I'm not sure whether that's a good thing or a bad thing.

Unfortunately, it's not the first time I've received a threatening text message.

CHAPTER THREE

At six, my workday ends. Except for when I'm driving to clients' houses, I'm on my feet all day, unless I'm doing a sit-down treatment, such as a manicure or pedicure, using the nail bar that I haul from place to place. It pays to wear decent shoes in my job and be strong enough to lift the couch and heavy boxes of nail colours, pots and bottles of cremes, toners and various other products I need for every treatment.

I wear my own branded uniform of black, fitted trousers and a black t-shirt with my logo. Noah designed it for me. It's pink and black with swirls around my business name – AJ Beauty.

Simple. Classic.

Some days, I don't finish till ten at night. They are rare occasions, but when I have a full day of treatments, it can easily happen. I do have one elderly couple who are very wealthy, and they pay me for the whole day from eight in the morning to eight in the evening. They have the full spa day treatment from me in the comfort of their own home, which is a mansion compared to my tiny flat. They feed me, ply me with non-alcoholic cocktails and then give me a generous tip on top of the cost of the treatments. I walk away with nearly five hundred pounds in total for a day's work. They do that every eight weeks. I'm very lucky to have secured their business, but both are well into their eighties now, so unfortunately, it's only a matter of time before my services are no longer required. It's a morbid thought, but over the years, I've lost more than my fair share of lovely elderly clients to the inevitability of death.

I've massaged celebrities too – I'm not allowed to divulge who, but I have a massive celeb crush on him, and now, thanks to meeting him in person, I think he's even more amazing. I also do bridal parties, hen dos and prom pampering sessions.

I drive into a car space in the multistorey car park, the closest one to the bar I'm meeting my friends at, and click my neck from side to side, popping a tight muscle.

There's no special occasion for our get-together, so it's just for a catch-up, which is long overdue. It's almost impossible to get all four of us together at once nowadays, thanks to parenting, work, and general life admin. It's a workday – Monday – so it's not like we can get wasted, but now we're all in our thirties, we prefer to go to a trendy bar where it's not heaving with university students or crowded with drunken people at weekends. We're more sophisticated now. More... mature. We like to sit down and drink, wear flats and hang out somewhere we don't have to shout to be heard or leave with a sore throat.

I lean over to grab the change of clothes I've left in the back seat. With nowhere private nearby, I awkwardly get changed in my car into my smart blouse and skinny jeans, which I do have to wrestle up my thick thighs, performing some very questionable movements and stretches in the process.

I slip on my trendy boots and then apply a top-up of mascara and pink lip gloss using the rear-view mirror. A shadow appears behind my car.

I angle my head so I can see better through the mirror. A woman is standing behind my car, facing it. I only see from her shoulders down. Is she watching me? Why isn't she moving or walking past?

Curious who it is, I glance over my shoulder, but she's already gone. I check left and right, up and down the rows of cars from where I'm sitting, but she's nowhere to be seen. A tingle tickles the back of my neck as I think about the message I got earlier. I'm still on edge from that.

I hastily finish preening myself, then climb out, sucking in my tummy as I squeeze between my car and the one next to me to avoid scratching either one with my bag. I'm running a few minutes late. The girls won't mind.

I spot them as soon as I enter the bar. They wave me over, and I slide into the booth next to Zoe, who looks spectacular.

'Your hair!' I squeal.

She shakes her head side to side, swishing and showing off her brand-new bob. 'Yep. I went for the chop.'

'And you were going to tell us about this, when?'

'Now?'

Georgina leans in, shoving a cocktail towards me. We always start off with a cocktail, but it'll just be the one tonight, as I'm driving. I could take a taxi home, but I need my car straight after I see Charlotte at nine tomorrow, so I have to drive it home. I live about a thirty-minute drive away, which is mostly spent sat in traffic lights. I could probably walk it quicker, to be perfectly honest.

I gulp down half the fruity, fizzy drink, stopping only for a moment as the icy liquid gives me brain freeze. Zoe tells the table about her sudden decision to chop most of her luscious locks off. She's like that, though; cool and spontaneous. She's single too, often introducing a new girlfriend every few months. The rest of us basically live vicariously through her.

Hayley and Georgina are the married ones. Hayley's husband works in finance, and they have two children, six and eight, and Georgina's other half is a graphic designer. No children yet, but they did start trying three months ago, so the girls and I are hoping for an announcement any day now.

I met the girls while on a beauty therapist training course, which I attended almost a year ago, only a few weeks after first moving to the area. I didn't know anyone and was just beginning to build up my client base, but meeting fellow beauty therapists was exactly what I needed. I'm happy to call these ladies my best friends. We may all have the same job, and some might say we are encroaching upon each other's businesses, but it's not like that at all. We're here for each other. If one of us gets approached by a new client who is a little too far for them to travel to, then they'll recommend one of us who lives closer. We help each other out, and because of that, I know I can depend on these women with my life.

'Well, it looks fantastic,' I say, finally taking a breather from my cocktail.

'Thanks! Charlie loves it too.'

'Who's Charlie?' I take another two big sips.

'My new girlfriend.'

I nod, knowing better than to press Zoe for more information. Zoe doesn't tell us a lot about her girlfriends because
they often don't stick around long enough.

'Bad day?' Georgina asks, eyeing my half-drunk glass.
The rest of them have barely touched theirs yet, and I've
been here less than five minutes. The strong concoction of
spirits is already making my head spin a little. Least I'm only
having one.

'Uh, no, not really. Just a weird text message that's
freaked me out.'

'Oooh. Spill!' says Hayley.

I shake my head and wave off her comment. 'No, no, it's
fine. Honestly. Probably just a wrong number.'

'Like last time?' asks Georgina.

'Yeah, I guess so, but without the dick pics.'

They know all about the issue I had with a previous boss
of mine, but it's going back a few years now, when I lived in
Portsmouth, not long after I first met Noah. I kept getting
random messages from an unknown number. Very explicit,
sexual messages and photos; close-up photos. And, when I
finally got fed up with them and messaged the person back, it
turned out to be the husband of my boss, Silvia. Things got
awkward fast when it all came out, and I couldn't work there
any longer, so I left and started working at another spa. How
he got hold of my number in the first place, I have no idea.
Afterwards, though, Silvia kept sending me threatening
messages, calling me a homewrecker and a slut, but she eventually stopped when I refused to bite back.

This message from earlier may not have been a dick pic,
but it's just as unwanted.

'Shame,' says Hayley with a giggle. The rest of us shoot
her a look. 'What?' she asks. 'He was pretty decent.'

'Anyway,' I say, ignoring her crude remark. 'It's just been the one message so far. I texted back and said they'd got the wrong number.' I fiddle with my engagement ring. It's small, a princess cut diamond, simple; perfect.

'How's the wedding planning going?' asks Georgina, spotting my fiddling.

'Uh, yes, wedding planning is going fine. Everything is booked, as you know, but... it may have to be a smaller ceremony than we originally planned.'

'Money issues?' asks Georgina.

'No, not really. In fact, Noah is in line for a promotion. He called me today with the good news, but... if he gets it, there's a possibility that he may have to move to a prison elsewhere.'

'Are you kidding?' asks Hayley.

The girls and I spend a few minutes discussing that and the implications of me having to start over with my business so soon.

'We seriously need to set a date for your hen do though,' says Georgina. 'I want to plan the biggest, most crazy hen do ever.'

I finish my drink and lean back in the booth. 'I know. I promise I'll talk to Noah soon and get it ironed out. He hasn't booked his stag either.'

'How is he?' asks Zoe.

'He's fine...' I answer slowly, like I'm not quite sure of the answer myself.

'But?'

'But... I think something happened a couple of weeks ago. I can't put my finger on what it is, but he gets so quiet when it comes to discussing work sometimes. Not always, but hopefully this promotion will help. I think this past year has been hard on him, working so many nights and long shifts, but it's all worked out now he's got his promotion.'

'You said you think something happened though? What do you mean?' asks Georgina, leaning forwards slightly. That's the thing I love about my friends. I always have their undivided attention when there's a problem, and I'd do the same for them too if the roles were reversed.

'I'm not sure,' I say. Now I've said it out loud, I can't even be sure what I'm trying to say.

I first noticed he was acting strange roughly three weeks ago, after he came back from a night shift. He seemed distant and grumpy for a couple of days afterwards. He wouldn't look me in the eye or offer any explanation for his bad mood.

My friends listen as I explain this, but then I notice them swap glances between each other, and I know they're all thinking the same thing.

'No,' I say bluntly. 'Noah would never cheat on me.'

They all bite their lips and look down into their drinks.

'He wouldn't,' I say. 'I trust him.'

Georgina is the first to speak. 'Then so do we.'

TWO HOURS LATER, I'm sober enough to drive home. After finishing my cocktail in record time, I then switched to Diet Coke. I say my goodbye to the girls and take my leave. As I walk through the multistorey car park, I take my phone out of my bag, checking for new messages.

There are none, just a few social media notifications, which I swipe away. It's a little after eight, so I'm glad I can make it back home at a reasonable time to celebrate with Noah.

Most of the cars have left the car park since I've been in

the bar. I check over my shoulder when I hear footsteps echo behind me. My thoughts jump to the woman I saw earlier, standing behind my car while I was changing.

Is she still nearby, watching me?

Could it have something to do with the threatening text I received?

Taking a deep breath to control the flutter of nerves in my stomach, I continue walking to my car, at a brisker pace than I would usually walk.

When I arrive, I stop in my tracks, frowning. Something doesn't look right.

'Son of a...'

My stomach drops as I take in the sight in front of me. It's the last thing I need, and I can't help but think that someone out there has intentionally waited around to deal this fatal blow.

CHAPTER FOUR

The left back tyre is completely flat, causing the car to tilt at a slight angle. I'm tired and want to get home to Noah. I also need to stop at a shop and buy some fizz, like I said I would.

I have three choices: be a super-powerful independent woman who doesn't need a man to help her change a tyre and do it all while wearing my skinny jeans and a low-cut top; call Noah for help, who will gladly come to my aid and do it in half the time and probably without breaking a sweat; or call the AA.

Decision made.

I call the AA. The woman on the phone says she will be with me within the hour.

It's not perfect, but it means I can still make it back home before ten.

I give her my location, then lean against the car to wait.

A young man gives me a strange look as he walks past. He glances down at the flat tyre and then averts his eyes, quickly walking away and taking out his phone. I guess he doesn't fancy helping a woman in need today.

I send Noah a quick text to say I've been delayed, but not to worry, I should be home in roughly an hour and a half. He replies with a thumbs-up emoji.

While I wait for the AA, I fiddle with my phone, attempting to distract myself from the bristling tickle of unease that's making its home at the back of my neck. At night, underground car parks are one of the creepiest places to be. All I hear are footsteps below and above me on the other levels, but the owners of the footsteps never appear, so it feels as if people are surrounding me, but staying hidden in the shadows. I check my watch. It's only been five minutes since I got off the phone to the AA. Time is dragging. I sit in my car for a bit, but I don't like the fact that my back is facing the pedestrian area. To check for the arrival of the AA van or keep an eye on any people approaching, I have to continuously check my rear-view mirror or glance over my shoulder.

Eventually, it gives me neck ache, so I get back out again. Now I have a clear view of the entranceway.

Forty minutes later, headlights approach, and I spy the bright yellow and black van driving towards me. Relief bubbles within.

The window rolls down, and a woman around my age looks out at me.

'Miss Jenkins?'

'Yes, hi. Thanks for getting here so quickly,' I say, even though the past forty-five minutes have felt like three hours.

'No problem. I was just finishing up another rescue when I got the alert through.' The woman gets out of the van. 'A flat tyre, huh? Not what you need at this time of night.'

'Tell me about it.' I point down at the tyre.

She bends and inspects it. 'Looks like you drove over a nail, and it deflated slowly while you were away.'

I attempt to swallow, but I can't. When I'd first seen the flat tyre, I thought it was some sort of sick joke, like the universe was toying with me, but now I find out it's a nail in the tyre, this changes things.

The woman who was here before, watching me... Did she intentionally drive the nail into my tyre? A cool breeze flows through the car park, but against my bristling skin, it feels like ice.

'I'll get this changed as quickly as I can and you can be on your way, although it might be worth getting a brand-new tyre soon, as these old ones in the boot can sometimes be a little brittle, depending on whether they've ever been used before.'

'Thanks. I will get it replaced as soon as possible.'

I watch in awe as the woman jacks up the car, removes the tyre, then swaps it over for the one in the boot, all within ten minutes. Once she's secured the damaged tyre in the boot, she wipes her hand on a cloth.

'You're all set,' she says.

'Thank you so much.'

As soon as she's driven away, I get into my car and take a breath, but as I do, a figure passes behind the back of my car. I turn just in time to see a woman walking past. I don't see her face, but it's enough to unsettle me again.

I tell myself to get a grip, then drive to the shops, grab a bottle of fizz, and head home, glad to finally be out of the creepy underground car park.

'YOU OKAY?' asks Noah as soon as he sees my face when I walk into the living area.

'Got a flat tyre.'

'Oh shit.'

'Called the AA.'

'Did you kerb it again?' he asks with a hint of humour in his voice.

I dump my bag on the kitchen counter. 'Haha. No, I must have driven over a nail, and it slowly deflated while I was at the bar with the girls.'

'Sorry to hear that. How are they?'

'They're fine, although they are all hounding me to set a date for the hen do.'

'The wedding isn't for another year.'

'Yes, well, you know how Georgina loves to plan ahead.'

Noah nods his agreement. 'But other than the tyre, have you had a good day?'

I hand him the bottle of fizz I bought. 'Let's not worry about my day right now. Let's celebrate your good news.'

Noah takes the bottle, pops the cork, pours the bubbly into two flutes he already had out on the side, and we toast to his promotion, each taking a tip simultaneously. The bubbles tickle my tongue, and I enjoy the sensation for a few moments before focusing my attention on Noah, determined not to let my strange and slightly unsettling day derail his hard work.

'So, tell me more about your promotion. What did Rob say exactly, and when are you expected to be promoted and start the new role?' Rob's the Custodial Manager at the prison. He oversees multiple departments and manages prison activities, people and resources. It's the job title that Noah is now eligible for.

Noah sips from his flute. 'It's not an immediate promotion. There are things going on in the background, like the course I have to attend, and uh... hoops to jump through. Rob hasn't fully decided whether he's leaving yet.'

'When will he decide?'

'I don't know.'

'And do you? Want to take over from him at the prison you're currently working in?'

Noah shrugs, taking another drink. He holds the liquid in his mouth for several seconds before swallowing it. 'I guess so.'

Is it just me, or has Noah's enthusiasm for his promotion suddenly dimmed? He's clamming up and I can't quite work out if it's something I've said or not.

I change tack.

'I'm proud of how hard you've been working. You deserve this.' Lord knows we could do with the increase in salary. Unless I had the ability to work twenty-four hours a day, I'll never earn more than thirty grand a year. I may not have rent to pay on a salon, but the expenses I do have are not cheap. Plus, I'm always trying to keep my qualifications up to date and go on various courses to ensure I can offer my clients the latest treatments and products. I'm currently in the middle of an online reflexology course, which I do whenever I have a spare moment.

I lean against the kitchen counter and sip the fizz, which is going down super-smooth.

Noah turns and pours another glass for himself, then tops mine up. 'And you won't be too disappointed if we have to move again?'

'Where would we move to?' I ask, bypassing his question.

'It depends, but there's a job up north that's available.'

'How far up north?'

'York.'

I almost spit out a mouthful of champagne. That's over a hundred and fifty miles away. The idea of moving so far away from my friends is not one I relish. I've already done it once before; left the familiarity of Portsmouth to live with Noah in Cambridge. He assured me that we were here to stay, to settle down, get married and save up to buy our first house, but now we may move to York, and it's all a bit... much.

'But the wedding is already booked, so would we cancel our venue and change it?' I ask. We chose a local church for the ceremony and a simple hotel function room for the reception. The idea of changing it all is enough to make me want to well up. We'd spent weeks deciding. We haven't sent the invites out yet, so friends and family aren't locked in with the location or date, but it would still be a huge upheaval.

'I'm sorry,' he says, clearly noticing my lack of enthusiasm for the move. 'I know it's not what we had planned.'

'Nothing is decided yet, right?'

He shakes his head.

'When will you find out more?'

'Uh... after I've done the course, I guess. I'm not sure.'

'Then let's not worry about it now,' I reply. I like to think I'm a positive person, always looking on the bright side of things, that everything always happens for a reason. If we have to put the wedding on hold for the move, then so be it. We can make it work somehow.

Noah sighs so loudly that I can practically see the weight lifting from his shoulders. 'Thank you for being so wonderful and understanding,' he says, moving in close and planting a light kiss on my forehead. I want to pull him in for a proper kiss, but he moves away too quickly.

It's gone ten now, so we finish the bottle, brush our teeth side by side with little discussion and then climb into bed. I go to give him a hug and maybe have a snuggle, but he already has his back to me, his knees pulled up to his chest. Guarded.

It feels like he's pulling away from me. I need to do something, say something, but what? I don't know what's wrong. As I lie in bed, staring at the dark ceiling, my thoughts from this evening's chat with the girls flood my mind.

It's true that since that night shift three weeks ago, he's been much more distant with me, but it's been so gradual I've only properly noticed it in the past week or so. I'm confident enough in our relationship to know that he'd never cheat on me. He isn't the type. I know a lot of women may say that about their boyfriends or husbands, but with Noah, it goes beyond certainty. The change in Noah lately is to do with something else. I'm sure of it.

Whether I like it or not, I'm going to have to ask him about it soon. I need to get to the bottom of this soon, before everything starts progressing with regard to our wedding plans and future living arrangements. But now doesn't feel like the right moment. If I push, he'll only pull away further.

I'm going to have to trust for now that, whatever it is, Noah can handle it himself and that when the time is right, he'll ask for my help and tell me what's going on.

I'M A LIGHT SLEEPER, so when Noah's alarm goes off at four the next morning for his early shift, it wakes me, but I don't say a word as he gets out of bed and pads into the bathroom. The tap runs. The toilet flushes. The shower turns on.

I listen with my eyes closed, curled up on my side. The alarm on his phone blares to life again, so I shuffle over, still half asleep, and switch it off, but as I do, my bleary eyes see a string of missed calls on the screen from a private number. Whoever it is has been calling him non-stop through the night.

What the hell?

Is it an emergency from work? Why would they ring him though? He wasn't on call overnight. Maybe something has happened at the prison, but surely, he would have seen the missed calls when he turned off his alarm the first time. Why hasn't he called them back?

I leave his phone where I found it and return to my side of the bed, feeling guilty yet confused, wrestling with the idea of asking him about it. In the end, I feign waking up when he emerges from the shower, a blue towel wrapped around his waist. He smells nice, looks even better.

'Morning,' I mumble. 'Everything okay?'

'Hey, sorry if I woke you. Yes, fine. Why?'

'I just turned your alarm off on your phone, and it looks like you had loads of missed calls.'

Noah's eyes flick to his phone. 'Oh, yeah, it's nothing. It's been sorted.' He leans over me and plants a soft kiss on my forehead. 'Go back to sleep.'

I smile as I close my eyes, but inside, my mind is racing.

Noah's hiding something. I can feel it.

CHAPTER FIVE

NOAH

I've always prided myself on my strong morals, my ability to stand up for what's right and wrong, to be capable, able to handle myself, no matter what. But that's not who I am anymore. I hate the man I've become. Hate him. I've changed, but it hasn't happened overnight. One person, over the course of the past year, since working at Blackmore Prison, has destroyed the man I once was.

Who am I?

I'm a liar.

But I'm not only a liar. I'm a horrible human being who doesn't deserve the love and trust I get from my future wife. She left everything to move to Cambridge with me – her friends, her father, her job – and now, because of my weakness, she may have to do it all over again. I call her Mills. Always have done. It was a pet name I gave her when we first met, and it's stuck ever since. Only I call her Mills. Her friends sometimes call her Milly. We got engaged two years ago and, finally, we've booked the date.

15th of August 2026. That's the day we're due to be married.

Three hundred and fifty-five days from now.

But I can barely see past the next few days, let alone that far into the future.

A lot has changed since we got engaged. It's not Mills' fault. She has no idea that I'm lying to her, and if she ever did find out the truth, then I doubt she'd believe me. No one would.

I don't want to cancel the wedding. It has nothing to do with Mills, but it would be so much simpler if she would just realise I'm a horrible person and leave me now. I'm too much of a coward to break up with her myself. It's too late to own up and admit what happened because, since then, my problem has taken off, growing exponentially, like a weed.

When it first started happening, roughly a year ago, it was easy to hide. Now, though, every day I fear the truth being discovered, so that's why I lie, because the more I deny it, the more I ignore it, the easier it is to believe – the version I've made up, not only to protect myself, but also the people I love and care about the most. They'll all be affected by this if it ever sees the light of day, which is why it needs to be buried down in the dark depths of what's left of my soul. I'm not even sure if I have one anymore. I've destroyed it.

It was nice to hear the excitement in her voice when I told her about my promotion, even though it's a load of bollocks.

That's the thing – I don't notice I'm doing it anymore. Lying, that is. I would say it comes as easily as breathing, but breathing is hard because every breath I take means I have to live a second longer with what I did, with what happened afterwards, because of one stupid mistake.

I have to tell Mills something eventually. I know she can tell something isn't right with me. She trusts me, and it sickens me that she does. But what do I tell her?

That's why I told her about the promotion and started drip-feeding her the crumbs that I need her to follow. Yes, we may need to move because I want to get as far away from this place as possible, but what if it doesn't help? What if I'm continually plagued by this for the rest of my life? I can't have Mills find out. Ever.

I'll do anything to take it all back. The fallout has been beyond anything I could have imagined. I thought I could just sweep it under the rug, hide it away, ignore it, pretend it didn't happen, but I can't. It's ruined my life, my career, and it will eventually ruin my relationship. Because there's no getting away from the fact that if Mills ever finds out, our relationship is over.

I didn't want to celebrate my good news last night, but Mills seemed adamant that we should. It's nothing worth celebrating because it's not true. I went along with it, but forcing my lips into a smile was almost as hard as breathing. I'm exhausted, as if the weight of the world really is bearing down on my shoulders.

Luckily, Mills isn't the type of woman to ask questions, to push me into difficult conversations. Maybe she should be. She's too trusting of me, and I hate that about her. Perhaps she shouldn't believe everything that comes out of my mouth. If she didn't, I doubt we'd still be together.

I am trying to hold on to her for as long as I possibly can, but she's slipping through my fingers with every passing day. It's probably for the best. She's better off without me. I don't deserve her. Other than earning money for rent and bills, I don't feel I bring anything to our relationship anymore. And that's my fault. I know it is, but I have no drive, sexually or physically, to make it work. To make anything work.

The lies just keep on coming. Relentless. Like torrential rain, and the water level is rising and rising, and I'm drowning. I'm not sure how much longer I can keep my head above the surface. If I even want to keep on fighting. What's the point?

I LEAVE Mills to sleep and drive into work, ready to start an early shift. The missed calls, voicemails and texts are still on my phone. I can't believe I was stupid enough to leave my phone on the bedside cabinet.

Stupid. Stupid. Stupid.

I haven't read or listened to any of them yet. I can't quite bring myself to do it.

I arrive at the prison, check in and toss my phone in my locker. Out of sight. Out of mind. If only that were true.

'Morning, Noah,' says Rob. He's not really like a boss. More like an ally, a friend. He's decent.

'Hey, Rob,' I say with a head nod.

'How's things?'

'Oh, you know... Fine.'

Rob doesn't buy it. He never does. He sees more than Mills does, that's for sure. He seems to care about me, about my well-being. I love Mills. I do, but she pisses me off sometimes with her lack of attention. Or maybe she just doesn't give a shit. This is the thing about me. One minute, I'm complaining that she doesn't pay enough attention to me, and then when she does, I push her away in fear of her getting too close and finding out more than she needs to know.

Rob and I are standing at the coffee-making table, which only consists of a kettle and a pot of instant coffee. For months, the prison officers have pleaded and begged for a proper coffee machine, but apparently, the budget doesn't stretch that far. Just like it also doesn't stretch to therapy and decent training.

Rob gestures towards the little room where we usually have our one-to-ones. It's the room where you know shit is about to get serious, when he doesn't want to be overheard. 'Shall we?'

My chin dips to my chest as I make my way into the room. I don't take a seat because I can't seem to keep still anymore. Always itching to stay active. If I'm still, my brain starts running away with me, and that's never a good thing.

'Noah... we need to talk.'

Ah, fuck.

CHAPTER SIX

I get up at seven, feeling a little groggy after the earlier wake-up. Plus, the half bottle of fizz late last night hasn't helped. I should have chugged a glass of water before falling asleep. It's always so quiet in the flat when I'm alone, so I ask my Echo Dot to play BBC Radio 2 to fill the silence.

The block of modern flats we live in was only built about a decade ago, so they are all still in decent condition. It's a two-bed flat with an open-style kitchen/lounge/diner. Perfect for just the two of us. The spare bedroom is used as a home beauty studio for clients to visit me. I have transformed it into a peaceful space, complete with motivational quotes on the walls and all my beauty products lined up on shelves. Everything has its own place. In a perfect world, all my clients would visit me and I'd never have the need to drive anywhere, but most of my clients prefer I come to them. It's more convenient.

For now, this flat suits us fine, but it's our dream to own a house one day. Although now, the location of this future house is up in the air. I'd love to own a home in Cambridge. Maybe not directly in the centre of the city like now due to the high prices, but somewhere on the outskirts, so I could keep the clients I have now. Moving to York would disrupt those plans.

I've spent the past year building my business and, now I'm earning roughly 25K a year, I'm finally earning a stable enough income to make the bank manager happy. If Noah and I wish to take out a mortgage together, then I need to have been self-employed for two years minimum and earning a decent wage for it to count towards the deposit, so I still have a year left to earn as much as possible.

Noah earns a lot more than I do, but not enough to take out the mortgage in his name alone, so it will be a team effort. One I relish, but it is putting a lot of stress on us lately. Money is always a topic of conversation that causes tension, so we try to avoid it.

I quickly check the treatment room is set up for my new client, Charlotte, and then do the washing up while the clock ticks towards nine.

At ten past nine, she still hasn't arrived, and I'm about to send her a message to ask if everything is okay when the intercom buzzes, making me jump. Noah always has it set too loud.

I hurry over and press the button. 'Hi, Charlotte?'

'Yes! I'm so sorry I'm late!'

I buzz her up, then open the door and leave it ajar, the tingle of anticipation I always get when greeting a brand-new client humming through my body. I'm not a shy or nervous person in general, confident in myself and my professional manner, but meeting a new client, especially ever since I had that awkward run-in with one a few years back, sets off a few nervous jitters. They dissipate after the first ten minutes, once I get a feel for their personality.

I like to plan an extra ten minutes for a first appointment to go through a short health questionnaire and consultation, checking for any allergies, skin conditions and the like, but with Charlotte being ten minutes late, I'm already running behind and we haven't started yet.

Footsteps pound up the stairs. Has she run the whole way up? Why didn't she take the lift? A red-faced woman finally appears round the corner of the stairway. She slows down, walking the rest of the way to my door.

I slap on a smile and extend my hand. 'Hi, Charlotte! It's so lovely to meet you.'

She returns my smile but actively avoids shaking my hand. Not in a rude way, but she's carrying several bags, so her hands are full.

'Can I help you with any of your bags?' I ask.

'Oh, no, that's okay! I'm so sorry I'm late. I... Well, time got away from me.' She sucks in a breath. I'm a little worried she may faint or stumble, so I allow her to walk ahead of me into the flat and softly close the door.

'You found the place okay?' I ask.

'Yes, no problem. I often pass this building on my daily walks. Oh, I'm a dog walker. This block of flats is on my route to the park.'

'Jesus Green?'

'Yes, that's the one. It's my favourite place to visit in the city, as well as the walks by the river.'

'It's so beautiful there,' I say. I smile and gesture down the hallway. 'My treatment room's this way.' She follows me without another word. I reach the door and stand aside to allow her to enter first.

'Can I use your loo before we start, please?' she asks. She then starts bouncing up and down on the balls of her feet.

'Yes, of course. It's just there on the right.' I point down the hallway.

Charlotte nods, sets all her bags on the floor outside the treatment room, then scurries off to the bathroom. Should I move all her bags into the room for her or leave them out here? I decide to move them. None of them is particularly heavy.

The treatment room has dim lighting and soft music playing over the sound system; a classical combination of popular pop songs and tracks from famous movies, all slowed down to a more relaxing tempo. Often, clients will be lying face down on the couch and then suddenly say, 'I recognise this tune!' and it'll be the piano music to "The Hanging Tree" from *The Hunger Games,* or *The Pirates of the Caribbean* theme tune.

While I wait for Charlotte to return, I can't help but glance at the clock on the wall. I'm now twenty minutes behind schedule, so I take a calming breath, determined not to let it rattle me. A lot has happened in the past twenty-four hours: the text message, the woman who was possibly watching me in the car park, followed by the flat tyre, not to mention Noah's revelation that we may have to uproot our lives again. It's all set me on edge, like I can't quite catch my breath. I'm not usually this anxious. I know as soon as I've finished with Charlotte, I have to be on the road to my next client. She's twenty minutes away, and that's in good traffic without hitting any red lights, something that only happens once in a blue moon.

The toilet flushes, but Charlotte doesn't appear straight away. Not even five minutes later. Time ticks by, but I patiently wait, crossing and uncrossing my legs while I sit in one of the chairs I have set out.

Finally, Charlotte enters the room. 'You have such a lovely flat,' she says.

'Thank you,' I reply, slightly taken aback.

Has she looked around the whole flat? I always shut the door leading to the main living area and the master bedroom so I keep my business and my personal space separate. There's no time to dwell on it, so I lead her through a quick consultation, marking things off on my client sheet. She hesitates when I ask her if she's on any long-term medication that I need to be aware of.

'Um, no... not right now, no,' she says without making eye contact.

I don't push her. I trust she's telling me the truth, despite the odd pause before answering. I have clients who are on all sorts of medication, from antidepressants, hormone replacement therapy and even one man who's going through chemotherapy, but I do need to know what they're on, in case they should react with any of the treatments or products I use. Everything is kept confidential.

She tells me the smell of lavender gives her a headache and she hates the smell of peppermint, but otherwise, I have everything I need to get started with her treatment. She chooses a sky blue for her nail colour and wants the nails' shape to be rounded at the edges.

As I start her manicure, I realise her nails are in quite bad condition. I'm going to need to file them down short to get the desired shape. Her cuticles are ragged and look like they've been bitten off in places, and the skin around the edges of her nails is red and raw. Not the worst I've ever seen, but certainly not in good condition, which means it's going to take me longer to sort out.

Charlotte appears more relaxed than when she first arrived and dives straight into asking me dozens of questions in quick succession about what I'm doing, why I'm doing that, but then moves on to asking questions about me. Usually, I like to be the one to steer the conversation, but Charlotte is full steam ahead, almost tripping over her words to get them out, then asking another question before I've finished answering the previous one.

'How long have you been a beauty therapist?'

'Where did you study?'

'Why did you decide to go self-employed?'

'Do you like getting treatments yourself?'

'You have such lovely nails.'

'What colour is that?'

'Oooh, maybe I'll try that next time.'

'What do you do for fun?'

At this question, I say, 'Well, I enjoy keeping fit. On Tuesday nights, I go to Everyone Fitness and do a spin class.'

'Oh, I love spinning! I also do a lot of running. I ran the London Marathon three years ago,' she says proudly.

'Oh wow! I'd love to run a marathon one day,' I reply, 'but it takes such a lot of dedicated training, and I never seem to find the time to go on long runs. I usually run early in the mornings or at weekends.'

'Have you done the park run in Cambridge?'

'Yes, several times.'

'What's your PB?'

I think for a moment. 'Gosh, I can't remember, but I think it's around twenty-six minutes.'

'That's really good. I'm more of a slow plodder myself.'

We then discuss Charlotte's background, and she tells me she's only lived in the area for a few months, having moved here after a hard break-up. She tells me she went to Lancaster University.

'Oh, my fiancé went there,' I say, my voice a little high. She looks around his age, maybe younger, so it's possible she may have been studying there around the same time as him, or maybe just as he was graduating.

Charlotte pauses to take a breath, then seems to lose her concentration and doesn't reply to my comment directly, but asks me what he did at university.

'He did a business course, I think,' I reply, slightly embarrassed that the actual title of his course alludes me. 'What about you?'

'Oh, I kept changing my mind about what I wanted to do and eventually dropped out.'

'Ah,' I say, although despite only meeting her less than half an hour ago, I'm not entirely surprised by this because her mind seems to jump from one thing to the next at the drop of a hat. She reminds me of my mother in a strange way.

I clear my throat and decide a change of topic is in order. 'So, you said you're a dog walker?'

'Yes! I love dogs. Don't you love dogs? You should get a dog. They are so lovely. I can't have a dog myself because of where I live, so that's why I decided to set up my own business and walk them instead.'

'That's lovely. I do love dogs, yes, but I'm the same. I can't have one in this flat, so maybe when we eventually buy our own house, we can get one. Lots of my clients have dogs, though, so I'll be sure to recommend your services to them. Do you have a business card?'

'Yes, somewhere. I'll grab some at the end for you.'

'Perfect.' I turn my attention back to her nails, which are now looking much healthier and shinier, although there's not a lot I can do about the red skin around the edges.

'Do you bite your nails?' I ask, hoping it doesn't come across as rude or accusatory.

'Oh, yeah. Sorry. Been a bit of a stressful time lately. It's a bad habit I need to stop, but... easier said than done, am I right?'

'Yes,' I say. 'Don't worry about it. I've managed to restore some of the strength that's been lost and tidied up the edges as best as I can. The colour looks lovely on you!' I've only got one more coat of polish left to set, then her nails are finished.

'Thank you,' says Charlotte. I glance at the clock, hoping she doesn't notice, but evidently she does. 'Have I made you run late?'

I shake my head. 'Oh, no, it's fine. I just need to make sure I leave enough time to pack everything in the car afterwards.'

'You have such lovely hair,' says Charlotte. The speed at which she changes subjects is enough to give me whiplash. 'I hope this doesn't sound rude, but what's your ethnicity? I sometimes say the wrong term, and I don't want to offend you. I've offended people before...'

Her forwardness surprises me, considering she seemed so anxious at the start. 'No, that's perfectly okay. I have a mixed ethnic background. My father is black British. Originally, his parents were from the Caribbean. And my mother is – was – white British.'

'How do you get your hair so straight?'

'I straighten it as often as I can.'

'Do you have an afro?'

I squeeze my lips together to stop from smirking because her fascination and enthusiasm are quite infectious, even though they would probably come across as rude to most people. But I'm perfectly fine with it. She's not said anything that would offend me.

I've had my fair share of racial slurs thrown at me over the years, including a woman who walked into the beauty salon I was working in at the time and told me, straight out, that she wanted to be treated by a white therapist. She didn't look ashamed or anything. I apologised to her, remained professional, and said I was the only therapist available for walk-in clients, and she kicked up a fuss and asked to speak to my manager, who, when she realised what was going on, told the elderly lady to get out of her salon and not come back.

'Not really, no, but it does go very frizzy in damp weather,' I reply with a smile.

Charlotte then tells me about her own hair, which is short and cropped, bleached blonde, but with dark roots. She has sharp cheekbones and a splattering of freckles across her nose.

'All done,' I say, sitting back and allowing her to take a look.

'Wow,' she says as she brings her nails close to her face, studying them. 'These are the most perfect nails I've ever seen. I mean, the shape is just lovely, and the polish is so neat. Thank you so much.'

'You're very welcome.'

'Can I book another treatment? This was such a lovely experience.'

'Of course. What treatment are you thinking?'

'I'd love a facial. Do you have any spaces next week?'

'Does Tuesday at ten a.m. work?'

'Yes, that's perfect.'

Charlotte pays for her treatment using my mobile card machine, picks up her bags, then follows me into the hallway, and we walk towards the front door. I open it and turn to find her staring at a picture of me and Noah on the wall. It was taken three years ago on our first official date. We don't look hugely different, bar one noticeable feature of his.

'Oh!' Charlotte exclaims. 'Gosh, I still think I preferred it when he had hair.' She laughs.

My mouth drops open. Noah has shaved his head ever since I've known him. I've only seen him with a full head of hair in old photos. 'Um... How did you know Noah used to have hair?'

She joins me by the front door, seemingly oblivious to my stunned expression. 'Huh?' she asks sweetly. 'I'm guessing he had hair once,' she responds quickly. 'It was lovely to meet you, Amelia.' She transfers the bags into one hand, then reaches into her pocket and pulls out some cards, handing them to me. 'Here are some cards for my dog walking business for you to hand out to your clients. Thank you. It's much appreciated.'

I take them, still completely stumped for words, barely able to get a word out edgeways. I want to ask her many questions about her throwaway comment, but my brain can't quite catch up to my mouth. I must have misinterpreted her. 'Thank you. Yes, I'll be sure to share these out to people with dogs.'

Charlotte nods. 'See you next week!'

And she's gone like a flash of lightning.

I stand, holding my front door open, listening to her footsteps trundle down the stairs. She hasn't used the lift again. I feel as if a tornado has hit the flat. I'm completely winded by her comment about Noah.

Is it possible she knows him from her time at Lancaster University? Why wouldn't she have mentioned it?

CHAPTER SEVEN

I close the front door with a soft click and stare at the picture of me and Noah, the one Charlotte looked at. I'm not overreacting. I haven't misremembered what I told her about him. We talked about our own hair, but I never mentioned anything about Noah other than that he went to Lancaster University. I didn't even tell her his name, but she made the comment about preferring him with hair, something he hasn't had on the top of his head for several years.

She did ask a hell of a lot of questions, and I must admit, I can't remember every one she asked, but I'm not crazy. She must have known him during the time he had hair.

There are no other photos of me and Noah in this hallway. In fact, the only photo of Noah when he *has* hair is in...

The master bedroom.

I walk fast down the hallway to the bathroom. The door has been left open, but that's not what concerns me. The door to our bedroom is further down the hallway, and that door is open too, but only slightly. It was closed when Charlotte arrived, which means she must have opened it, gone in, looked around and seen the picture of Noah.

What was it she said?

'Gosh, I think I preferred it when he had hair.'

So, either she knows him personally from when he *did* have hair, in which case it's odd she didn't mention it, or she went into the bedroom and saw this other picture, meaning she snooped around the flat when she should have been using the bathroom. No wonder she took so long.

Just to be sure, I push the door open the rest of the way and step into the master bedroom. Blood is pounding in my ears. My heart rate has doubled in the space of thirty seconds. I can barely catch my breath as I scan my bedroom.

There it is.

The photo of Noah in his graduation cap and gown, holding his certificate from Lancaster University. He may be wearing the cap, but his straggly, unkempt hair is clearly visible beneath it.

There's another picture on the wall beside it, of the two of us less than a year ago, taken as a selfie; me holding the phone. Both of us are grinning and we have our arms around each other, looking as happy as anything, but what the photo doesn't show is the tension brewing beneath the surface. We'd just had an argument. I don't even remember what it was about, but what had started out as a fun-filled day cycling along the river had turned into a moody storm of stress, and we ended up not biking to the pub we were aiming for. We'd turned around and come back home instead. He clearly had a lot going on at work, and I thought it would be good to get some exercise and fresh air, but it had been a horrible experience. I don't know why I framed the picture, because it only brings up bad memories whenever I look at it.

My eyes return to the photo of Noah in his cap and gown.

Charlotte must have been in here, but why? You don't go snooping around another person's living space, much less someone you met moments ago, unless you're looking for something or have another agenda. Or was she just being nosey?

I don't know her, but it's possible she knows my future husband.

I stand in the middle of the room with my hands on my hips, thinking. Something doesn't add up, doesn't quite sit right. Charlotte came across as a nice woman, a little edgy and slightly odd, perhaps. She asked a lot of questions, but then that's normal when you're meeting someone for the first time.

I take a breath and decide to brush it off as another weird experience. I'll ask Noah about her later. I should have left ten minutes ago to get to my next client. I don't have time to worry about Charlotte looking around my bedroom. Nothing is out of place. She didn't steal anything. The photo hasn't been moved.

I'll sort this out later.

THE REST of the day flies by, as it usually does, especially when my clients are spread over an area the size of Cambridge. I don't mind the travelling though. Plus, when I arrive at their houses, I get cups of tea made for me and get plied with biscuits and food. I can't complain.

I do sometimes make myself a packed lunch, but today

I've skipped it since I'm working over the lunch period. A granola bar and a smoothie keep my stomach from grumbling too loudly.

My busy day is enough to keep my mind occupied, rather than dwell on the weird events of the past two days, but as I finish my final client at five (an early finish for me), my phone lights up in my hand just as I'm putting it away after WhatsApp-ing Noah that I'm on my way home. He responds with a thumbs-up emoji and a heart.

But there's another text from an unknown number.

It's blank.

I open it to be sure.

No, it's not blank. Not completely.

A lot of clear space and then five words that send a cold shiver straight to the base of my spine and goosebumps rippling across the surface of my skin.

> It's all your fault, Bitch.

My mouth drops open. My hands tremble.

This must be a wrong number. I haven't done anything to anyone! The response I sent after the first message isn't in this thread. It's a new private number. Whoever has sent me these messages has two different phones or SIM cards.

My hands still tremble as my finger hovers over the reply button. No. I'm not going to respond again. That's what people like this want. They want to unsettle you, get a rise out of you. Well, whoever this is has certainly unsettled me, but they aren't getting a reply.

There's only one way to deal with this.

Block.

As soon as I block and delete the message, the tension

releases, albeit only slightly. I now need to go home and change. My spin class starts at six. Noah will be home already. He's always home around three when he starts the day with an early shift.

I stop at traffic lights, my fingers lightly drumming on the steering wheel in response to the upbeat song that's playing on the radio.

My mind keeps circling back to the text. Why is this playing on my mind so much? It's done. It's over. I haven't done anything wrong. It's just a random wrong number. There's nothing else I can do now.

A car horn blares from behind me.

Shit. The light's turned green and I haven't noticed.

My heart rate shoots up again as I hold my hand up to signal my apologies. I slam my foot to the floor to get away fast, but all it does is cause my poor old car to splutter and stall.

More car horns erupt from every direction.

In my haste to restart the car, I forget how to use the clutch, and it takes several attempts to get it started. All the while, horns blare, and people yell. It takes me right back to when I was learning to drive and I stalled seventeen times at a set of traffic lights. Granted, they were on a stupidly steep hill, but since that day, I've had a phobia of hill starts.

This hasn't helped my already high blood pressure. I'm not normally like this. I can handle a bit of pressure, but the combination of the threatening messages and everything else that's happened lately is getting to me, slowly chipping away at my usually calm, confident exterior.

Finally, my car grumbles and splutters to life, but by this time, the traffic lights have turned red again. To my horror, the man in the car behind gets out and storms towards my car. I can see him approaching in the rear-view mirror.

Oh shit.

'Hey!' he shouts through the window. I keep it closed. There's no way I'm opening it to speak to him. He raps his knuckles against the glass, hard. 'What the fuck do you think you're playing at? Don't you know how to drive? Stupid fucking women drivers.'

I ignore him. I don't particularly feel like having a confrontation with a man who looks as if he belongs in a boxing ring. Yet another person who's trying to get a rise out of me. Well, there also happens to be power in silence, so I continue to stare straight ahead, whilst simultaneously and surreptitiously checking to make sure my car door is locked.

The lights are changing, so as I pull away, I quickly slide him my middle finger.

His face turns red, and now he's the one left standing in the middle of the road, blocking it with his car while horns beep and people shout all around him.

My heart is still rattling around in my chest like a convict trying to escape the bars of a cell, but I feel momentarily pleased with my response, albeit a childish one. Perhaps not my finest retaliation, but my confidence is sparking back to life briefly.

I drive home on autopilot, feeling the sudden urge to have Noah's strong arms around me and his heart beating against my own.

I'M WRONG. Noah's not home when I arrive, which is weird, but I can't hang around because I have a spin class to get to. Noah walks in the door as I finish putting on my gym leggings and crop top. I rush out to tell him about the text message, the irate driver, and the whole Charlotte debacle, but as soon as I set eyes on him, I know something is wrong and decide against it. He's not in his work uniform. He looks as if he hasn't slept in a week. I know the early shifts can be a killer, but his skin looks grey. As a beauty therapist, I know he's in dire need of a face scrub and a rejuvenating mask, but he very rarely lets me do treatments on him.

'What's happened?' I ask.

He looks like a rabbit caught in headlights. 'Huh? Oh, nothing, why?'

'You look awful.'

'Gee, thanks.'

'No. Sorry. I didn't mean... What I meant is that you look stressed. Are you okay? Where've you been? I thought you'd be home before me.'

I don't mean to fire questions at him, and I instantly want to take them back and start again. Noah moves straight past without giving me a kiss hello. I watch him as he walks into our bedroom.

'I'm going to quickly get changed and join you at the gym, if that's okay. I'll do lengths in the pool while you're doing your class,' he calls out.

'Okay,' I say, frowning.

He's changed in record speed. Only then does he stop and give me a kiss hello. 'Have a good day?' he asks, as we step into the lift together.

'Um, yeah, it was fine.' A part of me wants to tell him everything that's happened, but I get the feeling he's not in the mood to listen. Sometimes it's worth picking and choosing your battles and not running headfirst into them with no plan of how to win. I haven't even told him about the first threatening text message yet. I usually tell him every-thing, but his reluctance to share details with me lately has made me reconsider whether he needs to know everything going on in my life, especially when it doesn't concern him. Although the whole idea of Charlotte knowing him does concern him.

We ride down in silence, but as we step out of the lift, I ask, 'Did you know anyone called Charlotte Whitmoore when you were at uni?'

He barely misses a beat before answering. 'Not that I can remember. Why?'

'My new client... she went to Lancaster University.'

'At the same time as me?'

'She didn't say when she attended.'

'What does she look like?'

'Um, quite pretty, short blonde hair with dark roots, brown eyes, my age.'

Noah shrugs. 'Doesn't ring a bell.'

'She said something odd that made me think she knew you from back when you had hair.'

Noah chuckles. 'What? What did she say?'

'She said she preferred it when you had hair. She caught sight of a picture of the two of us, the one in the hallway near the front door. In it, you obviously have a shaved head, which made me think she must have known you from before.'

'Did she say she knew me?'

'No.'

'Weird. I don't know what to tell you, Mills. I didn't know anyone called Charlotte Whitmoore back then.'

There's still a niggling ball of confusion settling at the base of my stomach. As much as I want to trust Noah, as much as I do trust him, there's something he's not telling me. Either he's lying or Charlotte is.

Noah drives us to the gym and takes off towards the changing rooms without so much as a goodbye or a 'see you later.'

I let out a long sigh. Maybe besting myself on the spin bike for forty-five minutes will help alleviate some of the weirdness and tension going on in my body, and I hope whatever Noah has going on, he leaves in the pool.

I was really hoping to talk to him about the wedding planning tonight over dinner because there are a few things we need to decide on and sort out. With every passing day, Noah seems to drift further and further away from me. Plus, there may not even be a wedding now if we end up having to postpone it due to the move.

I know he's suffered from depression in the past, back before I met him. I never knew him like that, so it's difficult for me to notice or recognise the signs, but there is *something* going on. I feel so helpless, like I should know what to do.

I need to talk to Noah tonight.

As much as I hate confrontation, there are some topics of conversation that shouldn't stay buried. My own issues can wait. I need to know that Noah and I are okay.

CHAPTER EIGHT

It's amazing what exercise can do for a bad mood. The endorphins flooding my body have a huge impact on my mental state when I walk out of the class forty-five minutes later. Yes, my legs are full of lead, I'm sweating buckets and feel slightly sick, but inside I'm as light as air. The fog in my head has lifted, and the tension in my shoulders has lessened.

I wait by the glass entrance doors for Noah, and as soon as he rounds the corner, there's a noticeable change in his posture and mood too. He practically glides up to me, kisses my cheek and taps my bum.

'Good class?' he asks.

I follow him to the car. 'My legs feel like lead, but yes, it was great. We did hill climbs and sprints. Good swim?'

'Forty lengths and ten minutes in the steam room. I feel like a new man.'

'You know, if you've had a bad day, you can talk to me about it.'

Noah pauses at the car door. 'I know.'

And that's all he says. He's never been hugely open to those difficult conversations, but there was a time he would talk to me in detail about his day, whom he spoke to, whom he met, what he did, but now I'm lucky if I get a full sentence.

As he drives home, my phone rings. It's Sally, a lovely client of mine whom I've seen every couple of weeks for almost a year now. She was one of my first clients who approached me when I started out as self-employed. She's due to visit me tomorrow.

'Hi, Sally. How are you?'

Her bright, happy voice chirps straight back. 'Milly! I'm very well, thank you. Listen, I'm just calling to ask a quick favour, but no worries if you can't squeeze it in. I know how busy you are. Is there any chance you can add a facial to my treatment tomorrow, or maybe change it from a massage to a facial? My skin is so awful at the moment. I've got blocked pores coming out my ears. Must be all the stress and hormonal changes.'

'Yes, that's not a problem. We'll have to change it from a massage to a facial instead, though, because I have another client straight after you and I can't fit both a massage and a facial in.'

'That's perfect. Thank you so much. Sorry for the short notice. We'll catch up properly tomorrow, yes?'

'Absolutely. Bye, Sally.'

'Bye!'

I hang up and take my business diary out of my bag, flip to the correct day and make a note next to Sally's name. It's not a big change. It just means laying out a few extra products. Sally is one of those rare clients whom I can call a proper friend. Yes, I'm friendly with all my clients, but Sally and I have clicked over our love of cocktails and running. We've met up for several runs over the past few months, even doing the park run together. She's a much faster runner than I am, but she stays at my pace.

'I don't know why you don't just put your client times and dates into your phone calendar,' says Noah.

'I told you. I prefer to write them down on paper.'

'Fancy risotto when we get home? I'll cook.'

My mouth salivates at the thought of food. I've barely eaten all day, and the exertion from the spin class has gone to my head, making me a little light-headed.

'Mmm, sounds great. Thanks.'

I sink back into the car seat as we lapse into silence once again. My mind is buzzing with the various ways I could try and speak to him regarding his change of mood over the past few weeks. I don't know where to start.

THE WARM, spicy aromas emanating from the kitchen when I step out of the shower are enough to make my stomach gurgle. Noah is a decent self-taught cook. I like cooking, but I need to be in the mood to make a meal from scratch, and I can't be under any sort of time constraint, otherwise I find it stressful. I did once attempt to bake a cake for Noah's birthday, but it ended up flat and chewy, not light and moist like the recipe promised. Turns out, I used the wrong type of flour and forgot to put the eggs in. I had to make a quick run to the shop to buy a cake. Noah's never let me forget that embarrassment.

Noah, on the other hand, uses cooking like therapy. One morning, I woke up to the warm smell of baking bread and found him in the kitchen pulling a loaf out of the oven after a particularly long night shift. I didn't complain. The bread was delicious, but he hasn't cooked anything like that for a while. Maybe I should suggest he takes the time to do some things he enjoys, such as cooking or swimming, because it's already proven to be a fairly effective method of lightening his dark mood.

I'm getting dressed after my shower when my phone lights up from where it's lying on the bed. I mostly have it on silent because of the number of texts I receive from clients. It would drive me nuts if it was on loud or vibrate.

Peering quickly at the screen, I notice several messages have come through from Charlotte. I inwardly sigh, not really in the mood for her fast-paced, hyper attitude, but I read them anyway.

Hi!

I just wanted to say I love my nails.

They are so well done.

Already looking forward to my facial next week.

Have fun at your spin class.

If you ever want to meet up for a drink, let me know!

Or not.

No worries.

> Bye!

> Charlotte xx

My eyebrows rise at the fact that she remembered I was going to a spin class this evening. I rattle off a quick text back to her.

> Hi, Charlotte. I'm so pleased you love your nails. See you next week! Amelia xx

Perhaps it's rude of me to ignore the comment she made about going for a drink, but the thing is, I don't make a habit of meeting up with clients for drinks or dinner or socialising. Sally is the only one whom I've broken that rule for. It's not that I don't like my clients and don't want to hang out with them outside of work, but most of them don't offer, especially so quickly after first meeting me.

Charlotte seems perfectly nice, but her comment about Noah is still niggling the back of my mind like an annoying, itchy insect bite, despite Noah's response of not recognising her name. Plus, she seems overly forward. That's not a bad thing, but I don't want to give her the wrong impression either. She freaked me out earlier. Maybe she has ADHD, or something like that. I have a couple of clients with mental health conditions, and I've worked with elderly clients with dementia in the past.

I know all too well how severely mental health can affect a person's life...

I brush away the memories of my mother, determined not to let them overwhelm me, like they tend to do, especially when I'm feeling low. It was a long time ago, and the stigma of mental health has changed a lot since then.

Charlotte responds with a thumbs-up emoji. I leave it at that.

Noah has cooked a delicious meal, so we sit at the table that doubles as a kitchen island, perched on the breakfast stools. He's got a beer bottle open.

'You want a wine?' he asks.

'No, thanks,' I reply, even though I could do with one.

We start eating.

'I'm sorry about earlier when I got home,' says Noah, picking up his cutlery. 'There was a particularly nasty incident involving a prisoner, and it... Well, it rattled me a bit. I got home from work at three and then just went for a long walk to clear my head. I guess it didn't really help.'

'I'm sorry you had a bad day. What happened with the prisoner?' I ask.

'He, uh... made some crude comments, and it kind of got under my skin a little bit.' Noah looks down at his plate of food, takes a sip from his beer.

My stomach flips. 'What kind of comments? Were they directed at you personally?'

'Yes, sort of. I just...' He pauses for a moment. '...took it the wrong way. That's all. They mentioned you.'

At this, alarm bells ring in my ears as I remember the texts I've received over the past two days. 'Me? In what way?'

'They... made horrible remarks about how you shouldn't be with a guy like me, how you should be with a real man. That sort of thing. It's a power play. Happens all the time.'

'Oh... I'm sorry.'

Noah avoids eye contact.

'Do you think they've got hold of my number somehow?'

Noah frowns, looking up at me. 'God, no. Nothing like that. Why do you ask?'

'I, uh... I've had a couple of weird texts. Yesterday, and then another today.'

'You have? From whom?'

'An unknown number.'

'Let me see.' He holds his hand out for me to give him my phone. I reach into my pocket and pull it out, scrolling to the first message I received.

'This is the first one. I deleted and blocked the second.'

He looks at the screen for a moment, says nothing. 'I don't think this is related to what happened today.'

'It's probably nothing, though, right?'

Noah shakes his head as he hands me back my phone. 'Maybe, but you can never be too careful. Are you okay?'

I smile, comforted that we're finally back onto the same page. Talking. This is why couples should communicate more and not hide things. Talking to Noah has already alleviated some of the tension, although the fact that a prisoner has made such horrible remarks upsets me. 'Yes, I'm fine,' I say, as I reach across the table and squeeze his hand. 'Are you okay?'

He leans over and kisses me lightly on the lips. 'Yes. It was just a prisoner trying to rile me up. Won't happen again.'

Noah can be very sensitive when it comes to his sexual abilities. We've had some issues in the past where he couldn't perform as well as he liked, leaving him feeling humiliated and unwilling to try again, but the last time we had sex, it was great and there were no problems. We've been going through a bit of a dry spell. It's not like I'm up for it every night of the week, but usually he is. Or he was, up until a month or so ago.

I've put it down to the stress, late nights and early mornings, but even I know that an engaged couple going through a dry spell is never a good sign. Every time I try to touch him, he sighs and says he's tired, or flinches and pulls away, so for the past couple of weeks, I haven't attempted anything. I was hoping that by giving him space, he'd find his way back to me, but all it's done is separate us further.

'I love you,' he whispers as he pulls away.

'Love you too.'

'I was thinking,' he says, going back to his food, a slightly chirpier tone to his voice, 'we should nail down the hen and stag dos soon, like you mentioned yesterday. What do you think? I know we may move, but I think it's important we stay focused on the wedding.'

I do my best to hide my shock. 'Sure,' I say. 'But until we know whether we are actually moving, we can't really make any further big decisions, especially if the wedding is likely to be postponed.'

'Who said anything about postponing the wedding?'

Shit. That came out wrong.

'Sorry, no. I didn't mean we should postpone it. I'm just saying that if we move, we may have to change the venue, and we may not be able to get that exact date.'

Noah looks as if I've just stolen his puppy. 'This is all my fault,' he whispers.

'No! You're getting a promotion. It's a big deal,' I say, jumping off my seat and moving to his side. I wrap my arms around his shoulders, but he doesn't adjust his posture to envelop me in a hug.

'All I'm saying is that until we know more, we should hold off on booking things, in case we need to change the date, okay? I am in no way saying we should cancel or postpone the wedding right now.'

'Okay,' he says quietly. I move away from him. He picks up his beer and takes a drink.

Things seem to have gone from bad to worse. Now, he's clammed up completely.

CHAPTER NINE

NOAH

Oh God. Everything is running away from me like a bullet train, and I can't keep up. To keep Mills happy and distracted, I thought I'd suggest planning the hen do, but it backfired massively. She wants to postpone the wedding. I know she does. Hell, I want to *cancel* the wedding. It would be easier for everyone if we did.

I'm a horrible person. A useless, pathetic excuse of a man, but if Mills really did leave me, or if I left her, I'd have nothing to live for. Even though she'd be better off without me, I can't let her go. I'm selfish. I know that.

There's so much going on at work that I can't afford to drop the ball. Rob has mentioned I should take some time off to get myself straightened out, but I can't. Not now. I need to be there to keep an eye on things. I need to stay busy. If I'm at home, I'll sit and fester and get in Mills' way. I don't want to be around when she has clients over. It's not a professional look if someone visits her for a massage and sees her lazy fiancé lounging around on the sofa. She's been on and on at me that she wants me to meet one of her clients, Sally, and her husband – what's-his-name – but I honestly can't deal with fake smiles and idle chitchat.

Plus, now Mills has had a weird, threatening text sent to her, similar to the ones I've been getting. It has to be related, which means I know exactly who it is who's sending them. And that scares the crap out of me because I don't know what's going to happen next, or whether I can keep everything under control.

When Mills asked me just before we went to the gym if I knew a girl called Charlotte Whitmoore while I was studying at Lancaster University, my heart almost stopped. I did know a girl called Charlotte back then, or Charlie, as she preferred to be called, but her last name wasn't Whitmoore. It was Kennedy. Obviously, it's easy enough to change a name nowadays.

I haven't thought about Charlie in a long time. An ex-girlfriend whom I wish I'd never got involved with, but we all make mistakes, especially while at university. We didn't end on good terms, and we didn't stay in touch.

But here she is, all these years later. She's tracked me down. I told her to back off a few weeks ago, when she approached me, wanting to make amends and catch up, like nothing ever happened. I didn't handle it well, but now she's befriending Mills, and that is something I need to keep an eye on. As if I haven't got enough problems with controlling women as it is.

That night, to try and keep up appearances, I pull Mills close to my body in bed. I haven't been this close, physically, to her in a long time, but as soon as I feel her body warmth, I realise I've missed her. It's nothing to do with her. I still think she's extremely attractive, from her jet black hair to her long, curvy legs. Her curves and dark skin. She's perfect.

Which is why I feel like the worst man alive as I hold her in bed, breathing gently on her neck as she falls asleep.

'I'm sorry, Mills,' I whisper in her ear. 'I'm so sorry.'

CHAPTER TEN

Noah and I don't have sex that night, and the air is still full of weird tension when we do go to bed, but he surprises me by reaching over and pulling me close, cuddling when we get under the covers. It's perfect. It's not a lot, and it hasn't fixed anything, but it's exactly what I need right now, and I think he feels the same way. We sink in each other's bodies, and I fall asleep to his gentle breath on the back of my neck.

There's still a lot of questions floating around in my head that I'm dying to set free, but I don't want to push Noah into telling me. Not until he's ready, but annoyingly, my brain won't stop making up crazy scenarios.

Despite me telling my friends that I'm adamant it's not an affair, the thought has crossed my mind on several occasions. It keeps popping up like an unwanted weed, and I don't know why. He's never given me any reason not to trust him when it comes to other women. He mainly works in a male-dominated profession, so it's never been something I've considered.

Once, when we were out for a date, early on in our relationship, he was at the bar ordering our drinks, and a very attractive woman slid onto the stool next to him and started chatting him up. I watched him with a smile across my face as he spoke with her for a few moments, then dealt the fatal blow. Her facial expression dropped into a frown, and she scurried away, throwing a vicious look in my direction as she did so.

He's an attractive man. I'm used to women side-eyeing him as he walks past, but I've never been worried about him acting on it.

But if it's not an affair, then what is it?

He hides his phone screen from me whenever he receives a message and takes his calls out of the room. He's distant and doesn't initiate sex.

I toss and turn all night, finally getting up at five to do some morning yoga in the lounge. I usually attend a class on a Sunday, but some mornings, my body is itching to move and bend and stretch. There's a constant hum or buzz all over me, but as soon as I centre myself and perform some stretches, releasing that outer and inner tension, it seeps away, leaving me feeling ready to take on the day. Whatever it may bring.

Sally is due to arrive at nine for her treatment, and I'm looking forward to seeing her. It's been a while since we've had a proper catch-up.

Noah leaves for work, a little more subdued than he was last night, but still better than when he'd first come back from work yesterday. I wish him a good day, and he gives me a light kiss.

Sally arrives promptly at ten minutes to nine, enough time for us to have a quick natter over a cup of tea before starting her facial. She says she's forty-one, but honestly, she doesn't look a day over thirty-five. She says her skin is stressed and in need of TLC, but it's practically flawless apart from some light congestion around her chin, which can be easily sorted out with today's facial.

Her luscious, long, chestnut-coloured hair could rival a model's. If she wasn't so lovely, I'd be jealous of her. I really must introduce her to Noah, especially as she's my favourite client. I keep meaning to, but either she's working or he's working. The timings just haven't worked out. Maybe I'll suggest meeting for a drink soon. She has a husband too, whom I haven't met yet. I make a mental note to try and arrange a double date.

Sally envelops me in a tight hug when she sees me. 'Looking gorgeous, as always.'

'Thank you. You too! Your hair is amazing.'

'Thanks. I visited the hairdresser's yesterday.' Sally walks straight in, down the hallway and into the kitchen, where there's a brew waiting for her. She's been here loads, and she's one of the only clients whom I happily allow into other areas of my home, and who knows the Wi-Fi code.

'So,' she says, leaning against the counter and picking up the cup, 'how are you? Sorry it's been so long, but...' She stops, lets out a long sigh. 'I've had a bit of stress going on. Old wounds re-opening and all that jazz.'

I take a sip of my tea. 'What's happened?'

'It's a long story, but do you remember me telling you about Aaron?'

'Your stalker?'

'Yes, well, sort of. There's something I never told you about him, and I feel a bit shit telling you now.'

My cup pauses at my lips. I have a feeling that if I took a

sip, I'd be in danger of spitting it out in a matter of seconds. 'Go on...'

'I slept with him.'

I lower my cup. 'You slept with your stalker? When?'

'Like a year ago. I'm not proud of it, and obviously, Hank didn't know at the time, but... Well, he's found out now, hasn't he?' She takes a big slurp of tea.

'Oh gosh. Are you okay? How did he find out?' Usually, I wouldn't be so forward with clients, asking all these personal questions, but it's Sally, and Sally's different. Sally's my friend.

'Aaron turned up at my door a few days ago.'

'No!'

'Blurted it all out, didn't he? Made me look a right fool.'

'I'm so sorry...'

'Anyway, Hank basically told him to fuck off, and now we're in a weird place. He hasn't left me, but something's changed in our relationship. It's my fault. I know it is, but it was a mistake. Everyone makes mistakes, right?'

I nod, but inside I'm thinking about my own relationship. What would I do if I found out Noah really had cheated on me? The thought doesn't bear thinking about, but I'm almost certain I'd end it with him. Trust is a hard thing to get back once it's gone. Even now, Noah is skating on thin ice with me. Something has changed in our relationship. I just don't have any idea what it is yet.

'Has Aaron been back in touch? He used to send you flowers and chocolates, right?' I ask.

'Yeah, and weird text messages too, but no, he hasn't started all that again. If he does, I may have to file for a restraining order against him. Honestly, I'm surprised Hank never noticed all this a year ago.'

'Would you have eventually told him if Aaron hadn't taken the decision out of your hands?'

Sally is quiet for a moment. 'I'm not sure. Is that wrong of me? Do you think I should have told him right at the start, when it happened?'

'Well, I'm sure it would have been better to hear it from you rather than the man himself, but there's nothing you can do about it now. You just have to remind Hank that you love him and he's the only man for you.'

Sally takes a deep breath and finishes her tea. 'You're right. Gosh, it feels good to talk about this with someone. I'm so sorry to burden you with this the minute I step in the door. You must think I'm a horrible person for cheating on Hank.' Tears flood her eyes, but she manages to hold them back.

I step forward, place my cup down and give her a quick hug. 'Don't be too hard on yourself. Like you said, everyone makes mistakes. Right, come on, let's go and start the treatment, and you can completely relax for a bit, yeah?'

'Sounds perfect. Thank you for being so nice.'

'What are friends for?'

Sally gives me a weak smile and then follows me into the treatment room.

I start her facial by giving her skin a deep cleanse. I thought she'd settle into a relaxing trance, staying quiet, but it seems she wants to talk more. But luckily, not about her affair. I listen quietly and respond when I need to, but deep down inside, I'm silently judging her, and I feel bad for doing so.

I remember, not long after I started seeing her as a client, she told me about Aaron, her stalker. We didn't know each other as well back then, so I admit I was slightly astounded by what she was telling me, but she went into detail about what Aaron, a guy from work, was doing and saying to her, all the while knowing she was a married woman.

She told me she liked the attention at first, something she wasn't getting from her husband, but then Aaron turned too full-on, and it scared her. I had no idea it went as far as her sleeping with him though. I expect it gave him the wrong impression, but then again, she wasn't getting the attention from her husband, so...

I try to put myself in her shoes. In a way, I am. Yes, Noah still talks to me, but up until last night, he's barely shown any sort of affection for a long time. It's enough to make me wonder if he's got bored with me. But then last night he goes and throws everything out the window and suggests planning the hen do and stag do, taking it badly when I say I'd rather wait and see what happens with his job. It feels as if I'm on a rollercoaster. One thing I know for sure is, even if Noah continues to be distant, I will never cheat on him. If I felt that our relationship was in that much trouble, that I no longer loved him, then I'd tell him, and we could work through it.

Sally settles into a relaxed silence as I put the deep moisturising face mask on, so I allow her to enjoy the moment as I work on releasing the tension in her shoulders, then perform a head massage while the face mask does its job.

When I peel it off, she lets out a long sigh. 'That was so good, Milly. Oh, how is Noah? You said last time we spoke that he was acting strangely.'

She's right. I haven't properly spoken to her since just after Noah started acting oddly, roughly three weeks ago. I told her that he came back home from work, refused to speak to me, and then went and stayed with his parents for a few days.

'Oh, yes. Well, to be perfectly honest, he has still been acting oddly. Just when I think we've turned a corner, something else happens, but he has had some good news. He got a promotion and will be attending a course soon. Rob, his boss, may even look at giving him his own job, but it's early days yet. If he doesn't get Rob's job, then there's the possibility that he may have to move prisons.'

'Oh, that's wonderful news about his promotion. But oh, please don't move away! I'd miss you so much.'

'Nothing's set in stone yet.'

'Good. Sorry, I know it's wonderful about his promotion, but what about your work? Your business? You'd have to start all over again.'

I sigh. 'Can I tell you a secret?'

'Of course!' She looks up at me from where she is lying on the couch.

I stand so she can see me. 'I'm happy about his promotion, but I really don't want to move again. I'm settled here. Our wedding is booked in a local church and hotel, and I love Cambridge. I've missed Portsmouth, but I'm finally feeling happy and settled, or at least I was until... I feel like Noah is pulling away from me, and I'm struggling to make sense of any of it.'

There's more I could tell her, but I'm not exactly being professional right now by telling her all of this while she's trying to relax.

'Oh, Milly,' she says, reaching for my arm and squeezing it. 'Sometimes these things happen for a reason. That's what I believe. Is there anything else going on? I feel like you're not telling me everything.'

I shake my head. 'No. I'm just not sure how to tell Noah that I really don't want to move. I'm just hoping against hope that he gets Rob's job.'

There's no need to tell her everything else with regard to Charlotte and the texts. In fact, since she's been here and we've been talking, I've barely given them a thought.

TWENTY MINUTES LATER, I say goodbye to Sally at the door, then return to the treatment room and prepare the couch and area for my next client, who is due in thirty minutes. I change the aromas in the room from lavender to juniper berry (because my next client prefers it) and quickly check my phone.

There are dozens of missed calls and messages from Charlotte.

Time seems to stand still as I stare at the screen, flicking through her numerous texts, which get increasingly desperate. There's even one in full capital letters that says CALL ME and HELP!

My heart rate shoots up as I consider what could possibly be wrong. Why would Charlotte call me? A woman she's only met once. I'm not a friend. If she's in danger or needs help, why hasn't she called someone else? A close friend. The police?

My eyes glance at the clock. I have time. I'm not a mean person. She'll see that I've opened her WhatsApp messages, so I can't pretend I haven't seen them.

I start typing out a message, but as I do, the phone springs to life in my hand and her name appears on the screen.

I accept the call. 'Charlotte? What's wrong? Are you okay?'

CHAPTER ELEVEN

Her high-pitched voice deafens me as it blasts through the phone. It's such a shock that I move the phone away from my ear for a moment. 'Amelia! Thank God! I'm so, so sorry to have called you. I didn't know who else to call. I shouldn't have called. I'm so sorry. You know what, never mind. I shouldn't have called—'

'What's happened? Are you hurt?' My heart hammers in my chest, my mind swimming with the possibility of having to phone the police or an ambulance. But I still can't imagine why she'd call me. Doesn't she have anyone else she can call whom she knows better?

'I'm not hurt. No. I was out for a walk with Jo-Jo, the dog I walk on Wednesday mornings, and I decided to take her to a different park today, but I had to take the bus. Her owner is fine with it. Jo-Jo loves the bus. Anyway, I get off the bus and we do our walk, and then I go to get back on the bus, and I can't find my purse with my ticket inside. It's gone. I've looked everywhere. I must have left it on the bus. I'm miles out of town and have no money for the bus, or an Uber, or anything. Jo-Jo can't walk that far. She's only little, and she's a bit too heavy for me to carry the whole way back. What do I do?'

She rattles off the words so quickly, it's a struggle to keep up, but I get the gist. I take a breath myself because her panic is sending my own nerves rattling. I've been known to be calm in the face of stress and turmoil, but this, on top of everything else, is enough to derail me.

'Okay, first of all, just take a deep breath for me, okay?' I hear her on the other end suck in a breath and then let it out. 'Right. Is there anyone else you know who lives nearby?' I ask.

There's a long pause on the end of the line. 'No, no one. I panicked and just called you because you were the first person who popped into my head. I'm sorry. I shouldn't have called...'

'No. Please. It's fine. I want to try and help. Whereabouts are you?' While I'm flattered that she thought of me first, my initial question still stands. Why me? I really don't want to have to drive and fetch her, but I can't very well leave her stranded when she's called me for help. It's a little odd and unorthodox, but now she has, I can't turn around and say no and leave her to fend for herself.

'I'm at Rochdale Park.'

Yeesh, that *is* miles out of town. Why the hell would she go all the way out there? She said she was visiting a different park, but it seems a bit strange that she'd catch a bus to get there when there are several other parks to choose from in Cambridge, all within walking distance and just as nice as Rochdale Park. I really don't have time for this, but I'm not sure what else I can suggest.

'Okay, I can come and get you in about half an hour. I

have a quick eyebrow wax in fifteen minutes, which only takes a few minutes to do, then I'll leave straight after that.'

'Oh! Oh, thank you. Thank you so much. Um, I'll walk Jo-Jo for a bit longer and then wait by the entrance.'

'I'll be as quick as I can and give you a text when I'm—'

'Oh!' Charlotte's squeal deafens me again. I lean away from the phone for a second, then hold it back to my ear. 'Shit, I am so, so sorry. I've just realised I never even brought my purse. I put my debit card and the ticket in my back pocket. I've just found it. Oh my God, I'm so fucking stupid. I'm so sorry to have bothered you. I do this sometimes. I forget things.'

It feels as if I have whiplash. My heart rate settles down, and I'm quietly relieved that I don't have to traipse across Cambridge to go and fetch her after all, but I'm blindsided by her sudden change of pace.

'That's okay,' I answer with a sigh. 'It happens to all of us. I'm glad you've found your ticket.'

'I'm so stupid. Stupid.' Charlotte mutters incoherently; most of the words I struggle to pick up. 'Bye, Amelia. Bye. Sorry. Bye.' She hangs up.

I stare at the phone in my hand, frowning. Charlotte certainly is a little scatty, but I've been in the same situation before. Once, I could have sworn I packed an important letter into my bag, ready to post after work, but when I arrived at the post office, it wasn't there. I searched my car and even called some of my clients I'd seen that day to check if I'd left it at their houses, but upon returning home, it was there on the countertop, ready to be packed into my bag. I hadn't even been in a hurry.

It happens.

I'm about to put the whole situation behind me when my

phone lights up with text after text from Charlotte. Ping. Ping. Ping.

> God, I'm so sorry.

> Silly me!

> Sorry again.

> Thanks though.

> Jo-Jo is very happy she doesn't have to walk home.

Following the messages, a photo appears of Charlotte kneeling next to a bulldog. I can't help but smile at the cute duo. I send her a message to tell her not to worry about it and to have a good day. Charlotte responds with a heart emoji.

I put down my phone just as another message appears. 'Bloody hell,' I mutter as I look at the screen, but as soon as I do, my frustration is replaced by fear. My blood runs cold, and I feel as if I've been slapped across the face.

It's another text from an unknown number.

It must be from another different phone because I blocked the previous number.

> Keep quiet, or you'll pay, Bitch.

What the hell? Keep quiet. Keep quiet about what? It must be a wrong number. There's no other explanation. Whoever it is must have realised I blocked them, and now they have a new number they can use to contact me. If I don't correct them, this will keep happening. Again and again. I can't deal with this. I have enough going on. I don't need the sporadic arrival of threatening messages appearing and derailing my life.

My fingers tremble as I type a short message.

> Who is this? I think you have the wrong number.

I press send and hold my breath. The fact that the texts have come through via direct text message rather than WhatsApp is weird too. Who doesn't have WhatsApp these days? I very rarely use text messages, even though I have an unlimited amount included in my phone contract. Gone are the days when I'd have to top up my phone to be able to send texts and make calls.

My phone flashes with a notification.

Message not sent.

I try again.

Message not sent.

The message came through only seconds ago, yet now I can't send one back. They must have blocked my number.

My thoughts spiral back to what Noah told me last night about the prisoner who upset him by using me as a catalyst. Noah told me the messages I've received wouldn't have anything to do with that because there's no way a prisoner would be able to get hold of my contact details. Noah says that prison officers always ensure they never speak about their private lives in earshot of the prisoners, yet somehow this prisoner knew about me.

The likelihood of these messages being related to that incident is slim.

I decide not to delete and block this message this time. I'll show it to Noah later. Maybe he knows how to trace the message or something. Talk about a stressful morning already. I don't have time to dwell on this message any longer. My next client is due any minute, and I need to finish tidying the treatment room. Thanks to Charlotte's unexpected and frantic phone call, I'm running behind again, and now I'm on edge thanks to the text.

Fat lot of good my early morning yoga session did. I don't know why I bother lately.

My life is turning into one giant stress ball of anxiety, and I'm finding it a struggle to keep myself grounded.

LUCKILY, for the rest of the day, everything runs smoothly. My clients are all on time. The traffic is kind to me, apart from one small road closure, which forces me to park further down the road than usual and walk up to the client's house, but luckily, I don't have a lot to carry, and I make it to all my clients' houses on time.

I end the day with an easy eyebrow wax for my next-door neighbour. I say *next door*. She lives on the bottom floor of the block of flats, but it's close enough. We always say hi whenever we see each other in passing. I get a lot of business from the residents of my building, thanks to Sally's ingenious idea of slipping my business card into every mail slot when I first moved in.

At quarter past seven, I say goodbye to my last client and head to the lift. While I wait for it, I take a scroll on Facebook, as I've had several notifications pop up throughout the course of the day, but haven't stopped to check them. To be honest, I rarely have time for Facebook or social media. Personally, it's not really my thing, but I can see the appeal and have made a business page on both Facebook and Instagram. I've left making the TikTok videos to the younger generation. As a proud Millennial, I'm happy to say that none of my antics from my younger days are streamed live on social media or posted online for the world to see. I don't have any personal social media accounts, only business ones, but I do follow all my friends and acquaintances from those accounts.

As soon as I open the app, I see my best friend Zoe's lovely smiling face in a photo with a woman next to her, planting a kiss on her cheek. It's a cute selfie. I assume the other woman is her new girlfriend, but as I look at it, a weird, uneasy feeling flutters in my stomach.

The woman.

She's tagged as Charlie Wilson.

Her hair is different, and her eye colour is different, but facially she looks awfully like Charlotte. Surely not...

Ping!

The lift doors open before me, but I don't step forward. I stay rooted to the spot, staring at the photograph of Zoe and Charlie, who is side-on in the picture, but her left eye is facing towards the camera.

Charlotte's last name is Whitmoore. Similar to Wilson. Charlie is usually short for Charlotte. If they are the same person, then why does Charlie have long, dark hair and blue eyes, whereas Charlotte has short blonde hair and dark eyes? Granted, it's easy enough to change appearances these days with contacts and wigs. Hell, maybe she has an identical twin.

But none of those reasons answers the main question that's flashing before my eyes.

Why?

The lift doors ping closed.

I don't re-press the button. I need to find out what's going on. Quickly remembering the photo Charlotte sent earlier of her and Jo-Jo, I bring it up on the screen and then swipe back and forth between the two photos, studying the facial features in each before swiping to the next. The resemblance is uncanny.

Which woman is the real one? Noah may not have recognised the name Charlotte Whitmoore when I told him, but maybe that's because her real name is Charlie Wilson. Perhaps he'd recognise that name if I told him.

But she's dating Zoe... It can't be a coincidence that Charlotte has appeared in my life at the same time as one of my best friends starts dating a new woman. This all must be connected somehow, but my frazzled brain can't seem to put the pieces of the jumbled puzzle together.

Alarm bells ring.

Charlotte can't be trusted. She's not being truthful.

Something's wrong here.

CHAPTER TWELVE

I try in vain to concentrate on the rest of my evening, but it's no use. In the end, when I'm standing at the hob and watching a pot of pasta water boil over, Noah steps up to me and takes the pot off the boil.

'Are you okay?' he asks, as he wipes up the spilled water with a dishcloth.

'Sorry... I've had another weird day.' I've forgotten all about the third message. I was going to tell him about it, but since I've stepped through the door, all I've been able to think about is Charlotte and the fact that she may be using an alias and dating one of my best friends. Not to mention the fact that she may or may not have known Noah while at university. It's time I got to the bottom of this conundrum once and for all.

'Another threatening text?' he asks.

'Yes,' I reply, 'but that's not why I'm distracted today. My new client, Charlotte, called me this morning, freaking out about being stranded, but that ended up being a false alarm.

But then I see a photo of Zoe and her new girlfriend, Charlie Wilson, and they look really similar.'

'Who do?'

'Charlotte and Charlie.'

'Let's see.'

I bring up both photos and show him, studying his facial expressions as he leans in. He looks at each one for a few seconds before scrolling over to the other.

'Hmm, yeah, I see what you mean.'

'Do you think they're the same person?'

Noah hands me back my phone. 'I can see the similarities, but their hair and eyes are different. I don't think they're the same. Just a random coincidence that they have similar-sounding names.'

I bite my bottom lip as I bend and take out two plates from the cupboard, keeping quiet about the fact that women can easily change appearances. Setting the plates on the worktop, I turn around and face Noah, who now looks a little pale.

'Are you sure you didn't know anyone called Charlotte while you were at Lancaster uni? What about Charlie Wilson?' I ask, taking his paleness to mean he's nervous.

'No, I didn't. Why do you keep on about it?'

His abrupt tone and defensiveness give me my answer. 'Because I know you're not telling me something!' I snap back.

'What do you want me to say, Mills? I knew a lot of girls at uni. Do I remember all their names? No, of course not. Maybe she *did* know me. Maybe she *was* in one of my classes, but if she was, I don't remember her, okay? Now, can you just drop it, please?'

My fists clench at my sides. I'm still not convinced, but

this argument feels like it will go around in circles if I don't back off for now.

'You said you got another text?' Noah asks, leaning back against the worktop. His tone has changed again. It's lighter, calmer. A clear ploy to change the subject.

I sigh and nod, scrolling through my phone again. I open the message, holding it up for him to see. He frowns as he reads it.

'Yes. I tried to send a message back asking who it was, but the message wouldn't send. They can send me messages, but I can't send them any. Plus, I think it's a whole other number from the previous couple I received because I blocked them, yet they are still coming through.'

'It's clearly a wrong number,' he says, turning to the hob and setting the pan back on the heat. He won't look at me.

'Noah... Do you know something?'

'Fucking hell!' He slams his fists down on the counter, making me jump away. 'I've had a bad day, okay? I really don't need this constant questioning from you.'

It feels as if I'm locked in a room with an angry lion. His mood and actions are unpredictable, and his sudden outburst has scared me.

'Fine. I'll back off,' I say. 'But there is something going on with you lately, and whether you want to or not, you're going to have to tell me eventually. If you don't, then...'

At this point, he turns to face me. His eyes are red, slightly watery. 'Then what?'

'Then... what hope is there for us in the future? We're not even married yet, and you're already keeping secrets from me?'

'They aren't secrets. I just don't see why you need to be involved in something that has nothing to do with you.'

'If it's to do with you, then it does involve me, because I'm your future wife, and you're my future husband. We belong together, but if you don't trust me enough to tell me...' I trail off, my own eyes watering.

I can't believe a few minutes ago, I was staring into a pot of pasta water, wondering if my new client is hiding something. Now, Noah and I are on the verge of a cataclysmic turning point in our relationship.

Noah rushes to my side and wraps his arms around me, lifting my feet off the ground in the process. He squeezes me tight.

'I'm sorry,' he says. 'I don't know why this has all got out of hand so fast. I'm dealing with it, okay? You don't have to worry about me. I'm doing my best.'

'I'm sure you are,' I say into the crook of his neck. He releases the pressure around my body, and my feet touch back to the ground. 'Just... whatever it is, if it's bad, you can tell me, and it won't change how I feel about you.'

Noah nods. 'I'll tell you soon,' he says.

I smile, but inside I'm screaming.

I don't believe him. And this is the first time I've realised that maybe Noah and I aren't meant to be together. He's pushing me further away with every passing day. All I want is for him to open up to me, but he refuses.

'What should I do about the text?' I ask, deciding to change tack. I don't have the strength or energy to carry on with our discussion.

He gulps. 'If it keeps happening, then you can always change your number.'

I let out a long sigh. 'That would be very detrimental to my business.'

Noah doesn't respond. 'I mean, it's clearly a wrong

number,' he says again. 'I'm sure eventually they'll get bored or realise that and move on.'

He then changes the subject to a funny story that Rob told him earlier today.

And that's the end of that.

We spend the rest of the evening together, watching Netflix and having a nice dinner, acting like our previous argument is all forgotten, but underneath the happy, relaxed exterior of our body language, where he lets me drape my bare legs over his lap, I know both of us are hiding something.

There's a lot of unspoken words, but neither of us knows how to say them.

THE NEXT MORNING, I have time to chill before my first client of the day, so I spend it catching up on housework and business admin while listening to one of my more cheerful playlists on *Spotify*. Something upbeat that I usually dance and shimmy to, but today I'm not in a dancing and shimmying sort of mood, so I allow the music to play, all the while knowing that no amount of catchy tunes will heal the hole that's opening up in my heart.

Once I've wiped the kitchen surfaces and run the hoover around the carpeted areas, I open my laptop, turn it on and sip my coffee while I wait for it to boot up. I need to update my Facebook business page and add some pictures, so I choose some recent photos of pretty clients' nails (taken with their permission), click upload, and navigate to the reviews that have appeared overnight.

I hate asking my clients to leave reviews, but it does help to make my page appear more professional to anyone who happens to come across it. I try and share my business page in local Facebook groups, but I hate doing it because I then get a bunch of spam comments or stupid questions in my inbox, like, "Can you travel to London?" No, I most certainly can't travel to London, considering it would cost me more than I'd charge to get there. Also, I make it very clear that I only see clients in and around Cambridge, a maximum of a five-mile radius.

I smile as I read a new review from Wilma. I didn't even ask her for one, but then my eyes are drawn to another new one, a one-star review.

I'm proud to say that every other review on my page is five stars. I don't pretend that my work is perfect, but I've never had complaints before. Well, not since that time with a client a few years ago who refused to pay, but that was before I worked for myself. As far as I can remember, I've not had any complaints from clients recently.

The review is brutal.

Do not go to this woman! She's rude, and her work is atrocious. A blind monkey could do a better job. My nails look like they'd been butchered. Do not recommend! Don't believe all these 5-star reviews. She clearly pays people to write them, or forces her friends and family to post fake reviews to boost her online presence. Stay clear of this Bitch!

The person has set their profile to anonymous.

My throat constricts and my pulse skyrockets.

I gasp, attempting to suck in a breath, but nothing happens. It feels as if I've been viciously and personally attacked. Who would say such a thing? Not one client I've interacted with has been any trouble. Is this just a troll who enjoys leaving anonymous reviews on business profiles for a laugh? I know they exist. My friend, Georgina, has had her fair share of trolls leaving horrible comments on her posts and sliding into her DMs, telling her to kill herself. She doesn't even know them.

This has to be what this is...

Unless...

Wait. Two months ago, I did have a new client – Gemma – who came to me for a manicure. She was very specific about what she wanted and wasn't as thrilled as my other clients at the result, but she smiled, and paid, and left without any fuss. She never made a second appointment.

If this is her, then why leave the review now, two months later, and not straight afterwards?

Then, another thought occurs to me as I read it and reach the end.

The word *bitch* jumps out at me.

Exactly the word used in the threatening text messages I've been getting.

Even the B is capitalised.

They've now moved on to trying to destroy my professional reputation and business.

I look for the delete and block button and press it, feeling a little better that the horrible review is now gone, but then I wonder if deleting it sends the right message. It makes me look guilty, like I'm trying to pretend that I'm perfect and can't take a bit of bad publicity.

I let out a long groan and rub my tired eyes. The stress of the past couple of days is grating on my nerves and I just want it all to stop.

Just stop.

I'm not sure how much more I can take until my mind starts breaking down on me completely. Tears bubble behind my eyes, but I take a deep breath, close my laptop, and walk away before they can escape.

AN HOUR LATER, I leave for work. For the first time in a long time, I don't want to talk to people. I don't want to slap a smile on my face and tell my clients how I am and ask them how they are. I don't care. I'm not okay. The bad review has rattled me more than it would have done if it had been an isolated incident.

As I reach my parking spot in the underground car park for the residents of the building, I check for another flat tyre. They are all fine, and a wave of relief washes over me. My heart is pounding as I slide into the front seat and check my phone.

No new messages.

I'm being paranoid now, expecting more texts to appear.

The radio blares at full volume as soon as the engine starts, not only making me jump but frightening the life out of me. I hastily turn it down and take a breath. I don't remember having it set so high the last time I was in the car.

What is going on with me right now?

My phone lights up, signalling an Instagram notification. I click on it, expecting to see one of my friends tagging me in a funny meme or a cute reel, but what appears on my screen instead is a direct message from an account I don't follow, asking if I'd like to be part of their new brand ambassador deal for jewellery, despite my profile clearly being about beauty therapy treatments and products. These types of messages annoy the hell out of me, and I instantly block and delete it, knowing full well two more of the same are likely to spring up again.

Just as I'm about to put away my phone, a photo message appears from a private number. I'm so used to receiving photos via WhatsApp that receiving one via text takes me back to the early 2000s. There's no message along with it. Not yet.

Just a blurry but instantly recognisable photo of...

Me.

My hands shake as I pinch the screen, zooming in.

It's definitely me. There's no doubt about it. I'm wearing my black work uniform, carrying my red shoulder bag, and I have my hair tied back in a loose ponytail. It must have been taken yesterday.

Then, while I'm staring at my photo, a message pops into the thread.

I'm watching you, Bitch.

A small squeak combined with a gasp escapes my mouth, and tears well up in my eyes.

This means that whoever is sending me these anonymous messages doesn't have the wrong number at all. They *are* targeting me directly. This is proof, along with the bad Facebook review. There's no doubt about it anymore. I can't get away with ignoring it, pushing it to the back of my mind. This person is threatening me, watching me from afar.

But why? It doesn't make any sense. I've never done anything to anyone. I'm not one for confrontation either. I hate it. It makes me break out in a cold sweat and my mouth go bone dry, yet this person clearly has something against me. They want to unsettle me with these messages, and now, they've made it clear that they want me to know they are watching me.

This has turned from confusing and creepy to downright scary and threatening.

I call Noah straight away. I know we're having problems lately, but he's the only person I want to speak to when I'm feeling this flustered and scared. He's at work, though, so I don't expect him to pick up. Prison officers aren't allowed their phones during shifts, not while they are working with the prisoners, but I call him anyway to distract myself. I leave a quick message, asking him to call me as soon as he gets this message, and then hang up before placing my phone in the cubby hole by the dashboard.

I don't even want to look at it.

Every time I do, my anxiety spikes.

The dashboard clock shows me I'm running late and, thanks to the traffic, I'm likely to not make it to my next client on time. I drive out of the car park, tears brimming in my eyes, scanning left and right, as if I'm expecting someone to be standing there, watching me with a pair of binoculars.

Because, for all I know, they are.

PART 2

CHAPTER THIRTEEN

NOAH

This cannot be happening. She has not only tracked me down, but she's now targeting my fiancée, coming into my home, pretending to be a new client. Why? What could she possibly want from me all these years later? As if I don't have enough to deal with, now I have Charlie stalking Mills. She wouldn't do anything dangerous, though, surely? She was never like that. She just enjoyed scaring people – mainly me. Only me. Everything was always about me, but now she's turned her attention to Mills.

I can't go through all that again. I'm barely keeping my head above water as it is. I know I should tell Mills the truth about Charlie, but that will mean everything I've worked so hard to bury in my past will rise to the surface again. I'm not ready for it.

I'm trying to convince myself that Mills is safe before I tell her about me going away for the week. She's not going to take it well. She's never been great at being by herself. No, that's not fair to her. She's more than capable of being by herself, but she tends to overreact to things and situations that she can't immediately explain.

Once, she thought Georgina, one of her best friends, was ignoring her because she didn't reply to any of her messages for three days. Turns out, Georgina broke her phone while she was on holiday and didn't reply to Mills' messages, or anyone else's. But Mills took it personally. She's like that though. Takes things too personally, thinks it's all about her.

I know that whatever these messages are that she's getting isn't about her, but I can't tell her because it will open a box of worms that I'm not ready to face. I'm not capable of handling it. Despite the morbid reason I have to leave for the week, I'm actually looking forward to getting away from here, away from work, away from everything, even Mills.

Last night, we were dangerously close to breaking up. I could feel it. That's why I ran to her and tried to make her believe me. I told her I would tell her soon, but that's not true. There's no way in hell I can ever tell her, and I'll do anything to keep it from her. Anything.

The more I'm around her, the harder it is to keep my secret. Every time I walk into the room, she's immediately on my case about something. I just want her to back the hell off. Give me some space to breathe, to sort my head out, but why would she? Mills doesn't know about my past, about who I was, what I almost did. She may know a little bit, but I've never shared the full story. I'm sure she keeps secrets from me too. Everyone does. No couple is one hundred percent honest with each other. If they were, then they wouldn't be a couple for very long. It's human nature to conceal things that may make us look bad.

I'm almost ready to leave work to return home and tell her the news about my dad. I'm sure she's going to want to come with me, support me during a troubling time, but I don't want her there. She'll be better off staying home. I hope she'll be okay for a few days while I sort this mess out. Maybe some distance between us both physically and mentally will do us the world of good.

My phone rings while it's in my hand. I stare at the screen. This time, it isn't Mills. She left me a voicemail, but I haven't checked it yet. I can't bring myself to call her back.

It's a private number.

I close my eyes, press accept, and hold it to my ear.

'Noah, I hope you haven't forgotten our little deal,' says the eerie voice of the person who's ruined my life.

'No, I haven't forgotten, but I have to leave for a few days. I'll be back as soon as I can.'

'The clock is ticking.'

I pause for a moment before asking the next question. 'Are you the one messaging Mills?'

'I have no idea what you're talking about. I don't care about your precious fiancée.'

There's no guarantee that they are telling me the truth. They never have before. 'B-But... Please...' Tears threaten to leak from my eyes while they're still closed, but I hold them back. I haven't cried yet. Not properly. If I start, there's a high chance they may never end. I'll cry until I'm dead. 'Just... stop,' I whisper.

'I'll stop when you give me what I want. Tick tock.'

The line goes dead.

I hang up, then rush to the nearest toilet cubicle and vomit into the bowl. I suck in several deep breaths as the last of the retching comes to an end.

I've never felt more alone in my entire life.

It needs to stop. I just want everything to fucking stop.

CHAPTER FOURTEEN

Noah doesn't call me back all day, which leads me to believe he hasn't had a chance to check his phone yet, because I know he'd call me if he heard my frantic messages. He always does. The tone and pitch of my voice alone on the voicemail would have been enough for him to call me straight away.

But today my phone remains silent. Like the grave.

I do check it in between client treatments and driving around, but he doesn't call, and no new messages pop up, not even from Charlotte. Not that I'm expecting her to text me.

My mind is so fixated on the photo, the messages, and the whole Charlotte/Charlie thing that I overrun with a massage because I'm not keeping an eye on the time. It's throwing everything off, and I have so many things buzzing around my brain that I can't work out which one to focus on and worry about more.

Should I be more concerned that I'm being followed by a deranged person who has a vendetta against me, or that

Charlotte could be Zoe's new girlfriend, and she also knew Noah from their university days?

Should I be more worried about the scathing bad review against my business and profession, or the fact that I'm being threatened via text message?

Should I be more focused on finding out what's going on with Noah, or getting to the bottom of who is doing all of this to me?

It's too much!

I'm out of breath merely thinking about everything, constantly trying to calm my heart rate, but failing. I've never suffered with anxiety before, but now I know how it feels. Hayley, one of my best friends, has anxiety, and some days she can't face stepping outside her front door to speak to people. That's how I feel right now. I don't want to be outside. I want to be locked away somewhere, where I know I'm safe, but is anyone ever really safe?

I'm late to all my clients, and I can't stop to chat or have a cup of tea because I'm constantly trying to play catch-up. I get asked several times if I'm all right, but I can't tell them the truth. If I was seeing Sally again, then maybe I'd tell her, especially since she has experience with a stalker.

Someone *is* stalking me.

It's a big word, a huge leap, but this is what this is.

I get the feeling that whoever it is, I've wronged some-how, somewhere along the line, and they are getting their revenge by making me feel afraid, but I still have no idea who it could be, other than possibly the client from a couple of months ago, who left the bad review. Or Charlotte. But the more I think about it, the more I disagree with that option because Charlotte is perfectly nice to me. I know people can be two-faced, but I only met her for the first time two days ago.

But then… if she does know Noah from years ago, then why not tell me?

Urgg. I can't deal with this. I hate the not knowing. It's bad enough Noah is keeping secrets from me.

By the time I pull into my parking spot, my head is thumping. I haven't stopped to eat or drink today. I sigh and rub my eyes, hoping to alleviate some of the pain and tension behind them. The bottle of water in the car I always keep filled is wedged in the car door, so I pick it up and drain the entire thing without stopping to breathe. The water is warm and stagnant, but it instantly helps me feel better, my mouth and throat a little less dry and scratchy. I stuff the empty bottle into my bag to refill it later and get out, locking the car behind me.

I begin a slow walk towards the lifts. Noah and I have two parking spaces in the building's underground car park, but his car isn't there. That's odd. It's gone eight in the evening. He should have been home by now.

There's still no word from him on my phone.

Something's wrong.

The lift is ahead of me, so I increase my pace, then glance over my shoulder as a noise comes from behind me. Are they here now? Watching me?

Footsteps sound.

I break into a jog, my eyes trained on the lift doors.

'Hey!'

I spin around, my heart practically trying to leap out of my mouth as a man's voice booms. He's jogging towards me, holding something in his hand.

'You dropped this,' he says.

I glance down at the phone in his hand. It's mine. How did... I could have sworn I put it in my bag, but it must have been resting on my lap as I got out of the car and then dropped to the floor. I didn't even notice. I was too focused on getting into the lift.

'I... Thank you,' I say as I take it with a shaky hand.

'No worries. Take care.'

The man walks towards his car. I recognise him. He lives in the building, but I have no idea what his name is. He gets into his car as I clutch my phone against my chest. Satisfied that he isn't following me, I head to the lift and press the button, only releasing my breath when I'm safely inside and the doors ping closed.

My set of keys has somehow sunk to the bottom of my bag. I wrestle with my bag, diving a hand inside, rooting around until my fingers touch the metal keyring. I pull the keys out and slide the front door key into the lock. No sooner has the door swung closed behind me than loud and what I can only describe as death metal blasts out of the Echo Dot speaker situated in the main bedroom.

I don't listen to death metal, and I certainly never play music inside at such a high volume. I'd been listening to my upbeat playlist before leaving the house earlier today.

I scream, drop my bag on the floor, and cover my ears with my hands. Leaving my bag and the items that have fallen out on the floor, I rush into the bedroom.

'Alexa, turn off the music!'

It's so loud that the system can't pick up my voice, so I race to the speaker and switch it off with the button. The flat plunges into eerie silence, but my ears continue to ring with the screeching of the vocals from the music. The ache in my head increases as I make my way back to the hallway, where my bag is lying on the floor. I scoop up the contents and traipse into the kitchen, walking straight to where we keep the medicine. I pop a couple of pills and down another glass of water. The water threatens to come back up.

My nerves are well and truly shot, and I can't stop shaking.

AN HOUR LATER, Noah walks into the flat and finds me with a glass of red wine in my hand on the sofa, and my feet tucked up underneath me. The second he sees me, he asks. 'Rough day?'

'You could say that,' I mumble. My headache hasn't gone completely; the lingering dull pain is still gnawing behind my eyeballs. I'm not quite sure why I thought I'd crack open a bottle of wine on a workday evening (something I never do), but here I am, the bottle half empty already.

'My mum called me today. Dad's sick. She needs my help for a few days.'

Rather than staying and explaining further, Noah backs away and walks straight out of the lounge and into our bedroom. A few seconds later, I hear drawers opening and closing, and the unmistakable sound of hangers being taken out of the wardrobe.

Frowning, I take my glass with me and stand at the entrance to the bedroom, watching while he packs a suitcase, which is laid out on the bed.

'Oh.' I'm momentarily taken aback. 'I'm so sorry to hear that. What's happened?'

'Pneumonia, Mum thinks. He's in hospital now, but Mum needs me at home to look after all the bloody animals and drive her back and forth from the hospital.'

Noah's mum and dad have five dogs in the house, two ferrets, three parrots, and a snake. Visiting their place is like going to a petting zoo, literally. They live about four hours' drive away up north. Both are quite spritely still, but his dad has never had the best of health; high blood pressure, high cholesterol, and a tendency to pick up chest infections in the colder months. His mum is an animal lover and often adopts stray and unwanted animals from the local shelter, no matter what they are.

I nod, taking a sip from my glass. 'Of course,' I say solemnly.

'Everything okay with you?' he asks. 'Any more texts?'

I stare into my now-empty wine glass. I can't tell him the truth, that someone really is following and messing with me. If I do, then he'll want to stay, and right now, his parents need him more than I do. I can handle myself.

'Did you get another message or not?'

I find myself tensing at his harsh tone and question. The alcohol flowing through my bloodstream is making me a little less amenable than usual, a little more impatient.

'No, I didn't,' I say. 'Did you get my voicemails and messages?'

Noah avoids eye contact, clearly not liking me turning the tables on him. 'Uh, yeah, I saw there was a message or two, but I haven't had time to listen to them.'

'Right. So... you're off to your parents', then.'

'Yes.'

Maybe spending time with his parents will be good for Noah. They know more about his low moods than I do. I should know more, but he's always been close with his mum and dad, always been able to talk to them about anything that's troubling him. I wish he were like that with me. I'm envious of the close relationship he has with them.

'How long do you think you'll be away? What has Rob said about work?'

'Rob's giving me compassionate leave for as long as I need it.'

'That's good,' I respond with a long, drawn-out breath. 'Listen... I am a little concerned about the text messages I've been getting, so I was considering calling the police and making a log of them.' It's the first time I have mentioned contacting the police about the messages, but since now I know I'm being targeted directly, it feels like I should do something more than just talk to Noah. I was mulling it over with my glass of wine before Noah arrived home.

'I don't think that's a good idea,' says Noah.

This stops me in my tracks. 'Why not?'

He looks up from placing some boxer shorts into his suitcase. 'Because they haven't done anything dangerous, have they? You don't even know for sure you're being targeted directly. Do you?'

I haven't filled him in on the photo I received yet, confirming the fact that I am being targeted directly. He's been so standoffish lately that it's making me not want to share details with him. A part of me thinks he wouldn't take it seriously if I did tell him, so I keep it to myself.

'Right. Yeah. You're right. They didn't exactly help the last time, did they?' I'm referring to the inappropriate pictures from my boss's husband at the time. Before I knew who it was, I went to the police about it, asking for advice, and they laughed at me.

Literally laughed in my face.

'Or the time I reported that break-in at our old place,' adds Noah.

We lived in a ground-floor flat. It was all we could afford at the time, and one day we came home from work to find the place ransacked. Someone had forced open the door and taken everything they could grab, including the television and Noah's Xbox. We reported the theft, and a police officer had come out, taken our statements, but nothing ever came of it. It wasn't deemed important enough, which I suppose is fair, especially if the police have actual murders to solve, but it hasn't cemented my faith in them.

I could log these messages and threats with the police, but one of the messages said to keep quiet. I can only assume that means no police. If I did speak to the police, then there's a risk of whoever it is escalating their threats. I've spoken to Noah about it, so maybe I need to be careful what I tell him too.

Noah finishes packing and drags his suitcase to the hall.

'Text me when you get there,' I say. 'I'll be asleep, but I'll see it in the morning. Let me know how your dad is.'

'I will.' He hugs me and squeezes tight before planting a light kiss on my lips. His body is stiff, guarded.

As I watch him walk out of the door, my bottom lip wobbles and my eyes brim with tears.

Why do I get the feeling that he's just walked out of the door, leaving me forever?

CHAPTER FIFTEEN

Deep sleep eludes me yet again, but not only because of everything that happened yesterday with the photo, the jump scare in the car park, and Alexa going all death metal on me, but because Noah isn't lying beside me. Even if he's been distant physically lately, having his still yet warm body next to mine as we sleep always brings me comfort, knowing he's within arm's reach. Now, it feels as if he's further away than he's ever been.

I do get a couple of hours of sleep, but it's light, broken. Cars are outside, their horns beeping. People shouting, walking around in the middle of the night for some unknown reason. Slamming of doors from the neighbours below. Raised voices. I think the couple below us are having relationship issues, not unsimilar to my own, but they also have a newborn baby to add to the mix.

Children were always on the cards for me and Noah one day, but now it seems more like a pipe dream. At this point, if something doesn't change with us, adding a child to our stressful, distant relationship would be like adding fuel to an out-of-control inferno. Some say having a baby fixes a relationship, but I've never believed that. It wouldn't fix anything with us. I've been told many times by my friends that I need to hurry up because I'm not getting any younger. They don't know what's going on behind closed doors with Noah and I, and if he doesn't start trusting me with whatever is going on with him soon, then I fear it may be over.

I don't want it to be over though. I want to stand and fight for our relationship, whatever that looks like, but if he's not willing to fight as well, then I'm in it alone, and that's a scary and lonely place to be. I don't want to spend the rest of my life with a man who shuts down, who keeps secrets from me and who doesn't trust me enough to tell me what's going on.

Eventually, I get up and pace the corridors, holding a cup of coffee that goes cold.

I need to think. About everything. Not just about me and Noah.

I *should* go to the police about everything that's happened. I should... It's what any normal, sane person would do, but what Noah said to me before he left keeps rolling around in my head. 'I don't think that's a good idea.'

This irritates me, to be perfectly honest.

It's not like this person is targeting *him*.

Why *wouldn't* he want the police involved?

It's almost like he's not taking these threats against me seriously, or he knows who it is and doesn't think it's worth telling the police.

My mind can't seem to make sense of anything right now. It feels as if I'm losing who I am in all of this. I'm strong, confident, independent, but whoever this person is who's stalking me is stripping me of my personality, turning me into a weak, scared individual who can't make a simple decision about whether to go to the police or not.

I'm due to leave to visit a client's house in fifteen minutes. Helen is elderly and doesn't drive, so it's easier for me to go to her. Stepping out of the shower, I tiptoe across the tiles and check out my reflection in the mirror. I think I've lost weight. My face is gaunt and tense.

My phone, which is lying on the side by the sink, lights up with an incoming call.

Helen is calling me.

My first thought is that something is wrong. My second thought is that Helen never calls me, so I scoop up the phone as quickly as I can. 'Helen, hi. Everything okay?'

'Hello, Amelia. I am just calling to say that I won't be needing your services any longer. There's no need to come over this morning.'

A cough gets stuck in my throat. 'Um... okay. Is there a reason why–'

'I've found someone else who is closer to me. I'm sure you understand. Take care.'

The line goes dead.

What the...

I lower the phone and rest it on the sink. Helen has been my client since I moved here. She's always been so sweet to me, and even told all her friends about me, some of whom I also see on a regular basis.

There's no logical reason why she'd drop me as a beauty therapist out of the blue. She's found someone who lives closer? It makes no sense. She knows it's never been a problem for me to drive to hers. I happily do it, so she doesn't have to worry.

The way she spoke to me was off too. Harsh. Direct. Normally, she's upbeat and chatty and goes off on random tangents, telling me about her grandchildren and how precious they are, or gossiping about the local Ladies That Lunch group she attends on a Tuesday afternoon. I want to phone her back, get to the bottom of her reason for not only cancelling her appointment last minute, the same appointment she keeps to every two weeks without fail, but dropping me completely. Not even rescheduling for another day.

As a self-employed beauty therapist, I have a twenty-four-hour cancellation policy in place. All my clients know this. If they cancel within twenty-four hours before their treatment is due to start, then they are expected to pay for it in full because it's unlikely I can fill a spot that quickly.

Helen didn't say anything about paying me. Now I need to send her an invoice, and it's going to be awkward. I hate this part of the job, but I must do it. Granted, Helen may not get the email, since she's not fully clued up on email and texts, which is probably why she called me instead. We've shared laughs before when she needed help to send a text message to her daughter with a photo attached. I had to show her how to use video chat once too.

I won't lie. I feel hurt and quite upset by this unexpected turn. I don't have another client for three hours. A whole morning of work is gone. I let out a sigh, get dressed, and then send Helen the dreaded payment invoice, explaining that I'm implementing the twenty-four-hour cancellation policy, thanking her for being a wonderful client, and wishing her the best in the future.

It gives me creepy goosebumps, so to distract myself, I

message Georgina, one of my best friends, asking her out for a coffee if she's free. I'm not sure why I haven't thought about calling my friends before now, but since Noah isn't here, and since he makes me feel unwanted when he is, I need to talk to one of my girlfriends.

She texts straight back, within seconds.

> Hey! Sorry, I can't this morning. I have a new elderly client and it's the first time going to her house. Don't want to get lost! I can message you when I'm done. xx

My jaw clenches and a lump forms in my throat. Oh my God, is she Helen's new beauty therapist? I go to message her back, asking if it is Helen, but change my mind, deleting the question and saying not to worry, I'll catch up with her another time and will message her later.

Confusion and betrayal simmer under the surface. No, maybe not betrayal. It's not Georgina's fault Helen has dropped me and chosen her, but the mystery remains as to *why* she's dropped me so suddenly. The bad review crosses my mind, but it's unlikely Helen would have seen it. She's not on Facebook (as far as I'm aware), and even if she had seen it, she never would have believed it or cared.

I do some yoga in the front room, even though it's proved pointless lately to calm my anxiety, then get some business admin done. I go and see my next client after lunch and finish my final client at a little after six. Both offer tea and biscuits and chat away like normal, making me feel more relaxed than I had been this morning. They enjoy their treatments and book in their next ones, but they aren't for weeks.

By the time I arrive home, I realise I haven't thought

about Helen, Charlotte, and my possible stalker all day. In fact, now I think about it...

I check my phone.

There's been no new threatening messages from the unknown number today.

Nothing.

It's Friday, and I've had messages every day since Monday. Four in total, but nothing so far today. Perhaps it's over and they've given up, satisfied that they've thoroughly freaked me out with the picture message, and are now content with their pathetic joke.

I stare at my phone, only now realising that Noah never messaged last night to say he'd arrived at his parents' safe and sound. I hadn't registered his lack of text either. It's been almost twenty-four hours since he left. There can't be anything wrong with my phone because it's been receiving notifications and texts all day. I send him a quick one, asking how his parents are, not bothering to complain that he didn't call, even though it irks me.

No blue ticks appear next to my message, so I put my phone down and make dinner for one. After eating and washing up, with nothing good on television, I open my laptop and do a little of the online course I've started on reflexology. A few of my clients have enquired about it, so I thought I'd add it to my repertoire of skills and qualifications.

But then I get distracted by browsing on Amazon in the Prime Day deals. I go to pay for a new nail bar, as my old one is second-hand and looking a little battered, but my account flags up with a warning saying my debit card is out of date. Damn it. The new card arrived a couple of weeks ago, but I haven't used Amazon in that time, so I haven't had the chance to update it. Sighing, I fetch my new card, input the new details, but then I'm prompted to put my Amazon password in to confirm it's me.

I try my usual password, but it's wrong. I reach into my laptop bag that I usually store underneath my bed, but is now beside me, and pull out a small notebook, which I use to write down all my passwords for the various online sites I use. I'm aware it's a security risk, and I'm sure there are safer ways of storing passwords, but I've never liked the idea of logging them all in my phone. Besides, I don't take my laptop bag out of my flat because there's no need. My dad always did it this way, and I suppose I've continued his old-school tactics.

I input the right password, confirm my new card, and order the nail bar.

Two hours later, Noah still hasn't seen my WhatsApp message. I send him another, just in case it's an issue on my end, but the tick remains solo and grey. Just as I'm about to put my phone away, face down on the arm of the oversized armchair I'm sitting in, it lights up with a message from Charlotte.

I open it. Then, more messages pop in one by one.

Hey!

Hope you're good.

Just checking in.

Jo-Jo and I got home okay.

How are you?

Fancy meeting up for a drink tomorrow
night?

Or not.

I don't mind.

Just a thought.

Okay, bye.

Charlotte xx

I screw up my nose and decide not to message her back.
I've not thought about her all day, and now my mind is back
on her. I'm sure she's just an overly friendly person. Maybe
she doesn't have anyone else in her life with whom she can
meet up for drinks, especially as she's new to the area, but
the idea that she's possibly dating my best friend, Zoe, and
she knows Noah keeps plaguing me.

I decide to message Zoe and get to the bottom of the
Charlie and Charlotte conundrum.

Hey. Just wondered if you were around for
a quick call? Xx

Zoe replies instantly.

Yes! xx

I call her and she picks up.

'Hey, how's things?' she asks in her usual chirpy voice.

'Hiya. Um, I've got rather a lot going on at the moment,
but that's a long story. I needed to talk to you about some-

thing quickly. This is going to sound really weird, and I'm sorry in advance if this is over the line, but... how long have you known Charlie, and do you know where she's from?'

Zoe laughs. 'Why are you curious about my new girlfriend?'

'It's just... I have a new client called Charlotte Whitmoore, and she looks strikingly like Charlie. I saw the photo you put up on Facebook the other day. Charlotte is giving me weird vibes, and I think she might have known Noah, too, from years ago.'

'Ooh, small world. Okay, yeah, so Charlie is from Ireland. Has a strong Irish accent, which is super sexy, and we only met like a month ago. She's a trained acrobat and does stunts and things in circus shows and some films.'

'Wow, that's cool,' I say.

'Yeah. As far as I know, she doesn't know Noah. Let's see the pictures.'

While still on the call, I WhatsApp them over to her and wait while she takes a look.

'I mean... there are some similarities, but I think maybe you're seeing things that aren't there.'

I take a deep breath in through my nose, thankful that someone has finally told it to me straight rather than dodging around the subject like Noah has been.

'You're right,' I say. 'I'm sorry. I didn't mean to accuse Charlie of keeping things from you.'

'It's fine. I get it. Is everything okay though?'

'It will be,' I say with a sigh.

We chat for a few more minutes about general topics, then say our goodbyes, promising to meet up again soon.

After I get off the phone, I realise I forgot to message Georgina back. There are too many thoughts spinning around my head. I can't concentrate, can't seem to catch them all and prioritise them. Everything is on high speed, like my thoughts are whizzing by at double the pace, making me dizzy, disoriented and slightly nauseous. This isn't normal for me. How have I let things get this bad? One day, I was doing just fine. Then, ever since Noah told me about his promotion, one thing after another has slammed into me, causing me to go off the rails, but at least I can now say with certainty that Charlotte is *not* Zoe's new girlfriend. She's not playing dress-up to try and infiltrate my life by dating my best friend.

It doesn't, however, answer the question with regard to her knowing Noah.

My fancy clock on the wall that I got from a charity shop chimes when it's ten o'clock, so I take myself off to bed, fully ready for this day to end.

Tomorrow is Saturday.

I don't have any clients until the afternoon, and I usually go for a run in the mornings, but that idea isn't exciting me as it usually does. The idea that the person is out there, waiting for me, is a real possibility. It's difficult to know whether I'm safe to step outside my own building. Are they watching me all the time, learning my movements, my routine, preparing to strike?

They could be out there this second, waiting for me, watching me with a pair of binoculars.

I brush my teeth, pushing too hard with the electric toothbrush so the red flashing light appears. I spit into the sink and see blood, watch it swirl around the plug hole, mixing with the foamy water.

That's it. I need to get a grip of myself. I don't want to stop doing what I love. I enjoy running. It's my Saturday morning routine. I normally run my usual route along the Cam tow path, then circle back a different way. There are a lot of isolated spots, narrow paths, and other runners and walkers use the path. There's not a lot of room to pass.

Screw it.

I'm doing the park run instead. It's safer. There will be more people around, but I won't be on my own, running down a narrow path alone. That's the main thing.

Safety in numbers, and all that.

CHAPTER SIXTEEN

At nine on the dot, surrounded by the hustle and bustle of eager Saturday morning park runners, I set off at my usual seven-and-a-half-minute mile pace, weaving in and out of the slower runners until I reach my perfect cruising speed. The sun is shining, but there's a light chill in the air, along with a steady breeze. A great running temperature. All around me, other people are chatting happily, and after waking up from a slightly better sleep to no messages from my stalker, I'm feeling lighter than I have all week.

Still no reply from Noah, although two blue ticks have now appeared on my sent messages, which means he's read them, yet decided not to respond. It makes me feel worse, because it means he's consciously deciding not to reply. Maybe something has happened with his dad, and he doesn't have the time. It's the only excuse I'll accept for his lack of response.

As I turn a sharp corner in the route, fast footsteps sound behind me. Crunch. Crunch. Crunch. I glance over my shoulder and see a man sprinting straight at me, a hard, direct look in his eyes. He's going to run right into me. I face forward and start running as fast as my legs can move, pumping my bent arms back and forth for extra momentum, but within seconds, the man has zoomed past me like a dart.

It's then that I realise my mistake.

He's the frontrunner and has lapped me already on this two-lap course.

'Kudos for trying,' says a female runner next to me.

I chuckle, my face burning. 'Seems I'm not that fast yet.'

I continue my pace, eventually finishing in a decent time of 26:13, only 17 seconds off my personal best. I scan my park run barcode, fetch my bag from the waiting area, and take a long, well-deserved drink. The water soothes my dry throat.

As I head back to my car, I spy the man who ran past me standing near it, chatting with a couple of other runners. He catches my eye and winks at me. I smile awkwardly back and shuffle to my car door just as he steps into my path.

'Hey,' he says.

'Hi. Listen, sorry about earlier. I wasn't trying to race you or anything.'

He waves off my comment. 'I didn't mean to scare you. Just wanted to make sure you were okay. I know I only saw you for a second or two, but you looked genuinely afraid as I came running past.'

'Uh, yeah. I mean, no, I wasn't. I just...'

'Anyway, great running today. See you next week, yeah?' He's already jogged back to his friends.

I stand by my car, fiddling with the keys. It was nice of him to ask, but my guard is instantly up as I'm questioning why he felt the need to check up on me. Even without me thinking about it, my hands have clenched around the car keys like a makeshift weapon.

I let out a long sigh as I get into my car. So much for a relaxing run.

When I get home, a call from Georgina comes in, so I answer it, switching to speakerphone while I wrestle to remove my sports bra. Every woman out there knows the struggles of taking one off while covered in sweat.

'Hey, sorry I couldn't meet up yesterday. You free for a coffee this morning instead?' she asks.

'Yes!' I reply. 'I'm just jumping in the shower.'

'Did you go for a run?'

'Yeah. Park run.'

'Time?'

'Twenty-six thirteen.'

'Nice. Meet you at Happy's in fifteen?'

'Yep.'

'Good luck getting your sports bra off.'

'Haha.'

She disconnects. I finally pull the damn thing over my head and dump it in the wash bin.

Wait a minute... How did Georgina know I was taking off my sports bra at that exact moment? Does she know me *that* well? Granted, we once did the park run together, and I went back to hers to shower and change because we were meeting up with Zoe and Hayley afterwards. She had to help me with pulling the too-tight bra off my sweaty skin. We'd laughed a lot.

But... it's a bit weird she mentioned it now. What the hell am I thinking? My best friend can't even make a joke without me being suspicious.

I ARRIVE at Happy's Hot Coffee with a sheen of sweat on my forehead after jogging through the busy Saturday morning streets. I forget that at the weekends, Cambridge comes to life with morning shoppers and coffee drinkers. You can't walk down a single street in the city centre without passing a cafe. Happy's is our new favourite independent coffee shop, not just because their coffee is some of the best I've ever tasted, but they also do an incredible iced bun that is just what I need this morning.

Georgina is already at our usual table by the window, overlooking the street outside. She has two cups in front of her, and two iced buns on a plate in the middle. Maybe she does know me *that* well.

She stands when she sees me, giving me a quick peck on the cheek. 'You look... Well, I was going to say you look great, which you do, but... what's going on? You look sick.'

'I do?'

'No, not sick, but something's not right with you. Sit.'

I sigh, take a slurp of coffee and a large bite of iced bun, then proceed to spill my guts about everything that's been going on like I'm attending my first therapy session. I don't mean to offload on her, but it all comes tumbling out of my mouth at the speed of light. I explain about Noah leaving to visit his parents and not replying to messages, and the weird messages and photo I've received. I skip a few things, including Helen possibly dumping me for her, but then I tell her about Charlotte, explaining that I first thought she was Zoe's new girlfriend.

'You did?'

'Yes, but I called Zoe last night and she confirmed I was just seeing things that weren't there. I'm still not convinced

Charlotte doesn't know Noah, even though he denied that he did. It's hard to believe anything he says lately.'

'Uh oh. Is there trouble in paradise?'

'It hasn't been paradise for a while.'

'So, hang on. If you think your new client knows Noah, then why hasn't she said anything? What do you think her reasoning is?'

'I don't know. That's the thing. She could be the one sending me the dodgy messages, but it's yet another example of something happening lately that I can't explain.'

'Why don't you believe Noah if he says he doesn't know her?'

I scratch the side of my neck. 'It's just... he's not himself, and he won't talk to me about anything. I feel like I'd get more information from a brick wall.'

'Have you gone to the police about the messages?'

'No. Noah said not to.'

'Hmm.' She takes a sip of coffee, staring over the top of her cup at me.

'What? What's hmm mean? You think I should? I haven't received another message since the photo, and that was on Thursday. Maybe they've given up.'

'Maybe, but it's clearly throwing you off your game. If you're genuinely worried about it, then yeah, go to the police. Fuck what Noah says. What's it got to do with him, anyway? You're the one they're targeting for some random reason.'

'I think maybe he's worried about work. He's been very disconnected lately, and now his dad being unwell isn't helping things, and he had to rush off so fast. We've had a few arguments lately and... I'm worried about us, Georgie.'

Georgina leans back in her seat, staring at me for a few

moments before saying, 'If there's one thing I know about marriage, or relationships in general, it's that it takes both people to make it work. It can't just be all one-sided. Babe, if Noah is pulling away, then there's a reason. His weirdness and distance started a few weeks ago, right? You said it's not an affair, so... maybe it's something else.'

'Like what though?'

'I hate to say it, but maybe he's sick.'

My insides clench. I hadn't even thought of that as an option. 'Oh my God. You're right,' I say, shaking my head. 'It would make sense, but I've tried talking to him. I really have, but he won't say anything.'

'Then you either need to trust that he'll tell you when he needs to, or you need to give him an ultimatum.'

I've never liked that word. It feels so... *final*.

'You're right,' I say. I stare into my coffee cup, at the frothy milk. I don't know what else to say. Georgina's comment about Noah possibly being unwell has thrown me off course, adding another stress to the mix.

Georgina clears her throat. 'Um, listen... slight change of subject, and I wasn't going to say anything, but I have this new client called Helen...'

My head pops up from staring into my coffee cup. 'Oh.'

'I get the feeling she doesn't know we're friends, because she started telling me about the beauty therapist she had before, and eventually I put two and two together and realised it was you.'

'Yeah, she cancelled on me with less than an hour's notice and hasn't paid me either.'

'Not cool,' replies Georgina. 'In fact, she was a bit out of order, the way she spoke about you, but I didn't want to let on that I knew you, so I listened.'

All the moisture in my mouth evaporates as I grip my cup, feeling the heat from the coffee seeping through.

'She said that she decided not to see you anymore because of some rumours about you burning your clients with wax... on purpose.'

'What?' I glance around at the nearby coffee drinkers, fully aware that I spoke too loudly. I return my attention to Georgina, whose face has turned pink.

'Obviously, I don't believe her,' she says quickly.

'I'm telling you, Georgie, someone is out to ruin me. I even got an awful review on my Facebook business page, telling people not to hire me.'

'Let's say it's not Charlotte. Maybe it's a previous client.'

'I did consider that option, but I can't for the life of me think who it might be. Unless... Oh my God, I've just had an idea. What if it's Silvia, my old boss?'

'Whose husband sent you the dick pics?'

'Yeah. She did send vicious messages to me for a while afterwards, blaming me for the breakdown of her marriage.'

Georgina shrugs, leaning back in her chair again, which squeaks badly. 'Maybe, but why bring all that up again? It's already been put to bed, hasn't it? How were things left in the end? Remind me.'

I think back. It's been several years at least, and yes, it did culminate in a confrontation at work. She didn't fire me. I left because I couldn't stand to work there any longer, especially when she spouted some racist slurs my way. No one should be expected to deal with that in the workplace.

'After I left the job, Silvia continued to message me, demanding to know details about our so-called *affair*. It was ridiculous. I'd never even met her husband. In the end, I blocked her, and I haven't heard from her since.'

Georgina doesn't respond. She sits and stares out of the window, watching a couple of hungry pigeons squawk and fight over a piece of dropped sandwich by a bin that's overflowing.

'Just be careful,' she finally says, turning back to look at me. She reaches over and grasps both my hands in hers, holding them tight. 'If anything else happens, if you get any other threatening messages, then let me know, okay? And we'll decide what to do from there.'

I should have told Georgina everything days ago. She makes me feel so much better, more like the old me. Confident and ready to take charge. The saying is completely true. A problem shared is a problem halved.

By that evening, having had no further threatening messages or jump scares from random people chasing me, I decide enough is enough and call Noah's phone. It goes straight to voicemail, so I call his parents' house, but there's no answer either.

It doesn't make any sense. Why wouldn't he call me back or at least send me a message explaining why he can't talk? He always lets me know where he is and what's going on. It's not like him to ignore my messages. I'm not the type of girlfriend to bombard him with texts, demanding to know where he is at every hour of the day, but it's getting to the point that not only is it irritating me, but there's also a flicker of worry and doubt blooming in the back of my mind.

For all I know, he had a car accident on the drive to his parents'. I don't know if he arrived there safely, which is why I was hoping to speak to his mum, but I expect she's at the hospital with his dad. If Noah had been involved in an accident, then I would have been notified about it, seeing as I'm his next of kin.

But if an accident isn't the cause of his silence, then something else is.

And that sends my worry spiralling once again.

Is Noah sick and hiding it from me?

CHAPTER SEVENTEEN

Sundays are my down days. No work. No exercise, except a yoga class sometimes. No stress. Except today is different. I find myself nothing *but* stressed, so I keep myself busy by cooking pancakes in my pyjamas, too lazy to go to yoga. I put on three loads of washing and clear out my wardrobe, which I've been meaning to do for the past several months.

It's amazing what a good clear-out will do. It's already spurring me on to do more, and before I know it, three hours have passed and I have two bin bags full of clothes and shoes to donate to the local charity shop. I dump them both by the front door, so when I next leave the flat, I can take them down to my car.

I'm making a cup of tea, my first break of the day, when my phone rings.

It's Noah.

I grab at it, almost sending it flying off the edge of the work surface. 'Noah!'

'Don't be mad.'

'What's happened?'

'No, I mean... Don't be mad at me. I'm so sorry I didn't reply.'

'Even a thumbs-up emoji would have been nice. I've been worried sick.'

'I'm sorry.'

'How are you? How's your dad?'

There's rustling on the end of the line. 'He's... uh... not great, to be honest. They've moved him into intensive care, and he's on a ventilator to breathe. It's so scary to see him like this, Mills.' Hearing the use of his pet name for me helps to settle my nerves. He's always called me Mills. No one else does.

'I'm so sorry to hear that. And your mum?'

'She's bossing everyone around, thinking she knows better than the doctors, as per usual, but otherwise she's okay. I'm just at home about to take the dogs for a walk up the fields.'

I smile at the image of a pack of dogs rushing around his feet, yapping excitedly. I don't hear any barking, which is odd, because usually those dogs love the sound of their own voices. It's always absolute chaos.

'How are you, anyway?' he asks.

'I – uh – did the park run yesterday, which was good, and met up with Georgina for coffee. We think we may have deduced who's been sending me those messages, but I haven't had another one since the picture message.' I remember too late that I haven't told him about that, but he doesn't question me.

There's a long pause. 'Who do you think it is?'

'Georgina and I think it may be Silvia, my old boss. She's the only person who possibly could have a grudge against me.'

'That all happened ages ago though.'

'True, but who else would want to destroy my business and scare me like this?'

Another long pause. 'You're right. Maybe it is her. Are you okay about it all though? You're not thinking about going to the police still, are you?'

'No, not right now. Do you know when you're likely to come back home?'

'Uh... Not for a few more days. At least until Dad is out of the ICU.'

'Of course. I understand, but please try and keep me updated. Just a text will do.'

'I promise. Sorry again. I love you.'

'I love you too.'

'Listen, Mills, I have to go. These dogs are getting restless.'

'Right. Okay, bye.'

'Bye.'

I hang up, frowning at the fact that I still hadn't heard a dog barking in the background.

MONDAY MORNING ARRIVES, and Charlotte is due any minute. It's only now I remember I never messaged her back on Friday night. She said something about meeting up for a drink on Saturday, and I ignored her because I was tipsy and freaking out about the picture message I'd received a few hours before.

God, I feel really bad now. Should I mention it when I see her or pretend I forgot about it? It's true, but she'll have seen I read the message, so there's no getting around it.

I open the door to see Charlotte standing in the hallway,

but she's not her usual upbeat self. Her hair is greasy, her skin pale and clammy, and there's no hint of a smile anywhere on her face.

'Hi, Charlotte. It's so lovely to see you again,' I say, holding the door open for her to step past me. She does without a word, cautiously stepping over the threshold, her eyes darting side to side as if expecting something to jump out at her. She looks like I did the other day.

'How are you?' I ask with a smile.

'F-Fine. You didn't message me back on Friday. Why?'

I'm taken aback by her bluntness. I didn't realise that by ignoring her message, she'd take such offence. 'I'm so sorry. Friday night was a bit manic. I saw it and then completely forgot to message you back. I was rather distracted. I do apologise.'

Charlotte stands awkwardly in front of me, shifting her weight from foot to foot. 'Distracted by what?'

My words catch in my throat. I don't know her well enough to tell her about Noah's dad being unwell, and I've still not fully got to the bottom of how she knows Noah, so I'm loath to tell her about the messages I've been receiving. I don't want to give her the wrong impression and make her think we're friends. There are a few things that don't add up when it comes to her, but I can't imagine she's dangerous, otherwise I wouldn't have let her inside.

'I was just having one of those stressful days,' I reply.

Charlotte nods, then stares at the bin bags by the door. 'What are they?' She points, her right arm outstretched, rigid.

I frown and scratch the back of my neck as a tickle of unease settles there. 'Oh, just some old clothes for the charity shop. I need to take them down to my car later.'

'I can take them for you!' she says, her voice rising an octave. Before I can summon a response from my confused brain, she rushes forwards and starts untying the first bag.

'Ooh, cute top!' She holds up a blue top that I haven't worn in years.

'Uh... Thanks.'

Charlotte shoves the top back in the bag and reties the handles together. Then, she stands up, a smile across her face, the opposite of what she looked like only moments ago. 'I'll take them to the charity shop for you. I'm passing that way.'

'Oh, no, that's okay. You don't have–'

'It's no trouble.'

Rather than letting this awkward conversation go on any longer, I nod. 'Thank you. That's very kind of you.'

Charlotte grins. 'And don't worry about not replying to my text. We all get distracted sometimes. Am I right?'

Thankfully, her change of tone and mood breaks the weird tension. 'Yes, you're right. Please. Come into the treatment room.'

'Thank you. I've been so looking forward to this back massage. I don't think I've ever had one before. Or maybe I have. I can't remember. I have a hard time keeping still for long periods of time. Also, I don't always like people touching me.'

We reach the treatment room, which is dimly lit with fake, flickering candles. Soft music is playing in the background, and there's a faint sweet aroma.

'That's okay. We can take it slow, and if you feel uncomfortable, just let me know.'

'Do I need to get naked?'

'No, not completely. You'll need to remove your top, but

you can keep your bra on if you feel more comfortable. Lie down on the couch with your face in the hole. I may need to unclasp your bra to ensure it doesn't get greasy from the oils, but I can work around it if you'd prefer to keep it on.'

Charlotte nods, rubbing the tops of her arms with her hands folded across her chest. 'Okay,' she says.

CHARLOTTE ENJOYS THE MASSAGE. At least, I assume she does because she doesn't stop me mid-way through or complain about anything. It takes several minutes, but eventually her muscles relax beneath my fingers and she sinks into the couch. I keep the pressure firm yet smooth, ensuring I don't travel too far down towards her bottom.

I leave her to get dressed, and wait out in the hall after washing my hands in the bathroom. When she emerges, she rolls her shoulders back and yawns.

'Oh, wow, my back feels amazing.'

'You may feel tired afterwards. Make sure you drink plenty of water throughout the day.'

Charlotte nods, then reaches for her bag. 'Um... shit.' She pulls a few items from her bag and holds them up whilst trying to pull out more. 'I seem to have forgotten my purse again.'

I almost laugh, but manage to hold it in. Is she a forgetful person in general, or is she doing this on purpose? I've had clients forget their purses or wallets before. It's not a big deal to me. It happens to a lot of people. But the other day, Charlotte had an issue with her purse, and now, it's happened again, which begs the question whether it's deliberate or not. Most clients are happy to pay. I've only ever had the one, years ago, who refused. Although Zoe has had a couple of clients who never paid her when they said they would.

'It's fine,' I say, even though I'm a little put out. 'I'll send you over my bank details.'

Charlotte nods. 'Thank you. Sorry. Urrgg, my brain is just... I'm having a weird week.' She stares at the wall, at one of the calming photos I have of a field of poppies. She stares and stares.

'Charlotte?'

Her head snaps round. 'Yes. Sorry. Thank you for the massage. I'll be in touch about booking another treatment. Is that okay?'

I swallow, attempting to summon some moisture to my dry mouth. 'Of course.'

She walks out of the treatment room towards the front door, where the two bags of clothes are still sitting. She bends down and picks them up.

I feel bad because, as far as I know, she doesn't have a car, so she's going to have to carry the bags either to the bus stop or to the nearest charity shop, which isn't that close.

'Are you sure you'll be all right carrying them? They are quite heavy.'

'I'm sure,' she says. 'I'll transfer over the money ASAP.'

'Thank you. Have a good day.'

'And you. Bye.'

I close the door behind her, a strange gurgling sensation in my stomach. Something tells me that I'm never going to see that money appear in my bank account, but I've been wrong about people before.

I've also been right about them.

CHAPTER EIGHTEEN

NOAH

Shit. She's now following Mills and taking her picture. I don't have time for this. It's exactly what she did to me. It never went any further, but how can I be sure she's not going to escalate things? I don't know what to do. If Mills goes to the police, then my life will get extremely complicated. No, that's the wrong word to use. It's already complicated. My life will be destroyed, even more than it already has been. I'm trying to juggle everything, putting out fires wherever I can, but each time I do, another one starts. It won't be much longer before I run out of water, and I'll be left to burn. Maybe that's the way it should be. Maybe she's right. I would be better off dead, then I wouldn't have to deal with any of this.

Staying in my family home is not helping things. Mum is constantly on my case whenever I'm around, and now I have to worry about Mills and how she's coping back at home. What about me? What about how I'm coping? No one seems to give a shit about me.

Rob does, but I get the feeling from him that he's tired of

fighting my corner. He wants me to admit what happened, tell the truth and get it all out in the open, but if I do that, I'm a walking target. I may as well put a sign over my head with an arrow, alerting everyone to who I am and what's happened to me. I can't do it. I can't. I'd rather die.

I suppose that's why I'm here. Rob keeps calling me every day to check up on me. I'm not a fucking child. I wish he'd leave me the hell alone so that I can focus on why I'm here.

I'm sure Mills is questioning why I told her not to get the police involved, but it's the last thing I need right now.

My phone remains off for most of the day because I can't afford the distraction of it lighting up every five minutes with another desperate text from Mills. I do check it regularly, but mostly she wants to know why I haven't messaged her back. She's irritating me, getting under my skin. I hate to do this to her, but she has no idea what I'm going through. It's better this way; to keep as far away from her as possible. She doesn't realise I'm doing it for her own good.

The worst thing is, I have no idea how to keep it from her for much longer. I think maybe I've been deluding myself for a long time. Too long. Something as big as this is impossible to hide, especially now Mills is being targeted too. I know the person behind this is targeting Mills, trying to scare me, trying to scare her. How far will she take it? I'm not sure if I can risk it any longer. If Mills gets hurt, then I'll never forgive myself. It will be my fault because I didn't speak up. I'm a coward. I've always known that.

I'm keeping quiet, refusing to cooperate with the HR investigations and the court proceedings. What more do they want? There's nothing else I can physically do. I know what they really want me to do, but I'm not strong enough to go through with it. Not yet. But I will, because if I don't, then my life is over. Mills' life is over. Our life, our future, is done. Finished.

I'm going to admit to everything. I just need to get this week out of the way, then I'll return home, go back to work, and put an end to everything. Just say it was all my fault. I did it. That's what they want. That's what they'll get. Then they'll stop going after Mills. Of course, I'll be hauled off to jail and my name will be dragged through the mud.

But if that's the price of keeping Mills and my secret safe, then it's what needs to be done. I hate it though. I hate the thought of admitting it was all my fault when it wasn't. But I have to, because I'm the man. That's supposed to mean I must protect the woman, right?

Ha.

It makes me sick to think...

'Hi, Noah!' calls someone up ahead.

I lift my head, which feels as if it weighs a tonne, and give them a wave back. I've just arrived at my destination, but every fibre in my body keeps telling me to turn around. I hate hospitals almost as much as I hate places like therapists' offices.

'Hi,' I say. I've forgotten the bloke's name, even though I met him yesterday. He's a decent enough guy, but he's a little too in-your-face with his problems, as if he's the only one going through difficulties. Give me a break.

'How's it going?' he asks.

'Uh, yeah, not bad.' I should probably ask him how he is, but I really couldn't care less.

'Oh,' says whats-his-name, 'before I forget, someone left you a message at reception.'

'They did? Who?'

The guy shrugs. 'No idea. Just passing on the message that there's a message for you.'

'Cheers,' I reply, walking straight past him and in through the hospital doors.

I reach reception and give the person behind the desk my name. She hands over a hastily scrawled note. I take it, not thanking her.

Sorry to hear about your dad. Hope he's on the mend soon. xx

What the hell...

They know where I am.

CHAPTER NINETEEN

I send Charlotte my bank details and wait for the notification from my banking app to tell me it's been paid, but five hours later, the money still hasn't appeared. The blue ticks are next to the message I sent her, telling me she's seen it, but she hasn't responded in any way.

My mind races. I should have made her pay me there and then via a bank transfer, standing over her like a bank manager. My fingers hover over my screen. I'm debating whether to message again to remind her. This is another part of being self-employed I hate. A few of my clients don't pay me straight away, and I do have to send them reminders, which is fine. We have a laugh about it, putting it down to busy lives, but Charlotte is different. She's new. I don't know her well enough to send a jokey message, asking for my money. She's also done more than one thing recently that's put my guard up and made me question her authenticity and honesty.

It bugs me all day. Noah sends a quick message to say his dad is stable but still in the ICU. It's short and to the point.

No kisses at the end, and he doesn't ask how I am. By the time I've made dinner, eaten it and washed up, Charlotte still hasn't replied to my message or sent the money. On the plus side, I've had no threatening message today either. It's been three days since the last one. The heavy pressure on my chest has lightened considerably, enough to enable me to walk across the car park without jumping at nearby footsteps. When a car horn blares nearby, I don't flinch and worry that it's directed at me.

That evening, I settle in the oversized chair and pick up my phone. Just as I do, an odd sound appears from the hallway, by the front door. It's odd because it's a sound that shouldn't be there.

A child giggling, like from a creepy horror movie.

It sends my whole body into freeze mode. I can't move. Can't even draw in a breath.

'Hello?' I call out timidly, hoping to God that no one answers, because if they do, I may just throw up or pass out from fear.

The giggling stops.

I scooch forwards and sit on the edge of the armchair, leaning as far as I can to see down the hallway just outside the living area door, but I can't quite see that far. I need to move if I want to check there is no evil child standing in the hallway.

The sound doesn't come again.

'Hello?' I squeak. My throat constricts. If I don't take a proper breath soon, I'm going to hyperventilate.

No giggling, but a very long, loud creak sounds, like someone has stepped all their weight onto a squeaky floorboard. We don't have floorboards. The hallway is carpeted.

'This is ridiculous,' I say out loud. I feel stupid for

thinking someone is out there, because it's impossible. The front door is locked. The chain is bolted across. No one can sneak through the open window in the bedroom because we're on the second-to-top floor of the building.

That's when it hits me.

The Echo Dot in my bedroom.

I get to my feet and pad into the hallway, turning left into the bedroom.

'Alexa, turn off sound effects.'

'Turning off sound effects.'

What the bloody hell is going on with that device?

The Echo Dot is still on, so I reach down and switch it off at the wall. There. That settles it. Stupid thing. I don't even know why Noah got it for me. I've never liked the idea of a piece of technology listening to conversations and answering back like a human being. It's creepy and weird. It's hooked up to my Amazon account apparently. Noah set it up. It can do all sorts of things, including adding items to shopping lists and reminding me to do things that I've forgotten, but I've never heard it play sound effects before. I'll need to get Noah to check the settings when he gets back. Only he and I have access to the login and passwords.

Relieved I got to the bottom of the weird noises, I go back to my phone, scroll straight to Charlotte's chat, and send her a direct, but polite, message, reminding her about the payment due before I talk myself out of it. It's time to be direct.

To my surprise, she messages straight back.

I'm so sorry!

Today has been manic!

> Doing it now.

> ... ...

> All done.

> Sorry again.

> Do you happen to have any space free for me tomorrow?

> I have a party this weekend and wouldn't mind my eyebrows getting touched up.

I check my work diary for a space. Annoyingly, there is one. Eyebrows take only minutes to do, so I could easily squeeze her in between my other clients who are coming here, but the idea of seeing her again so soon unsettles me. Maybe it's because whenever I see her, something weird happens that freaks me out. It's clearly not her fault. She just unnerves me in a way that sets my teeth on edge and, especially with Noah being away, I don't feel strong enough to deal with her right now.

I send her a reply, saying I'm sorry, but I can't fit her in. She won't know any better.

A minute later, a bank notification pops up, informing me she's paid her invoice.

That's a weight off my chest.

Charlotte responds with a string of further texts.

> No worries!

> I know it's last minute.

> Have a great week.

> I'll book in again soon.

> xx

I send her a thanks.

I'm fully intending to do some more of my online reflexology course, but decide to go to bed instead. The scare with the strange sounds has made me want to curl up under my duvet and hide like a child.

I send Noah a goodnight text, and he responds straight away with a line of cute emojis that make me smile like a teenager. Despite his dad being unwell, I'm glad he seems more like his old self, even though I can't help but notice that emojis aren't real words. It's like he's doing his best to avoid talking to me, even in text form.

I brush my teeth, get into my oversized t-shirt I sleep in, and climb into bed. I'm about to plug my phone in to charge overnight when I see a new message on the screen.

At first glance, it appears to be empty, but it is from a private number.

My heart leaps in my chest.

No. No. No.

I thought they'd stopped...

My hands shake so badly as I type in my passcode that I keep hitting the wrong pattern. It takes three attempts before I'm in and can navigate to the new message.

> That was a cute top you had on today, Bitch. Have you missed me?

They were watching me again.

But... I wasn't wearing a normal top today, only my black beauty therapist uniform. The text doesn't quite make sense, but then, whoever they are, they're not doing it to make sense. They want to unsettle me. They want me to know that they're watching. Still.

The words *cute top* flash in my mind.

Charlotte said the same thing earlier when she rooted around in the charity clothes bags. She held up an old top of mine. Is that a coincidence or... Holy shit. What if it really *is* Charlotte who's doing this to me? Is she casually dropping hints on purpose to make me suspect her?

Now, my suspicions are back on her.

If I reply and ask who they are, that will prove they are getting under my skin and give them what they want: validation that I'm afraid.

In the end, I don't reply, but I do get out of bed and double-check the front door is locked and bolted before climbing back into bed and attempting to sleep.

I fail miserably.

CHAPTER TWENTY

I get out of bed the next morning groggy, like I drank too many glasses of wine last night. My tongue sticks to the roof of my mouth as I reach for the glass of water by my bed. Except it's not there, which makes no sense because I always fill up a glass with water before I go to bed. It's one of my night-time rituals, but last night I clearly didn't because I'd been too distracted by that stupid message and creepy giggling. This isn't me. I keep forgetting things, and it's all down to my life turning upside down and multiple things going on, none of which I can control. I don't like being out of control. That's why I'm not a very good car passenger, nor do I enjoy rollercoasters.

I sigh and check my phone. Another message has arrived overnight, but it's from Lucy, a client who is due to visit me first thing for four hours' worth of treatments.

> Hi, Amelia. I'm so sorry to do this last minute, but I can't see you today. Something has come up. Hope you understand. I'll be in touch soon to rearrange. xx

I huff with annoyance. Seriously, another last-minute cancellation? It's not merely the short treatments that are being cancelled. It's four hours of my day I can't fill at short notice. It's almost two hundred pounds' worth of treatments gone. Just like that.

I close my eyes, tilt my head to the ceiling, and count to ten before typing out a message that's, again, both polite and direct. I can't fill those four hours, and she's cancelling within the twenty-four-hour period, so I have to charge her the full amount. Obviously, I hope it's nothing serious that's come up, so I add that to the message to make myself feel a little better and less like a bossy, money-driven salesman.

This is getting serious now. Without clients, I don't get paid. It's as simple as that. If I don't get paid, then I have no money for bills, and it won't count towards my yearly earnings. I also can't help to save towards a house deposit or the wedding. It's not like I earn tens of thousands of pounds a year being self-employed, but when I started, I set myself a target to reach, and for a short while, I was reaching twenty-five thousand a year. If things keep going the way they are now, though, there's no chance of me even hitting half that.

I'm losing my business.

Sometimes, it feels as if clients don't understand this part of working for myself. Yes, I'm there to provide a service to them, but if they cancel so close to their appointments, then I don't earn a wage.

Lucy messages back within two minutes, and when I

read her message, my blood runs cold, and a jolt of pure shock and fear shoots through my heart.

> Amelia, while I understand that cancelling last minute is an inconvenience to you, I am NOT paying you for a service you haven't provided. I'm afraid if that's the way you're going to treat me, then I won't be using you again in the future. Take care. Lucy.

The phone slips from my trembling hands and bounces on the covers before dropping to the floor. I'm glad I'm in bed because otherwise, I would have sunk to the floor. Nausea swirls in my stomach, and a lump gets stuck in my throat. Part of me wants to reply, fight my corner, the way I would usually if this happened, but all the fight, all my confidence has shattered. It was on shaky ground before this, but now it's been shoved right off the edge of a cliff and exploded into a million pieces.

I'm broken. There's no point in getting out of bed this morning. I don't have a client until after lunch. It'll be just my luck she cancels too. Leaving my phone on the floor where it landed, I sink into my pillow, grab Noah's from next to me, cover my face, and scream into it.

It helps. A little.

After a long, internal pep talk, I replace the pillow, get up, make the bed and pour myself a cup of tea. I could call my friends, see which one of them is free. I could go to the gym or out for a run, but if I leave, there's a chance my stalker will see me. I don't know what I'm supposed to do. I can't stay in my flat forever and only have clients come here, like some agoraphobic hermit. This is ridiculous. I can't live like this!

The only other option is to carry on and pretend everything is normal, when clearly, it's not. That's just as terrifying because I'm losing money daily from clients cancelling, and I know for certain someone is watching me. Granted, they haven't threatened me again, but they are out there. Somewhere. Planning God only knows what next.

To make myself feel better, I return to my phone and message the client who is due later today to ask if we're still on, then text Charlotte, saying I am free for a treatment today after all. It's not a lot of money, but screw it, I need every penny I can get right now, and since I'm losing so many clients, I need to try and keep the ones I do have.

Charlotte replies straight away.

> Yes!

> What time suits you?

I tell her to come in one hour.

Then, my other client replies and confirms her appointment for later. Thank God for that.

CHARLOTTE ARRIVES ON TIME. I have a plan. Rather than tiptoe around the subject and pretend I'm fine with not knowing whether she does or doesn't know Noah, I'm going to find out a bit more about her. It's time to stop acting like a victim and start facing this thing head-on. Despite her ability to talk for ages, she's never revealed too much detail about her personal life. Does she have a partner? I know she's a dog walker and she's new to the area, but what's her background? Does she have any close family nearby? How does she know my future husband? Maybe I'll not blurt that question out, but I can discover the years she attended Lancaster University. I've set myself a mini mission. No more pottering around. I'm going in straight for the kill.

'Would you like a cup of tea?' I ask Charlotte as soon as she enters the flat. 'I've had a cancellation today, so I'm in no rush.' Sometimes it's good to keep your enemies close. That's the wrong word. *Potential stalkers* close.

'Oh, okay, then yes, please!'

'Come on through,' I say. I've made sure to close the door to my bedroom.

'This is a beautiful flat,' says Charlotte as she enters the spacious kitchen/dining/lounge area. I've always loved having an open-plan living space, complete with double doors leading to a tiny balcony overlooking the city below. In the past, I've tried to make it a green space but struggled to find plants that thrive in pots on balconies, especially since we're on the wrong side to catch the full sun during the day.

'Thank you,' I say, flicking the kettle on and prepping the mugs.

'Have you lived here long?' asks Charlotte, walking to the balcony and peering out at the traffic below.

'About a year. Noah and I decided to move in together. Start small. We're saving up to eventually buy our own house.'

'That's nice.'

'What made you move to Cambridge?' I ask, keeping the tone light and friendly, switching the topic back to her. 'You said before that you were new around here.' The last thing I want is for her to think I'm interrogating her, which I am, but she doesn't need to know that. I need to get her focus off me for once.

'Oh, you know, this and that,' comes the curt response.

That's a red flag. This woman normally can never shut up talking about nonsense, yet when it comes to information I've asked about herself, she slams shut like a trapdoor. I decide to try a different approach. Direct.

'Do you have a partner?'

'Well, I did, but...' She stops. Her back is still turned.

I wait patiently. The kettle boils and switches off on its own. Only then does Charlotte turn to face me and, to my horror, her face is bright red, and tears are streaming from her eyes.

I rush forwards. 'Oh, my goodness, I'm so sorry! I didn't mean... Whatever I said, I'm sorry.'

She shakes her head. 'No. No. It's not anything you've said. Ignore me. Everyone else always does.' She turns her back on me again, attempting to hide, and wipes her face with the sleeve of her jacket.

I place a hand on her shoulder, but it's the wrong thing to do because she flinches sideways and scurries away from me.

'Please. Come and sit down. Let me make the tea.'

Charlotte sniffs loudly and nods before walking slowly to the nearest sofa and perching on the edge. She's not comfortable and looks as if she's ready to bolt at any minute. I feel her watching me as I make the tea.

'Uh, how do you take your tea?' I ask.

'Black, please. No sugar.'

I nod. This hasn't gone the way I planned. She wasn't supposed to break down in tears, but maybe this is a good thing. Maybe she'll open up if I can make her trust me. I'm good at this sort of thing, talking with clients and being a friendly, listening shoulder to lean on.

I still have no idea whether she is or isn't my stalker, and maybe I'm putting myself in danger by having her in my flat again, but I have to know what's going on. This must end somehow.

And it will. My life and livelihood, my business and future marriage depend on it.

CHAPTER TWENTY-ONE

Charlotte is still perching on the edge of the sofa when I bring over a cup of steaming tea and place it on a small, round table next to her. She's squeezing her hands together on her lap and bobbing her knees up and down, bouncing on her toes. Constantly moving. She looks so small, so delicate and troubled, like a lost soul in need of rescuing. Either she's very good at the game she's playing, or she truly is struggling with something, like I am.

I don't like the person I've become lately. Suspicious of everyone. Never believing them straight off the bat, but until I'm able to prove otherwise, my guard is up around Charlotte and must remain that way if I'm to protect myself. It can't be a coincidence that everything started happening, started going wrong, the day Charlotte walked through my front door.

'I'm sorry. I don't mean to break down in tears in front of you. It's just... you're easy to talk to, and I've had such a lot going on lately. It all piles up. You know?' Charlotte blinks at me with wet eyelashes and then shakily reaches for her cup of tea.

Funnily enough, I know exactly how she feels, but I don't want to go down the long and winding road of telling her about my troubles. My plan is for her to tell me hers.

'I know,' I reply with a soothing tone. 'Maybe it would help to talk about it? I've been told I'm a good listener.'

Charlotte takes a sip, realises it's too hot, and replaces the cup on the side. She lets out a long sigh, allowing her shoulders to sink several inches. 'I've tried talking about it, but... Oh, I should just give up. What's the point anymore? I should be punished for what I've done.' Charlotte leans over her knees and covers her face with her hands, sobbing like a hysterical child.

I take a step back, unsure what to do.

Bloody hell, what has she done to warrant her saying that?

For a moment, I wonder if she's about to confess everything. Tell me she's known Noah all along and has been stalking me for some strange reason.

I shuffle out to the bathroom, fetch a couple of clean tissues and return to Charlotte, holding them towards her.

'Here,' I say. I don't know what to say to her now. We still have a treatment to do, but she's hardly in the right state to lie still and have her eyebrows waxed. I'm so close to discovering the truth. I'm sure of it.

Charlotte looks up and gives me a weak smile as she takes the tissues. She blows her nose and dabs her eyes, then tucks the used tissue up her sleeve.

'Thank you. You're such a good friend. I'm so sorry about this. I shouldn't have said anything. I know better than to be around people when I'm like this. It's my fault.' She stands up abruptly, brushing herself down. 'I should go. I'm sorry for wasting your time.' She goes to leave the room, but I quickly step in front of her. She can't leave. Not yet!

Her eyes grow wide. She's like a rabbit caught in headlights. Shaking.

'Charlotte,' I say in as calm a voice as possible, although my heart is beating so hard in my chest I'm surprised she can't hear it. 'Whatever it is you've done, I'm sure if you talk to someone about it, it will get better.'

'We'll see,' she says. 'I'm sorry, I don't think I'm in the mood to have my eyebrows done now.'

'It's fine,' I reply quickly.

'I'll be in touch.' Her eyes swivel towards the exit.

She's afraid of me, eyeing the exit like she's about to bolt for freedom.

I step to the side, allowing her to leave, and stare at her back as she walks through the hallway and out the front door, closing it softly, taking any chance of me finding out the truth with her.

The flat plunges into eerie silence. I run to the door and slam the bolt and chain across before leaning my back against it, sinking to the floor. I don't know what to think, but I do know Charlotte has done something bad, something she's clearly feeling guilty over. Whether it's to do with me is yet to be seen. I grab my phone from my pocket and call Georgina. I don't expect her to pick up, but she does.

'Hey, babe. You okay?'

'Uh, yeah. Hi. I've just had Charlotte in the flat for a treatment, but before we got to it, she broke down in tears and now she's just left.'

'Huh. Weird. Oh, that reminds me, I think I saw her

walking a dog early this morning. I recognised her from the photo you showed me.'

'You probably did. She's a dog walker,' I say.

'Right, but... I could have sworn she was wearing a top of yours. You know, that cute blue one. It made me do a double-take.'

'What? She was wearing my top?'

'That's what it looked like. Did you give it to her?'

'No, it was in the bags. She offered to take them to the charity shop for me. She even had a look inside and mentioned the top. She must have taken it for herself before handing in the bags.' There's a silence on the line. I check to make sure we're still connected. 'Georgie?'

'Babe, that's weird. Also, why'd you get rid of that top? It was cute!'

'I hadn't worn it for like a year. I'm surprised you even remember.'

'I'm sorry, but this Charlotte woman sounds sketchy as fuck. Who the hell checks through charity bags in front of you, then proceeds to take an item and wear it before heading over to see you? She was probably wearing it when she saw you just now. Stalker alert!'

I shake my head, even though Georgina can't see me. 'No, she wasn't wearing it, but... she was wearing a jacket, so she could have been wearing the top underneath.' I pause for a moment. 'Shit... This doesn't feel right, does it? I've been back and forth about whether I still suspect her, but...'

'I mean, maybe she's skint and can't afford new clothes,' replies Georgina.

'But she's had a couple of treatments from me now, including a ninety-pound massage. She can't be *that* skint.'

'Touché.'

I rub my temples. 'Uh, what the hell is going on? I had another creepy message this morning, and it even mentioned me wearing a cute top yesterday, but I didn't wear anything other than my uniform. Plus, another client cancelled on me, and when I asked her to pay, she freaked out and dropped me as a therapist. I'm losing clients left, right and centre.'

'Yeesh.'

I wait for a further response from her, but it doesn't come. 'I thought you'd at least have some good advice for me.'

'Yeah, I have some advice, but you're not going to like it.'

'Go on...'

'Go to the police.'

'I knew you were going to say that.'

'Well, let's be honest. It's gone past a few annoying texts, hasn't it? This chick is threatening you, following you and taking pictures.'

'I can't decide if I think it's Charlotte or not.'

'Okay, but... will you at least call the police so there's a record? That way, when you end up stabbed to death in the street, or found dead inside your flat, I can say, "See, I told you so!"'

I stifle a laugh, but in all honesty, she's right. I should, as a minimum, log a complaint with them, so they're aware. I don't need to inform Noah that I've told them either.

'Okay,' I say. 'I'll contact the police. You're right. It's got to the point now where I need to tell someone.'

'Cool. In the meantime, call me whenever you need, but try not to let this affect your everyday life.'

'It already has. I barely have any clients left booked in this week, and the week after is looking sparse too.'

'Send out a blanket message to every client in your book,

asking if they'd like a treatment this week. Couldn't hurt, right?'

'No, I suppose not. Thanks, Georgie. You've been a great help.'

'What I'm here for. Gotta run. I'll text you later to make sure you're still alive.'

'Haha.' I hang up and sigh, leaning my head against the door behind me. Should I call the police now or walk into the nearest station and do it in person? Perhaps it'll be better face-to-face. They might take me more seriously that way.

CHAPTER TWENTY-TWO

It takes me fifteen minutes before I can pull myself together enough to walk out the front door. I scurry to my car, slam and lock the doors, and only then take a deep breath. My legs shake as I push the clutch down and drive out of the car park.

It takes me ten minutes to get to the nearest police station, and there's one visitor parking spot left, so I pull up, switch off the engine and quickly check my phone in case Noah has messaged me. He hasn't, but there is a new message from another number I don't recognise.

> If you speak to the police, then things will get a lot worse for you very fast, so don't even think about it, Bitch. This is your final warning.

My head snaps up, and I'm scanning the car park. Is she out there right now? Either Charlotte has somehow followed me on foot or... I gulp as a new realisation hits me squarely between the eyes, knocking me off balance. There's only one person who knows I had plans to tell the police. Granted, I didn't tell her I was doing it today, but she knew I was telling the police. Hell, it was *her* idea.

Georgina.

No. Surely not.

This changes everything.

Icy shock floods my veins, and I swallow back thick saliva as my heart rate spikes. This can't be happening. It can't be Georgina... it can't! I won't let myself even think it. It must be Charlotte or someone else like my old boss, Silvia. If I can't trust my best friend, then I have no chance.

From where I'm parked, I can't see the entrance to the car park, so I'm unsure if anyone else has driven in behind me, but I took the only parking spot left. When I called Georgina, she didn't say where she was, so she could have been outside my building, waiting for me, ready to follow.

Then, just to settle my rising panic, I swivel round in my seat and check the back seat. Empty. My eyes water, and tears leak out of the edges, trickling down my cheeks. I have two choices. Either I ignore the message, march into the station right this second and report this, or I drive out of the car park, go home and deal with this by myself. Somehow.

I'm suspecting everyone, so I have no idea how I'm supposed to sort this mess out. I'm paranoid, delusional. Georgina and I have been friends for a year. Granted, it's not that long in the grand scheme of things, but in that time I've come to think of her as a sister. All the girls are like family to me, but Georgina is special. She and I are a little closer to each other than anyone else. There's no way she's behind this. The only weird thing that's happened with Georgina lately is Helen leaving me for her, but that wasn't her fault. Unless... Georgina has been sabotaging my business to poach all my clients from me. She has plenty of her own, though, so I expect she hardly needs to steal mine.

Still, with tears in my eyes, I restart the car and drive slowly out of the police station car park. I sniff and wipe my tears and snot on my arm because I don't have a tissue nearby. I can barely see anything. The tears won't stop. It's like the floodgates have finally opened.

They stream down my face, blurring my vision.

I need to stop. It's too dangerous to keep driving like this. I sniff again, then erupt into even bigger sobs. Oh God, what is happening? I don't remember the last time I cried this hard.

Then, it happens in the blink of an eye.

A long car horn sounds.

SMASH!

The car is shoved from behind. My neck snaps forward. The airbag deploys. The force of hitting the airbag sends the back of my head bouncing off the headrest. I see stars. My vision swims, and a loud ringing erupts in my ears like that time I had tinnitus. Lots of shouting. Car horns.

A few seconds later, my car door flies open, and a man reaches in, touching my arm. 'Lady, are you okay? Can you hear me?'

I reach my fingers to my forehead where it hit the airbag. There's no blood. I don't think I'm hurt, but I'm dazed, confused.

'No, I'm... Yes, I'm fine. I think,' I say, attempting to focus my vision. 'What happened?' Clearly, I hadn't been paying attention to the road, but I don't know what happened exactly.

'You were stopped at the lights, and a car drove up behind and slammed into you. I saw the whole thing. You hadn't noticed the green light. He beeped his horn and then bam! Didn't even wait for you to notice the light had changed. Just drove straight into you. Wanker.'

'Is he okay? You said it was a man?'

'To be honest, I didn't see them. It was an educated guess. They've driven away though. Sorry, I didn't get the whole numberplate. Started with a K though.'

I reach over and unclip my seatbelt, my hands shaking so badly it takes me a couple of attempts to press the button. 'That's okay,' I say. 'Thank you for stopping to help.'

'No worries. I've called an ambulance. You should get yourself checked over. The police will be here, too, I expect. Your car will need moving eventually, but I think it's still drivable.'

I nod, taking it all in, but unsure of what to focus on first. Then, one of the words jumps out.

Shit. The police. They're on their way.

This car accident has nothing to do with my stalker, so even if they are watching me, they'll have no reason to...

Wait a minute.

Only moments before, I'd received a message threatening that things would get a lot worse if I tell the police, and then a car rams into the back of mine.

My final warning.

The kind man helps me out of the car, and I hobble to the side of the road. Not injured. Just shaken, dizzy, like I've been put through a spin cycle. Horns blare, but I hardly notice. Clearly, I've inconvenienced a lot of people by not reacting to the green light as fast as I should have done. It's not my fault someone slammed into the back of me.

'Thank you,' I say, leaning against a low wall near a shop.

'Can you explain again what you saw? Did the car slow down before they hit me?'

'A bit, maybe,' replies the man. 'I'm not sure it was them who blared their horn. May have been someone else. It all happened so fast, but when I saw them ram into you, then drive away, I knew I needed to stop and help.'

'Thank you again.'

He nods. 'I'm Derek.'

'Amelia.'

'I'll hang around and give a statement to the police.'

Derek does more than that. He meets the paramedics as they get out of the ambulance and leads them over to me, explaining what he saw, then leaves me with them while he helps a couple of other people who have stopped to push my car off the road so it's no longer blocking traffic. There's plenty of pedestrians and other cars driving past who are stopping or slowing down, hoping to get a good look or maybe a shot of a bloody, disfigured body, but they're out of luck.

The paramedics check me over, ask some questions, shine a light in each eye, and take my blood pressure. Other than a whack to my forehead and a sore neck, I'm in one piece. But I do have a headache and am still dizzy. My blood pressure is also high, but then I'd be surprised if it wasn't.

The police talk to me, taking my statement. I explain what I can, but I blabber on, repeating the same thing over and over. *I don't know who hit me. I didn't see them. It all happened so fast.* My car is towed to the nearest garage. It is still drivable from the looks of the outside, but it needs to be checked over for internal damage. Plus, the rear bumper is hanging off, so that'll need fixing. It's also a little dented.

Unfortunately, due to the accident, I'm in no state to see

my client this afternoon, so I cancel her appointment last minute, which fills me with shame and embarrassment, but I don't have a choice. I don't have access to a car now, which begs the question: Was the accident deliberate? Perhaps the person who's trying to ruin me has now moved on to the next phase of destroying my business. Not only have they started taking away my clients, but now I have no transportation to get to the ones I do have. Without a car, I'm confined to my flat to do treatments. I have many clients whom I visit, including Wilma, Trish and Susanne, all high-paying clients whom I can't afford to lose.

Satisfied that I'm not about to keel over, the paramedic gives me a list of symptoms to keep an eye out for over the coming days. She asks if someone can drive me places or help with day-to-day chores and errands, and I say yes without thinking, only remembering Noah isn't home when I say thank you and watch her walk away.

Derek offers me a lift home, but I decline and say that I'll walk. The idea of getting into a car with a strange man fills me with even more dread. It's not far to my building. Maybe the walk will do me good.

As I turn and shuffle in the direction of home, my bag clutched against my chest, I suddenly feel as if I have a target on my back. Without thinking about my tired, beaten body, I run home as fast as my legs can carry me, only feeling somewhat better when I slam the front door shut and bolt it.

CHAPTER TWENTY-THREE

I call Noah after I've taken a long, hot shower and washed off the sweat and grime from my body. Despite feeling slightly more human afterwards, I'm still shaking as I wait for him to answer, sitting down on the bed to keep myself from toppling over. He picks up on the third ring.

'Hey,' he says. 'You okay?'

'Yes. Um, no. Not really. I've just been involved in a car accident.'

I tell him everything in detail, even admitting to almost telling the police about the messages.

'I'm coming home,' he says.

'No. Please don't,' I say with a sigh. 'Your parents need you more. I'll call one of the girls if I need anything. The car is in the garage to be fixed. I'll get a call when it's ready. I'm going to call the insurance company later.'

He pauses a moment. 'Are you sure you don't need me there?'

No.

'Yes. How is your dad?'

'He's awake, which is good, but still in the ICU. On lots of drugs too, so he's a bit out of it when I'm there. Mum stays with him as much as she can.'

'But he's getting better?'

'I think so, yeah. I told Rob I'd be coming back to work Friday, so I'll be home Thursday at some point.'

'Okay,' I say, relief flooding over me. I'm glad there's a time frame for his return. I'll feel safer at night with him by my side. I can survive another couple of days on my own. It's not like I have anywhere to go now I don't have a car. There's enough food in the fridge and cupboards to keep me going. Not that I feel like eating any of it.

I finish the call with Noah. He sounds better in himself. He's concerned about me, offered to come home early. I'm glad I've told him everything, although now I think about it, I realise I didn't mention my suspicions about Georgina.

I pop a couple of painkillers from the packet, washing them down with a glug of water. There's nothing for me to do for the rest of the day except sleep and recover, so that's what I do. I curl up in bed, still fully dressed, and pass out from sheer exhaustion.

I WAKE up the next morning at seven, groggy and confused as to why I'm wearing normal clothes and not my pyjamas. It takes a few seconds for my brain to click into gear.

The car accident.

It's wiped me out, but I am feeling better. My headache is gone and so is the ringing in my ears, but my body feels as if I've done a heavy weight-lifting session. The back of my neck is sore too. Whiplash. My muscles ache and, to be perfectly honest, the thought of speaking to people, even in the confines of my own flat, is enough to make me break into goosebumps. I know I *have* to see people, speak to them, interact with them – it's my job – but whoever this person is who's threatening me is taking away the part of me who really enjoyed all of that.

I don't feel like me anymore.

I have a single client booked in at ten this morning and one after lunch, both of whom are due to come to the flat. Not the busiest of working days, but by the end, I'll have a little under a hundred pounds. I don't dare look at my bank balance. I'll be lucky to scrape a thousand pounds this month. I expect I'm already in my overdraft.

I still need to call the insurance company about my car, but again... speaking to people. No. Not right now. I only want to talk to Noah. The door buzzer sounds.

That's odd. My client isn't due for another hour. Luckily, I'm dressed and ready, but I haven't prepped the treatment room.

Shit.

I rush to the intercom and press it. 'Hello?'

'Amelia! Thank goodness you're in. I need your help.'

It's Charlotte.

My heart jolts in my chest. I don't answer, not straight away. My finger pauses on the talk button. I don't want to let her in, and I feel positively horrible about it, but whatever this is has gone on long enough. I don't know what her deal is, but it's enough to put me on edge.

'Um... Hi, Charlotte. I'm sorry, but I have a client soon, and...'

The door buzzes through the speaker. Someone in the

building has let her in. I back away from the intercom. She's on her way up right now! I double-check the chain is in place.

I'm not about to put it past her that she wouldn't bust the door down and attack me. Everyone is a threat.

A triple knock sounds.

I peer through the peephole. She's there, red in the face, probably from running up the stairs. Why doesn't she ever take the lift? Is she afraid of enclosed spaces?

I can't pretend I'm not in. We've just spoken via the intercom. If I ignore her, then she's going to get suspicious and take it the wrong way. Maybe I want her to take it the wrong way. Maybe then she'll get the hint and leave me alone.

Oh, this is stupid.

Get a grip, Amelia!

I unlock the door and open it. 'Hi, Charlotte. Listen, I'm really sorry, but...'

She's standing on my doorstep, holding a lead in her hand. At the end of it, sitting at her feet, is an enormous, fluffy dog that looks half wolf.

'Um...'

Charlotte lets out a long sigh. 'Thank God. I'm so sorry, but I really need a favour. I completely forgot I had a doctor's appointment this morning, and it's super important. I can't reschedule because I'm desperately in need of a repeat of my medication. I'll only be an hour. Maximum.' She holds out the handle of the lead towards me.

'Wait... You want me to look after this dog for an hour?'

'Please,' she says. 'I wouldn't ask, but I'm desperate.'

'I... I really can't. Noah is allergic to dog hair, and—'

'But he's not here.'

'No, but... I have a client in an hour. At ten.'

'I'll be back by then. I swear.'

Before I can open my mouth, she shoves the end of the lead at me and bolts down the stairs.

What. The. Actual. Fuck.

CHAPTER TWENTY-FOUR

NOAH

Fuck.

I didn't think things would go this far. Mills has been involved in an accident because she almost went to the police. I should be home with Mills, looking after her, reassuring her everything is okay, even though it's not. I'm out of my depth, and I know I should be doing more, but how can I without revealing what really happened? If my secret gets out, it's over. I won't be able to recover from it. Nothing will withstand the fallout. Not me. Not Mills. Not our relationship. Not my job.

Everything is escalating. Getting worse with each passing day. Even if I was at home, there wouldn't be anything I could do to stop it. It's like a snowball rolling downhill, gathering speed. Eventually, it's going to reach the bottom and smash against something, destroying it.

That will be me.

She said nothing about hurting Mills. What if she had been seriously injured or killed? It's a warning. There's no doubt about it. Mills will think it's either an accident or a warning for her, but I know it's a warning for me. But I've had enough now. I get it. I'm not going to risk Mills' life for another second.

I make a call and wait for it to connect. There's no sound on the end of the line, but I know they're listening.

'I told you to stop going after Mills,' I say sternly.

'I don't know what you're talking about.'

'Don't give me that shit,' I reply.

'Noah, I can assure you that I had nothing to do with whatever has happened to Amelia.'

I shake my head. 'No, it has to be you.'

They hang up.

Time is running out. They are increasing the pressure, ensuring I don't back out of our agreement. I feel as if I've been pushed into a corner.

There really is no way out for me other than... ending everything.

The truth will still get out though. Mills will find out and will be forced to deal with the aftermath without me. Ending my life will only make things worse for her.

But at this point, it's looking like the easiest option, and that scares me.

It scares me a lot.

Because I've come close to choosing that option before.

It looks like they're going to get what they've wanted all along.

CHAPTER TWENTY-FIVE

My body is frozen to the spot, unable to move a muscle. My legs won't work. I can't even blink. I'm so stunned by what's happened it doesn't feel real, like a dream. No, a nightmare.

And it's arrived in the form of a fluffy dog-wolf.

It sits staring at me, whining. It's a Siberian husky, or maybe a cross between a husky and something else fluffy and enormous. It can't stay out here. This building doesn't allow dogs. I'm breaking the rules merely by having it here, breathing heavily and wagging its overly fluffy tail in the main hallway. It's very cute, though, with its tongue lolling out the side of its mouth and its dark chocolate eyes.

'Fine,' I say. 'Come on then. Come in.' I glance at the corners of the main stairwell, wondering if there are CCTV cameras installed in the building.

The dog-wolf wags its tail, woofs loudly, then bolts straight through the open door behind me, yanking the lead out of my hand.

'Stop!'

It barrels down the hallway, skidding on the carpet as it rounds the corner and into the lounge.

Crash!

I make it into the living area in time to see the potted plant in the corner roll across the floor, spilling soil in its wake. The dog-wolf has one of the pillows from the sofa in its mouth, shaking it violently from side to side.

'Stop it!'

I rush forwards but then take a moment. This is an unfamiliar dog. It looked friendly enough at the door, but now it's turned into a crazed lunatic, tearing into my favourite pillow, the one I use to snuggle up against in an evening.

I'm not a dog person. I like dogs, don't get me wrong, but I'd never own one. I'm more of a cat person. Noah isn't allergic. I only said that as an excuse, but he loves dogs. He takes after his mum in that way, which is why he always enjoys looking after her pack whenever she asks.

Charlotte didn't tell me the dog's name, in too much of a rush to bolt down the stairs and leave it with me, so I can't even try and call it to get it under control. I'm going to be hoovering up dog hair for the next month at this rate. Tufts of white and grey fur float through the air and stick to my sofa cushions, then start gathering in the corners of the room.

'Come,' I say in as stern a voice as I can muster.

The dog-wolf tilts its head to the side, looking adorably cute despite its menacing size. It's wearing a thick red collar. Maybe its owner's details are on its tag. I can call them, explain what's happened. Charlotte would take it badly. It would make her look very unprofessional, but that's not my problem. She has no right to leave this dog with me. No right.

We aren't friends. This isn't normal, rational behaviour.

What makes her think this is okay? It's preposterous and, when she does come back, I won't be taking it lying down. Enough is enough.

'Come here,' I say, holding out my hand for the dog to sniff.

The dog-wolf stops jumping on the sofa and bounds towards me. It weaves in and out of my legs, sending me off balance. Righting myself, I grab for the end of the lead and manage to catch it, but it's strong, too strong, pulling me over to my knees. It thinks I'm playing a game.

I clench my fingers around the collar and stop it from running in circles around my feet. 'Calm down. I just want to check your collar. I don't even know if you're a boy or a girl.' There's no tag attached with its owners' details. 'Damn it,' I mutter, but I do find out its name because it's engraved onto the thick collar in gold lettering.

William.

'That's an odd choice of name for a dog,' I say, ruffling its huge head. I take the lead and walk William to the kitchen, where I find a big plastic bowl, usually used for salads, and fill it with water from the tap.

I place it down for William, who laps up huge mouthfuls, splashing over the sides and onto the tiled floor. If I didn't know any better, I'd say the dog has never had a drink of water in its life, the way he's gulping it down.

William drains the bowl, then starts prowling around the kitchen, sniffing every nook and cranny, licking the floor where I spilled sauce last night and didn't clear up properly.

I check my watch. My client arrives in forty-five minutes. There's no way I can have this dog in my flat while I'm doing a treatment in the other room. It's going to destroy the place, not to mention it may bark, disturbing the ambient massage.

I'm angry, but I don't know who I'm angrier at: Charlotte for dumping this dog on me, or myself for letting her dump this dog on me. But she turned up at my door unannounced, let herself into the building, practically threw the end of the lead at me and ran away.

It's the last thing I need.

Thirty minutes later, I make the hard decision to cancel the client. I give her a call because texting so close to the appointment seems like cheating my way around a confrontation. She's probably already on her way here, but I've had no contact from Charlotte, despite sending several messages, none of which have been delivered, let alone read.

'I'm just about to leave the house!' Jenny says, annoyance clear in her voice.

'I'm so, so sorry,' I say, as William bounces around the flat. He still hasn't settled, and I'm beginning to wonder if he ever will. 'Something has come up and I can't get out of it.' I daren't tell her it's because of a massive dog-wolf invading my home. 'I can reschedule to any time you want another day.'

'Don't bother,' she snaps. Then hangs up.

I close my eyes and count to ten. 'Fuck's sake,' I mutter.

Maybe I shouldn't have cancelled, and instead dealt with the fallout of locking William in one of the other rooms while I did her massage, but God knows how much damage he would have caused in ninety minutes. He's already midway through destroying the living room and has knocked over one of the dining stools by the breakfast bar, breaking one of its spindly legs.

It's doubtful Charlotte walked him before she dropped

him off with me. His energy is through the roof. I should take him for a walk, but controlling him is going to be tricky. There's a small park at the back of my building, where I see people taking their dogs; more like a green space situated in the middle of the city. It's only across the road. I can take him there for a bit. There's not a chance in hell I'm letting him off the lead, but hopefully it'll help lower his energy levels.

Plus, I don't want him cocking his leg on any of my furniture.

William and I take the lift to the ground floor and head outside. He's not too bad on the lead, walking politely beside me, but as soon as he sees the patch of grass and another dog, he lunges forward with the strength of a horse and bounds over, almost yanking my shoulder out of its socket. I'm still sore from the car accident, so it rattles me a little, but I cling on for dear life as my brain rattles around in my head.

Somehow, I manage to hold onto the lead as he half-drags me across the park towards a tiny dog and its owner. Oh God. I'm done for. He's going to attack this poor little thing, and then he'll have to be put down, and I'll be in trouble, even though he's not my dog, and—

'Aww, what a lovely dog,' says the lady.

I take a much-needed breath.

Thankfully, William is a good boy, and he and the tiny dog sniff each other, their tails wagging. 'Uh, thanks. He's actually not mine,' I say, slightly breathless.

'Are you a dog walker?'

'I guess today I am, yeah,' I say with a sigh. 'You wouldn't happen to have a spare doggy bag, would you?'

The lady looks at me, probably wondering what kind of

dog walker comes out without a doggy bag. She reaches into her pocket and hands me one.

'Thank you,' I say, my face heating.

The lady and her tiny dog eventually move away, leaving me and William to do a couple of laps of the small park. I keep glancing around, searching for anyone nearby. Charlotte. She could be out there, watching me, enjoying my awkwardness. She's probably finding it hilarious.

Twenty minutes later, William has done countless wees and one large dog turd, which I pick up using the bag and place in a nearby bin. We return to my building. I make him walk up the stairs to tire him out some more. His little adventure outside seems to have done the trick because he's more subdued when we reach the top floor.

We enter the flat, where I refill his water bowl and set it down. He drains it for a second time. Looks like I'll be taking him out again soon...

Where the hell is Charlotte? It's been almost an hour and a half since she left. I call. Text. But she doesn't reply. I feel like a pressure cooker ready to explode. It wouldn't surprise me if steam was escaping out of my ears. My next client is due in just over an hour.

If Charlotte's not back by then, I'm screwed. My blood pressure is rising with every passing minute as I keep calling Charlotte, but it goes straight to voicemail every time. She's turned off her phone. It's like she has no clue what she's doing to me, how she's inconvenienced me.

William finds a sunspot by the balcony, finally succumbing to exhaustion. He's lying on his side with his eyes closed, not a care in the world, oblivious that he's royally fucked up my entire day. It's not his fault. It's my fault for being so stupid, so trusting of Charlotte, who is, after all, a practical stranger.

I call Georgina, but she doesn't answer, so I leave a voice-mail. 'Call me.'

I call my other friends, Zoe and Hayley, but they don't answer either. There's no reason to call Noah because he's not close by, so he won't be able to help me. The blood pounds in my ears as I hang up. Another headache is forming behind my eyes, this one from stress, so I head to the kitchen and pop a couple of painkillers, gulping them down with a glass of tepid water from the tap.

I decide to keep busy and prepare the treatment room for my next client, all the while wondering if I'll need to cancel again because time is ticking by and Charlotte still isn't replying.

In my head, I repeat what I plan to say to her when she eventually arrives. William belongs to someone who will be expecting him to be returned at a certain time, I assume, so she'll come back for him eventually.

Now, though, my mind starts second-guessing Charlotte. It's possible she's not even at a doctor's appointment and is sat nearby, watching the building. Hell, maybe she's else-where, drinking a coffee in a cafe, laughing at me from behind her cappuccino, having fun at my expense. I can't avoid it any longer. I need to confront her, and this time, no amount of her tears will make me back away and change my mind.

An hour later, I'm forced to cancel yet another treat-ment. This time, my client is more understanding, but I still feel unbelievably guilty about it.

I take William for another wee break, but as I walk back

across the road towards my building, a familiar figure stands outside the door, pressing the buzzer.

CHAPTER TWENTY-SIX

Charlotte turns abruptly as I shout her name, spots me and William jogging towards her, and waves over-enthusiastically. She's smiling like a Cheshire cat and greets the dog by bending to his level and ruffling his thick fur, giving him fuss and attention. William is beside himself, wiggling his fluffy butt side to side. I can barely hold onto his lead. In any other situation, I'd think it was adorable, but not in this instance.

'What the hell are you playing at?' I shove the lead at her. Charlotte manages to catch it before it falls to the ground. She stands up, a look of pure horror on her face. The smile she wore a moment ago has slipped.

'W-What?'

I laugh, but it comes out slightly menacing, like that of a crazed psychopath. I'm finding this anything but funny, but if I don't laugh, I'm worried I might cry or scream.

'Don't try and pretend you don't know what I'm talking about, Charlotte. You promised me you'd be back in less than an hour. I've had to cancel two clients today. Two! I've lost out on over a hundred pounds' worth of work. Do you realise how much you've inconvenienced me?' I glare at her, nostrils flaring, eyes blazing, but she stares blankly at me, her mouth open.

'I-I was only gone an hour. I thought you wouldn't mind looking after him. You said you love dogs.'

My fists clench at my sides. 'You've been gone almost *four* hours, Charlotte! But that's beside the point. If you'd given me a bit of notice and asked me to look after him, then I would have said yes, but you didn't. You turned up at my door, practically threw his lead at me, and ran away. You didn't even stop to consider I might be busy. You only thought of yourself.' My raised, angry voice is drawing attention from a few passers-by. I don't care. I've reached boiling point. Breaking point. Whatever you want to call it. I'm there. She's pushed me too far this time. Everything that's happened over the past week has finally brought me to this moment, and I can't hold it back any longer. I'm scared, frustrated, confused, and I need to get to the bottom of this once and for all. She knows exactly what she's doing to me, and I want to know why.

Now.

Charlotte grips the dog's lead tightly in her hand, wrapping it round and round her wrist. If Williams bolts, then he's going to drag her along with him or severely damage her hand in the process.

'I told you, I forgot I had a doctor's appointment. I couldn't cancel at such short notice, Milly.'

'Don't call me Milly,' I snap. 'We're not friends, Charlotte. You don't get to call me by a pet name. I had two clients booked in for appointments, and I had to cancel them both.' I grab my head, certain it's about to explode. 'You didn't even think!'

'I – I'm sorry...' She looks at the ground, tears filling her eyes.

Oh great. Not this again.

'That's not good enough. And another thing–' But before I can get my next word out, Charlotte lets out a huge sob, turns and runs across the road, William jogging beside her. 'Wait!' I call out.

But she's already gone.

Damn it.

A man watches her run away, then turns and glares at me, tutting as he shakes his head. It instantly makes me shrink towards the front door of the building. I hastily fish my keys from my pocket and let myself in, slamming the door closed with such vigour that I worry for a moment I may have damaged the frame.

I take a slow breath, the only proper one I've taken for the last few minutes, since I started yelling at Charlotte. Now that the red mist is subsiding, I can clearly see I've over-reacted, but I don't think I was in the wrong to have a go at her. I was too harsh, and I could have been a little more tact-ful, a little less aggressive, but what the hell did she expect? That I would say, 'Oh, it's no bother, don't be silly, of course your doctor's appointment is more important than me earning a wage so I can afford to buy a house and get married to my future husband.'

I stomp up the stairs, my foul mood still simmering, bypassing the lift because I'm too agitated to keep still, and re-enter the flat. My body is vibrating with adrenaline, as if I've jumped out of a plane. I don't know how to calm down or how I'm supposed to feel. I've made a grown woman cry and run away from me. Never in my life have I ever been that aggressive towards someone.

But I don't owe Charlotte anything. She's practically attached herself to me for some reason. It's not my fault she's taken things too far. For all I know, she's been playing this game with me from the start. Even if she isn't my stalker, she's still crossed a line, and I'm the one who's come away looking like the villain.

Before I tackle the mess that William caused in my living room, I flick the kettle on. No clients. No clients tomorrow either. I'm not seeing Sally or Wilma or any of my other wealthier clients until late next week. I need more income. Usually, if I am going on holiday or taking planned time off, I book clients back-to-back for at least two weeks beforehand to earn as much money as possible, so I can take the time off and not worry about the lack of money coming in.

But this time off isn't planned.

Well, not by me. *Someone* has planned it.

The threatening messages.

The car accident.

The bad review.

Clients cancelling back-to-back.

Clients calling and dropping me for no reason.

Someone has planned it all right, and it's bloody working. I barely have any clients left, but I have an idea. I don't often do it, but Georgina is right. I can't afford to be picky.

I quickly type out a professional yet short text to my remaining clients, explaining that I've had some recent slots open up over the next couple of weeks and can offer a discount of 10% for any spend over eighty pounds.

Feeling momentarily better, certain my most trusted and valued clients will jump at the chance of cheaper or earlier appointments, I make a cup of tea... and wait for the texts to come through while I clean up.

Three hours later, not one client has responded.

Not one. Not even to say no, thank you.

My left eye starts twitching, and I'm seriously considering cracking open a bottle of wine.

Being stuck inside is driving me crazy. I've never been one to stay in because keeping busy and active is like a drug. Sure, I enjoy a good chill day from time to time, where I can slob out on the sofa and watch Netflix, but give me the option of working or being outside doing something, and I'd jump at the chance every time.

I want to venture out, go for a run, clear my head. Do something. *Anything.* But every time I go to take a step outside, I wonder if she's watching me. Charlotte. My stalker. Georgina. Hell, even my old boss, Silvia. There are too many suspects to make sense of anything. Every time I discount someone, another clue pops up, and I start suspecting them again.

Telling the police is not an option because my stalker has threatened to make things even worse. How much worse can things possibly get? I'm already afraid to go outside, been involved in a car accident and lost most of my business income.

I glance around my flat, my thoughts whirring. A question pops into my head and, try as I might, I now can't get it out.

How has this person been able to find out so much about me?

They can't be watching me all the time. They'd learn next to nothing just by watching the building, so they must have devised a way to watch me even if they aren't around.

...

My Echo Dot.

Leaping to my feet, I race to the bedroom and bend next to the listening device. It's switched off at the wall now, so it might not be working anymore, but it would have been working for a while beforehand.

I'm not tech-savvy, but I know the whole idea of an Echo Dot is to listen and learn. But how would someone other than me or Noah be able to access it? My eyes travel to my laptop bag, which is pushed underneath the bed. It wouldn't be enough to connect to the Wi-Fi, which anyone could do with the password, but...

Everything clicks into place.

My laptop bag holds my password book, the same book that holds the Wi-Fi code *and* my Amazon account password, which connects to the Echo Dot.

It's my fault.

Noah told me so many times not to keep my passwords in a physical book, but I told him it was more dangerous to have them stored on my phone. He was the one who convinced me not to use the same password for everything, so how else was I supposed to remember them all?

It makes sense now.

Charlotte snuck into my bedroom the very first time she entered my flat while she claimed she was using the bathroom, probably took a photo of all my passwords in the book, logged into the Wi-Fi router and connected to my Echo Dot, then has been using it to freak me out with sound effects, all from the comfort of her own home. Maybe she's even been using it to listen to conversations. It's possible the signal wouldn't reach that far, and perhaps I'm making all this up, forcing situations to fit, like shoving a square peg into a round hole, but it would explain so much.

What if she took things further?

She's been in my flat a few times now. I made her a cup of tea. In that time, she could have planted a bug or a camera in the lounge.

To satisfy my paranoia, I spend the rest of the day searching my flat high and low for anything out of the ordinary. I pull furniture out from the walls, even all the plates and saucepans out of the cupboards, which makes no sense, because even if there were a camera in there, it wouldn't be able to capture anything with the cupboard doors closed, but I'm a woman on a mission. A woman possessed. Everything gets moved and searched.

I don't stop to eat or drink for the whole day.

At nine that night, the buzzer echoes from the hallway. My hair's a mess, sticking up like I've electrocuted myself; my natural hair making an appearance, sticking to my sweaty face.

I race to the door and press the video feed. It's Georgina.

'Um, so are you going to let me in or what?' she asks.

I bite my lip and step back. I've made up my mind that it's Charlotte who is stalking me, so what's the harm in letting Georgina in? She's the only person who knows everything that's been happening, although now I think about it, did I tell her about the car accident?

I don't know. The timeline of events is blurred. They've all rolled into one, and I can't remember when all this even started. What day is it? I hate this!

I press the buzzer to let her in and unlock the front door. My anxiety skyrockets while I wait for her to use the lift and join me. Something isn't right. I don't feel normal or stable.

The lift doors ping open and Georgina steps out, holding a bottle of red wine. 'Hey, what's going on? Why haven't you messaged me back?' she asks.

'What?'

Georgina stares at me. 'I've sent you like a dozen Whats-Apps, none of which have been read. I got worried and thought you might have been murdered in your flat or something.'

'So you came over and brought wine?' My eyes drop to the bottle in her hand.

'Yeah, on the off chance you *weren't* dead. There's clearly something going on... so, I thought wine would be a good option. Why are you all sweaty?'

I let out a long sigh and beckon her inside. 'Just come in and I'll explain.'

Georgina follows me and closes the door. When she reaches the lounge and kitchen area, she whistles, scanning the array of mess and destruction. 'You've been busy, I see. Why do I smell dog?' She heads to the glass cabinets above the worktops, reaching for the wine glasses like she's done a hundred times before.

Once the wine is poured, I tell her about Charlotte and William and the car accident, which, apparently, I had *not* told her about, momentarily forgetting the place could be rigged with secret hidden cameras and microphones.

'And the fact your place looks like a bomb site is because...'

I down the last dregs of my second glass of wine. 'Because I thought maybe she's bugged the flat with a hidden camera. She's already connected to the Wi-Fi and my Echo Dot. Do you know how to change the password?'

'Right. Now is the time to go to the police. Frankly, I'm shocked you haven't already.'

'The message said not to, or things will get worse.'

'Fuck the message! The police can deal with it. Hell,

they can put a guard outside your door if they must, but you *need* to tell them.'

I hold out my glass and she refills it with the last of the bottle. I blink back tears as I stare into the red liquid, which looks horribly like blood. My stomach swirls and gurgles. 'I can't. I'm afraid if I do, something bad will happen. I've lost everything,' I say with a whimper.

Georgina is sitting next to me on the sofa. She squeezes my knee. 'Hey. You haven't. I promise. It's all fixable. When is Noah getting home?'

'Tomorrow.'

'Okay, and he can't come back any sooner? What's he said about this? Have you even told him?'

'Yes... Some... I didn't want him to worry. His dad's sick.'

'Yes, and you have some crazed stalker who's after you. He'd want to be here with you. It's turned you into some crazed, paranoid hermit.'

'I'm still no closer to finding out why she's after me. Charlotte, I mean. I yelled at her earlier, and she ran away crying. She doesn't seem like the type of person who'd do this sort of thing. Something doesn't add up. She knows Noah, I'm sure of it, but I have no idea why she'd be after me like this.'

'Maybe you need to confront her, but maybe not shout at her in a public space. Do you think she's dangerous?'

'I... I don't know. I mean, the threatening texts are pretty... Well, threatening, but that's all they are. Threats.'

'How about you invite her over to make amends? I'll be here for moral support. Backup, if you will. How's that? Then, if things get heated, I'll attack her with a kitchen knife.'

My lips twitch into a smile. 'Maybe leave the knife out of

it, but I think you're right about inviting her over to clear the air. I don't want to see her as a client again, even if she is one of the only ones I have left.'

'Great. Message her now. Tell her to come over tomorrow at nine. I'll be here. We'll sort this out one way or another. If she doesn't give us the answers we want, then we'll go to the police. Threaten *her*. See how she likes it.'

I do just that. At first, I try calling her, but she doesn't answer. Not that I expect her to want to talk to me after the way I shouted at her, but she does read my text, and messages straight back in her usual style of sending one short message after another in quick succession.

Hi, Amelia.

You scared me today.

I am sorry.

I didn't realise the time.

Yes, I can come tomorrow at nine.

I can explain everything.

See you then.

Charlotte xx

Georgina reads the messages. 'Well, let's hope she can explain everything, or she's going to get a foot up her butt from me.'

CHAPTER TWENTY-SEVEN

The next morning, Georgina arrives at half past eight, and I'm wired on my third cup of coffee. I can't keep my body still. During the night, I tossed and turned constantly, trapping myself within my duvet, then freaking out when I could barely move my legs. It felt as if someone was holding me down, trapping me within my bed sheets.

By the time the door buzzer goes at nine, I'm a frantic mess, pacing up and down the hallway like a caged lion. Georgina helped me straighten the flat last night. I accidentally broke a few things while I tore the place apart, and I had to hoover the carpets at least three times to remove the dog hair from the fibres. The blasted stuff got everywhere. She helped me change the password for the Wi-Fi and my Amazon account, and for good measure, I changed every other password I could think of too. I also destroyed the password book, ripped up the pages into dozens of tiny pieces and put them in separate recycling bags. Obviously, I didn't tell Georgina the new passwords and, if I forget them every time I try and log in, then so be it. I'll have to change them every time. It's a small price to pay.

I never found any cameras or microphones in the flat, but I did find the phone charger I lost six months ago and my favourite hairbrush that mysteriously disappeared several weeks ago. It had wedged itself down the back of the sofa cushions and slipped through a tear in the fabric.

When I open the door to Charlotte, she smiles at me, her face lighting up, but it quickly fades when she sees Georgina with her arms folded, leaning against the lounge doorway. My own personal bodyguard.

'This is Georgina,' I say calmly. 'A friend of mine.' Georgina clears her throat. 'Best friend of mine,' I add.

Charlotte is clearly not comfortable with her being here. Maybe she thought she'd be here alone with me again.

'Nice to meet you,' says Charlotte, avoiding eye contact with both of us. 'Look, I just want to apologise again for yesterday with the dog. I... I had the doctor's appointment I forgot about, and it really *was* an emergency. I'm on a specific type of medication, and I'd already missed several doses, so I wasn't quite myself. Afterwards, I just... just forgot I'd dropped William off with you. I forgot where I was and...' Charlotte stops, tears brimming in her eyes.

I gesture for her to take a seat on my sofa while giving Georgina a glance out of the corner of my eye. She's frowning. Charlotte sounds genuine, but how does someone simply forget something like that?

Charlotte sits down, and I take a seat nearby, but not too close. 'Charlotte,' I say firmly, 'this medication you're on... Are you genuinely unwell? Like... are you sick?'

Charlotte shakes her head. 'It's nothing like that. It's for my head...' She looks up at Georgina, wary, but continues. 'I have borderline personality disorder, and I'm bipolar.'

And, just like that, everything clicks into place and starts to make sense, like slotting in a missing piece of a puzzle.

Guilt hits me like a freight train, because I should have realised, noticed the signs, but I didn't. I made it all about me, thought she was targeting me because she had a personal issue, but it's not like that at all.

I should have known.

Because my mother had the same disorder.

I take a deep breath, trying to calm my racing heart. 'I'm sorry,' I say.

'Don't be sorry. It's my issue, not yours. I know I can come off a bit... odd sometimes, but when I first met you, I really liked you, and I thought we hit it off as friends. I can get a bit obsessed when I meet new people I connect with. I struggle to hold on to any kind of relationship, be it friends, boyfriends, girlfriends. I'm bisexual as well, so that can be confusing for me, but I don't fancy you or anything. For years, I struggled with finding my identity. I guess I still struggle with it. Anyway, I'm now blabbering and talking nonsense, so I'll finish by saying that the medication I'm on doesn't always keep me steady. Sometimes, I can spiral and become irrational, forgetful and a bit... scatty, I've been told. It's not an excuse, but it is a reason.'

I shake my head, sighing. 'I should have realised...'

'Why?' she asks directly.

'Because... ' I really don't feel like telling her about my mother and the hell she put me through as a child. Even Noah doesn't know the full truth, because it's too painful to think about. 'I thought you were targeting me,' I say instead.

'Huh?'

'I feel so ridiculous now,' I say, standing up. I need to move, shake off this nervous energy. I turn back to her. 'A lot of things have been happening with me lately, and I thought...'

Charlotte stands up. 'What? What's been happening?'

'It... it doesn't matter. It's not your concern. I'm sorry I blamed you for it, though, and I'm sorry for shouting at you yesterday, but I've been losing all my clients, and I had to cancel two appointments yesterday, so I lost out on a lot of money. I was angry and–'

Charlotte holds her hand up. 'No, I'm sorry. I don't usually tell people about my disorder because I know they'll look at me differently when I do. I'm only telling you now because I've genuinely upset you, and I'm sorry.'

I give her a weak smile, feeling like the worst person in the world. 'Thank you.'

'I... I hope we can still be friends?' she asks timidly.

'Yes, I'd like that.'

Then, she steps forward and gives me a hug. I don't really know how to respond, so I lightly put my arms around her, throwing Georgina a quick glance. She looks as flabbergasted as I do about this whole revelation.

'Wait, Charlotte. Can I ask you a direct question?'

'Of course.'

'Do you know Noah from when you were at Lancaster University?'

Her eyes flick to the side again. 'I... Yes, but not well. He was on a different course. I only met him a couple of times. I used to date one of his friends.' Her voice wobbles at the end.

'Okay,' I say. 'Thank you for telling me, but why didn't you tell me before?'

'I've not been good at taking my medication. My mind

has been... all over the place.' Her bottom lip trembles. I don't want to push her too far.

'I understand.'

'Thank you,' she replies.

A few minutes later, I say goodbye to Charlotte at the door, then gently close it once she's disappeared round the corner. I turn to Georgina.

'Well, that was unexpected,' she says after letting out a long exhale. 'Do you believe her?'

Her question knocks me off guard. 'W-What? Of course I do. Why? Don't you?'

'I don't know...'

'Yes, I believe her. My mother had the same disorder. I'm kicking myself for not recognising the signs before. I should have known better.'

'I remember you telling me a while ago about your mum. You only told me a little, though, and I never pressed you for more details because I know how badly it affected you.'

'Yeah...' I say sadly. 'I don't like to talk about it, but... she... she was... not herself a lot of the time. Her moods would swing from one extreme to the other in the blink of an eye. One minute she was my best friend, laughing and joking with me, and the next she was screaming at me for ruining her life, calling me names. She'd forget to pick me up from school and, when I finally got home, I'd find her asleep in bed. One time, she walked out on us for two weeks, then returned and acted like nothing had happened. Dad struggled with it. He was worried about how it was affecting me. She kept trying to blame him for everything, then apologised, grovelling at his feet, begging him not to leave her. In the end, Mum made her own choice... and she left us for good when I was fifteen.'

Georgina steps closer and wraps her arms tight around my body. I burst into tears, smushing my face into her shoulder. I have unresolved issues when it comes to my mum, something I should have dealt with in therapy years ago, but I had no idea just how much it would affect me in the long run. Charlotte revealing her diagnosis has opened old wounds I thought were healed, but the scars from my mother's mental illness run deep in my own skin, have moulded me into who I am today. I didn't understand her condition. I still don't, because I've never taken the time to understand it. Not fully. I've blamed her. Resented her. Hated her. And I know I shouldn't have done, because it wasn't her fault.

I used to beat myself up daily, blaming myself for my mother's condition. Dad told me that these types of disorders stem from a trauma of some kind, usually from childhood. When I think about Charlotte, all the issues with my mum come flying back, almost smacking me in the face. If Charlotte has the same condition, does that mean she's suffered through trauma, too, in the past?

Georgina can't stay for too long, but she gives me a warning to be careful before waving goodbye.

Once alone, my mind spirals. Now I know it's not Charlotte who's been targeting me, my thoughts snap to who else it could be.

I'm at a loss as to what to do for the rest of the day.

It's then I realise I haven't collected the mail from my cubby hole downstairs in the foyer for several days. Usually, I check it every time I walk past, but I've been too distracted each time, so I've forgotten.

Grabbing my keys, I head out the door, pull it closed, and walk down the stairs. I need the exercise. I've barely been out of the flat for days, apart from walking William yesterday. Crossing a suspect off my list has mellowed my anxiety slightly now that I understand Charlotte's actions a little more.

But, as I reach into my mail slot, my anxiety skyrockets again when I pull out a single sheet of A4 paper. On it, in large red letters, are the words.

Guess again, Bitch.

CHAPTER TWENTY-EIGHT

Dizzying fear sucks all the air from my lungs as my eyes zone in on the words on the page.

It has to be Georgina. No one else could have known I no longer suspect Charlotte. I searched my whole flat from top to bottom and found no cameras or listening devices. Georgina had been standing next to me the whole time while Charlotte and I had been talking, clearing the air. It's her. There's no doubt about it now.

I've made up my mind. I can no longer avoid telling the police about this. They'll know what to do and can advise me on what to do next. It's Thursday today. Noah finally comes home. When exactly, I have no idea, so I walk slowly back up the stairs to my flat, going over my plan.

Before I speak to the police, though, I want to speak to Noah. I'm glad his dad is on the mend and out of the ICU. I assume he'll be making a return trip to visit them soon, but for now, the worst seems to be over. I need us to be on the same page. I want him to understand that me going against his wishes and contacting the police doesn't mean I don't trust his judgment. But it's gone too far now. My best friend has infiltrated my life and is targeting me. Surely, Noah will understand my decision to involve them.

I don't want to pile more stress onto Noah. He's always been quite emotional and susceptible to it, and I can't imagine his time away looking after his parents has helped.

The only client who texted me back to take me up on my offer was Sally and, I must admit, my heart leapt a little at the thought of seeing her. She's always been a great friend as well as a client, so I've booked her in for tomorrow morning. I'm not sure when I'll be going to the police, but I'm hoping I'll be able to get it over with tonight. It all depends on what time Noah arrives home.

The day drags on and on, and there's still no sign of Noah. My phone remains silent, and the door locked. I dare not step outside. I make dinner and am straining pasta over the sink when keys sound in the lock. My heart rate spikes. I've left the chain bolted across the door, so he can't get in.

'What the...' I hear from the hall.

'Hang on!' I leave the pasta on the side and jog to the door, sliding the chain across.

Noah pushes the door open. 'Hey,' he says with a tired smile.

I wrap my arms around him, squeezing him around the middle and burying my face in his chest. He rests his chin on the top of my head. I've always loved that he's over six foot tall to my five foot five. Instantly, my body seems to relax against him, soaking up his warmth and strength.

'I missed you,' I say.

'I've missed you too. I'm sorry I haven't called much. How's it all been here? How are you feeling after the car accident?'

We break apart and walk together into the main living area, where he takes a seat on a nearby breakfast stool while I return to serving dinner.

'I was a little stiff afterwards, but I'm okay now. The car is at the garage having its rear bumper replaced. The police haven't been in touch yet, but... I need to speak to them anyway about something else.' I slide a plate of food over to him and sit opposite with my own.

I take it slow, explaining everything in as much detail as I can. I explain about Charlotte and the dog, and then her revelation regarding her mental health. I show him the note I found in the mail slot and the messages on my phone. I think I remember everything, and when I finally stop and take a bite of food, Noah stands up, pushing his own plate away, which he's barely touched.

'This is my fault. I shouldn't have left. I shouldn't have told you not to tell the police.'

'But she warned me not to tell the police too.'

'Yeah, and then what happened? Someone crashed into you and drove away. And the police haven't caught them yet?'

'Not that I'm aware. They've not been in touch.'

Noah scratches his chin, then runs his hands over his bald head. 'You really believe it's Georgina?'

I nod my head. 'This feels personal. I'm convinced it's her. She used the phrase "cute top" in one of the messages. I'm certain of it.' I gulp back a mouthful of saliva.

Noah's eyes widen. 'Out of the three of your friends, she's your closest, though, isn't she?'

'Yes, but... there's been certain things that have happened only when she's been around. She also used the phrase *cute top*. She's been in the flat, so had access to the

Wi-Fi code and my password book if she knew where to look. She was there with me when Charlotte revealed her disorder. She also took one of my long-term clients and could easily be the person who's spreading bad reviews about me to all my clients. She's the one I've been telling everything to, and the latest message says, "Guess again," which she could have slid into my mail slot on her way out earlier.'

'Okay, so say it is her... Why? What have you ever done to her to make her turn against you like this?'

I take a step back, perching my bum on the edge of the kitchen stool. 'I have no idea.' And that's the truth. Again, I could be trying to make all these clues fit somehow, but something tells me Georgina is targeting me.

'Maybe stay away from both of them. Georgina and Charlotte, I mean. It sounds like Charlotte is a bit of a loose cannon anyway. Sorry, I don't mean to be insensitive, but seriously, dropping off a huge dog at the flat? If the landlord found out, we could have been kicked out.'

'I know, but... Noah, you don't understand. I barely have any clients left. Sally, Wilma and two others. That's it. I can't afford to turn clients away. Charlotte isn't the one behind all this.'

'How do you know that for sure? She could have been lying and made it all up. You can't trust her.'

This makes my skin bristle with goosebumps. I left out the part about her admitting she knows him because I wanted to test him, and he's failed. Miserably.

'I believe her,' I say matter-of-factly. 'And that's all that matters. I'm not turning her away because of what's happened to her and who she is. I just... I need all this stalking stuff to be over.'

'Yes, of course. You're right.'

I wait to see if he's going to expand, but he doesn't. He's refusing to admit that he knows Charlotte, and even though I'm not worried about her anymore, I'm still convinced Noah is hiding something. He's never been the best at hiding things from me. Like that time he promised to go sugar-free for a month to improve his health, and I found a plastic wrapper of biscuits in the bin. I asked him outright about it, and he blurted out the truth before I could even prepare the response to his lie.

'Noah... What's going on?'

'What?' His eyes are like saucers. 'Nothing's going on.'

'Do you know who's behind these messages? Do you think it's someone other than Georgina?'

'No! Why would I?'

'Is it something to do with your work?' Noah backs out of the room, but I follow. He's not getting away that easily. 'Noah!'

'Mills, I don't know, okay? I'm tired and stressed from being with my parents, and the long drive, and the fact that I now have to go on a night shift.'

'What, now? You've just got home.'

'Yes, but Rob needs me to cover and I can't say no now, can I, especially since you're not earning much lately. It's not a dig at you. I'm just stating a fact.'

I rub my temples. 'I need to get my clients back, or at least find new ones, but I can't if this person is still out there and wants to destroy me.'

'Give me twenty-four hours,' says Noah as he takes off his clothes, preparing for a shower. I watch him undress, taking note of his tall, toned physique. He's lost a lot of weight lately. Muscle mass too. He's been working out at the gym, but clearly hasn't been eating enough.

'Twenty-four hours,' I say. 'What for? Why do I need to wait twenty-four hours before contacting the police?'

'Because... I don't want you to ruin your friendship with Georgina before you have all the facts, okay?'

'But...'

'Trust me. I'm going to speak to some people at work. In the meantime, just stay in the flat. Don't go out. Don't do anything. Don't speak to anyone. Please.'

I stare at him, unblinking. What he's asking of me is ridiculous, and I can't wrap my head around why he'd want me to do it. He's giving me an ultimatum. He may not have said it in as many words, but either I trust him this once, or I go against him and potentially ruin not only my friendship with Georgina, but my relationship with Noah too.

'Twenty-four hours,' I say again. 'And then I'm going to the police. I'll deal with whatever consequences come after that.'

Noah nods. He's only in his boxers now. He notices me looking at him, then backs away towards the bathroom. I frown as he closes the door, almost as if he doesn't want me looking at him any longer.

I put my mouth close to the door as I say, 'I was thinking of sending some flowers to your dad and giving your mum a call. I don't want them to think I don't care about them.'

The door opens. 'No! Don't do that. They're fine. They know you love them. Don't send flowers or speak to them either.' And he slams the door.

Okay, now I *know* something is wrong. There's not a doubt in my mind.

Noah knows something about what's been going on, and I'm more determined than ever to find out what it is.

CHAPTER TWENTY-NINE

I go over what Noah said after he leaves for work, how he reacted when I not only spoke about contacting his parents, and what he said about giving him twenty-four hours. What if Georgina comes after me tonight? She knows where I live. For God's sake, she knows everything about me, personal stuff I've never told Noah. The details she knows about my life are enough for her to have complete control over me if she wants to. The fact that I've changed all my passwords is a relief, but now she *knows* I've changed them. She was there! I've been so convinced all along it was Charlotte, or Silvia, at one point, that I pushed the more obvious choice – it was Georgina – out of my mind, certain one of my best friends wouldn't betray me.

I have no idea what her final plan is or whether she wants to hurt me. Perhaps she wants to destroy my business, but then why mine and not Zoe's or Hayley's? Everything has been building up and up. This isn't going to end unless I take a stand.

By the time I go to the police, it may be too late. Will

Noah call me tonight, or am I doomed to spend the whole day stewing by myself, repeating all the worst-case scenarios until I've driven myself crazy from stress and anxiety?

Noah's reaction to me sending his parents flowers was weird too. I've never been particularly close to either of them, but it's the least I can do. They may think it strange that I haven't contacted them and asked how they are directly. It would make me feel better if I did call them. Perhaps I can ask his mum a few details, like what to do when he won't talk to me or even look me in the eye. She must have dealt with it when he suffered with his own mental health in his youth.

With nothing else to do, my mind settled on a plan of attack, I grab my phone and call his parents' landline. If his mum doesn't answer, then I'll try her mobile. She may be at the hospital or out for a walk with the dogs.

'Hello,' comes the familiar voice of his mother, Deborah.

'Hi, Deborah. It's Amelia.'

'Amelia! How lovely to hear from you. How's things?'

'Um, yeah, I'm okay, thanks. I actually called to ask you how you're doing and to ask after Mike. Noah says he's out of the ICU now. That's great news.'

There's a long pause. Then, a nervous chuckle.

'I'm afraid you must have got your wires crossed, love. Mike wasn't in the ICU. He's fine. In fact, he's out on a fishing trip with some old college friends, so I've got the house to myself for a change, other than the animals, of course. It's bliss.'

'B-But... Noah came to visit you this week to look after you while Mike was sick in hospital.'

'Noah has been staying with us, yes, but it's got nothing

to do with Mike being in the hospital. Is that what he told you?'

I slowly lower the phone from my ear, staring blankly ahead. I hear muffled words coming from the speaker, but nothing registers apart from the fact that Noah has flat-out lied to me. Not only that, but he's made up a lie about his dad being at death's door.

'Sorry,' I say into the phone. 'Um... you're right. I've got my wires crossed. I'm so sorry.'

'Amelia, are you sure you're okay?'

'Yes. No. I...' Oh God. Tears flood my eyes, streaming down my cheeks before I can register what's happening.

'Is everything all right with Noah?' Deborah asks, keeping her voice calm.

Nothing like mine, which comes out all squeaky when I say, 'He's been acting strange... I – I think he might be depressed, but he won't talk to me, and... Well, he told me his dad was dying in hospital, and he went to visit you all last week, but clearly that's not the case, so...' I stop, take a breath, wondering if it's the right thing to do to blurt all that out to Noah's mother over the phone. I don't mean to drop Noah in it with his mother, but I'm at a point now where I can't depend on anyone, not even my best friend or my future husband.

Everyone's lying to me. Everyone knows something I don't.

'I'm so sorry to hear that. I know how difficult it was for him, back then. He can spiral if not caught early. Do you want me to try and have a word with him? He seemed fine when he was staying with us. Perhaps a little quieter than usual.'

'I... Thank you, but I'm going to try and talk to him myself, or at least find out why he lied.'

'Why do you think he lied to you?'

Her words almost knock me backwards. It's a question I haven't allowed my brain to think about yet because the possible answers are too terrifying. Yes, why was he staying with his parents if it wasn't for his dad being sick?

'I don't know,' I say sadly.

'Listen, love, we can't force this with Noah, okay? If you push too hard, then he'll only react worse.'

'Worse than lying to me? What if... Deborah, I know we've never spoken about Noah's depression in the past, but I think it's time to tell me what happened. If there's something you think I should know, then you need to tell me. Otherwise, I'm never going to understand what's going on with him. Is he a danger to himself? Should I be worried about him taking his own life? Why did he stay with you last week? Is he sick?' I almost choke on the words, but I splutter them out.

Deborah sighs at the end of the line. 'It's really not my place to tell you, Amelia.'

'Deborah, please.'

'I will say this though. I don't think he's at risk of taking his own life, nor is he sick, but if something has happened that's set him off down a dark path, then he needs guiding back to the light.'

I grind my teeth, realising I could be here all day, arguing with his mother over the phone. She's clearly not going to tell me. How am I supposed to help him if I don't know what's going on?

'I'm sorry, love, but I truly think it will be better for

Noah if he's the one to tell you. If he doesn't tell you, then maybe that's because he doesn't trust you enough to do so.'

The accusation in her voice is clear. She's always been pleasant, never said a bad word against me as far as I know, so this is the first time I'm hearing a note of negativity. I don't fight her on it because she's right. He clearly doesn't trust me enough to confide in me, and that hurts more than anything. I've always trusted him. Always. But now he's giving me every reason not to, and I'm sick of it. Sick of being used and lied to.

Yes, I've been keeping certain things from him this past week, but only because I thought he was at his parents', looking after his mother while his dad was in the hospital. I was doing my best to shield him from what was going on with me. I've been taken for a complete fool. I told him everything when he got home, yet he's done nothing but shut me out, tell me not to do things. Don't go to the police, don't call his parents. He'll handle it. Trust him. But how can I?

My guilt has now been replaced by anger. I know what Deborah said is true, about not pushing him too hard, but my life is on the line, my business and reputation.

'Yes, you're right, Deborah. Listen, I have to go. Thanks.' I hang up without waiting for an answer. She doesn't call back.

I immediately call Noah, but it goes straight to voicemail. He's on a night shift, so his phone will be off. I toss my phone on the countertop and watch it clatter and skid across the surface.

The constant gnawing worry in my gut starts giving me a stomach ache. I want to release a primal scream, yell, punch something, do anything to relieve this stress, this build-up of tension in my whole body. I have no one I can call. No one I can trust.

I've never felt more alone than I do right now. Everyone has turned against me. There's only one person who can help me. One person who can get me out of this mess.

And that's me.

I go to bed, triple-checking the lock on the door.

Tomorrow.

Tomorrow is the day that I find out the truth.

I don't care what it takes, even if my relationship falls apart because of it.

I deserve to know the truth.

CHAPTER THIRTY

NOAH

I've been forced into a deadline. I only have twenty-four hours to finish this. If Mills calls my parents, then it's all over. The unveiling of my lie will be enough to unsettle her, force her to take action, make her ask questions she won't like the answers to. She'll start digging around, and, before long, she'll find the skeletons I've been desperate to hide.

I know all too well what she's like. Once she gets an idea in her head, nothing will remove it or satisfy her until she's figured it out. It's endearing, really. Or at least it would be in a normal, everyday situation, but this isn't your normal, everyday situation.

She has no idea what she's about to uncover if she continues down this road. I need her to trust me. Will she, though? I have no idea. The way she looks at me now tells me she doesn't. Trust me, that is. There's nothing I can say or do to regain that trust because the more I push back, the more I ask or tell her not to intervene, not to speak to my parents, not to go to the police, the more she'll want to do all those things.

The fact is, if Mills finds out that my dad wasn't in the ICU, then she's going to want to know where I was and why I was staying with my parents if it wasn't to help my mum. The truth is that yes, I was visiting the hospital each day, but for a completely different reason.

Mills has a strong head on her shoulders, but I bet it's not strong enough to know the truth about what I've done, about what's happened. Every time I think about her finding out, a little part of me breaks inside.

I've told Mills I'm going to work on a night shift. That's not true. I said it to give myself twenty-four hours to sort this out, so for me to do that, I need to put my plan into action; write my statement, finalise it. I need somewhere quiet to sort my head out. I know what I need to say, but I'm not sure I'll find the right words.

The person who's ruined my life wants me to take the blame for everything so she can get away without any issues, but it's already gone too far. Some people at work are asking questions too. Rob has figured out that I've been blackmailed into changing my statement.

I need to try and head this off and get it done before Mills finds out. My thoughts are all over the place. I'm unable to keep any in order. I call my mum. She knows more about my past than Mills does. It's not Mills' fault. I want the woman I'm about to marry to know me inside and out. Of course I do, but how can I show her the real me? I thought I'd put all my dark feelings behind me, left them in my university years, but if this past month has taught me anything, it's that no matter how you try and hide, how far you run or how often you bury your head in the sand, the darkness inside always finds you. Somehow, it always does.

That's what I've been trying to keep at bay, and only my

parents know what really happened back then. But they don't know about what occurred at work. They can't know that. Ever. It's humiliating. My mum wouldn't know how to look me in the eyes, and my dad... he'd be ashamed of me. I know he would.

'Hi, love. How was your journey back home?'

'Hi, Mum,' I say, as I look both ways to cross the busy street. I'm on my way to my thinking spot. The place I go to be alone. 'Listen, if Mills calls you, then please–'

'She's already called me.'

A solid lump forms in my throat. 'What did you tell her?'

'Well, I had to tell her that your dad was fine. Why didn't you tell me that you were lying to her? I assumed she knew everything. You told her your dad was in hospital. Honestly, Noah, that's an awful lie to use.'

'I'm sorry, okay? She never calls you, and you guys hardly speak, so I didn't expect... Listen, that's not the point. She knows I lied now. What exactly did you say to her? What did she say to you?'

My mum sighs loudly. 'She's worried about you, Noah. She wanted me to tell her about your dark time at university, but I didn't. There's no need to bring all that up again, is there? But she did say something that worried me. She asked if you were at risk to yourself. You're not, are you?'

'No, Mum. I promise I'm not. You don't have to worry about that, okay? Just... give me time.'

'Very well, Noah, but know it never bodes well to hide things from the person you're going to marry. It doesn't promote a healthy relationship.'

'Thanks, Mum.' I hang up abruptly.

Like I need her to tell me what I should or shouldn't tell Mills.

I need to clear my head. I want as much space as possible between me and the world. There's a place I go when I need peace and quiet.

It's time to make a plan.

CHAPTER THIRTY-ONE

I wake at seven and check my phone; an automatic morning reflex. Noah didn't call or even text during the night. In fact, no one has messaged me at all. No notifications. No Whats-Apps. No nothing, not even from my friends. Nothing from any clients either. Everyone appears to be on radio silence.

Even Georgina is quiet.

I don't like it. Something isn't right.

Just to be sure there's nothing wrong with my phone, I switch it off, then on again. But not a single message comes through, other than a couple of spam emails, which I immediately delete.

I have Sally booked in this morning, and a part of me wants to call and cancel because my head isn't in work mode anymore. I've turned into a hermit, someone who'd prefer to hide away than face the world head-on. The past couple of weeks have taught me that even confident exteriors can crack, even those who think they have it all sussed out, all planned, can lose everything if they're not careful. I've done everything to hold on to some resemblance of the old me, but Georgina hasn't only wanted to destroy my business. She has made it personal.

However, despite this, my business mindset tells me I can't afford to cancel Sally's treatment, but as soon as she's left, I'm going to follow through with the plan I came up with last night. Noah only has until the end of the day, and then I'm going to the police with all the evidence I have, which isn't physical or substantial, other than the text messages, but it's all I've got. When I explain she's threatened to make things worse, hopefully they will make sure I'm safe.

I text Sally, saying I'm looking forward to seeing her soon, and she replies with a cheery message. Maybe she can distract me for a couple of hours and tell me more about her stalker and her affair. Perhaps her problems are worse than mine, and I can disappear into someone else's world for a while and forget about my own, which I'm slowly drowning in as the days go by.

I want it to be over. However that's supposed to look.

Today, something is going to happen. I don't know what, but today is the day.

I buzz Sally up and wait by my open front door as the lift ascends the building. The doors ping open and she steps out, holding a bouquet of dead flowers. A frown is etched into her face as she walks towards me.

'I saw these in your cubby hole downstairs. When was the last time you checked your mail slot? They look like they've been there a while, or they were already dead when someone dropped them off, but then, that's a bit morbid, isn't it?'

'I only checked it yesterday,' I say, reaching out and taking them.

Sally follows me into the flat. 'They could do with a water,' she says.

'I think they're well past saving now.'

'Is there a note?'

I check in between the dead, rotting stems and pull out a small white card.

> Speak to the police or tell anyone else about me, and you'll be as dead as these flowers, Bitch.

'Oh God...' The flowers tumble to the floor as I wobble sideways, slamming into the wall for support. Sally shrieks and leaps to my aid, grabbing my arm and keeping me from collapsing completely.

'Amelia, are you all right?' She walks me into the living area, leading me by the arm like I'm an elderly person crossing the road, where I crumble in a heap on the sofa. My legs are like jelly, no longer strong enough to support me.

Sally races to the kitchen and fills a clean glass with water from the tap, returning to my side and holding it out for me to take. I do, but I only take a sip.

'What's going on?' she asks.

I glance at the clock in the kitchen. 'W-We need to get started on your massage...'

'Fuck the massage. Is this something to do with that stalker you told me about last time? Are they from him?' She points towards the dead flowers, which are still on the floor in the hallway by the door. Out of sight, but not out of mind.

I shake my head, squeezing my lips together. I can't risk

saying anything out loud anymore. She's got me cornered. She knows I'm speaking to people. My eyes fill with tears, and they overflow, spilling onto my cheeks. I shake my head over and over until I'm dizzy.

'I-I can't explain...' I say weakly.

'Try.'

'I... I can't.'

'Is this the same person who's been sending out texts to all your clients?'

I stare at her, unsure at first if I've heard her correctly. 'W-What? How do you know about that?'

Sally lifts her bag onto her lap and rummages through it, eventually bringing out her phone. She navigates to the text messages and clicks on one.

I look at the screen and read the multitude of texts, all from the same number.

> Amelia is a lying whore. Do not use her services. She's a scam artist.

> Do not use Amelia anymore. Your health is at risk.

> She burned me with hot wax and laughed. She's a bitch.

> Amelia is unprofessional and expected me to pay for a treatment I never received.

There's more, but I can't bear to read them. I turn away from the screen, shame washing over me. The thought of all my clients getting messages like this is humiliating. How can I ever explain to them that someone is targeting me? Will they believe me? It doesn't take a lot these days for people to believe anything. Often, proof isn't needed.

Sally puts her phone away. 'Listen, who is this person? Luckily, I know a scam when I see one, so I ignored them.'

'Most of my other clients have dropped me.'

Sally puts a soft hand on my arm. 'Oh, I'm so sorry. I should have told you sooner. Like I said, I've been ignoring them. It's only when Janice told me she'd been receiving them, too, I realised it wasn't a fluke. That it wasn't only me they were sending them to. Don't tell me Janice has dropped you as well?'

'No, but I haven't heard from her for a while. I sent out that blanket text to all my remaining clients the other day because I'm desperate, and you're the only one who respond-ed.' I quickly clamp my mouth shut, realising I'm talking, and she could easily be listening. I must have missed a bug when I searched the other day. How else would she know who I'm talking to? 'I'm sorry, Sally, but you have to go.'

'I'm not going anywhere. We need to get to the bottom of this. Do you have any idea who it might be? Why are they doing this?'

'I think I know who it is.'

'Who?'

I don't answer, afraid of revealing my hand.

Sally sighs. 'Where's Noah? Can he help?'

'He's... No, he can't.'

'He is back from his parents', though, right?'

I nod. 'Yes, but...' I stop as my breath catches in my throat. I try to swallow, but my tongue sticks to the roof of my mouth. 'H-How did you know Noah went to his parents'?' I ask, attempting to keep my voice on an even keel.

Sally shrugs. 'You told me.'

I think back to our previous conversations. 'No, I didn't,' I say.

The silence stretches between us as fear creeps up my spine, sending all my nerve endings tingling. Sally stands up and steps away from me.

'Ooops,' she says with a smile.

PART 3

CHAPTER THIRTY-TWO

'Oops?' I repeat, then pause as my breath threatens to run away from me like a steam train. 'What do you mean, "*oops*"? How did you know... Wait...'

The cogs and wheels in my head spin faster and faster. Too fast for me to make sense of any of it. It's a good job I'm sitting down because otherwise, my legs would have buckled by now. My hands are numb as I clench them, squeezing the sofa cushions beside me. I try to take a breath, but I can't. My rib cage constricts my lungs tighter and tighter.

Oh God...

Sally has her back to me, her head craned to look at the ceiling. 'You know, I was hoping to stretch this whole thing out a little longer, make you suffer a little more, but I guess I let the cat out of the bag a little early, huh? My mistake.'

She turns to face me, no longer looking like my friend and client. Her face is different. Changed in the blink of an eye. Gone is the kind smile, replaced by wide eyes, pure burning hatred behind them. Her fists are clenched by her sides, her whole body rigid, as if she's fighting back the urge to attack.

I shake my head. 'No. You? It's been *you* this whole time?'

'Guilty,' she replies with a sing-song voice. The fact that she's making light of this startling revelation riles me up, and I instantly see red.

'But why?' I jump to my feet, but it's a bad move. My legs are too wobbly and in no condition to hold me up, but somehow, I fight with my body and remain standing.

'Ha! Wouldn't you like to know.'

'Yes, actually, I bloody well would!'

I thought I'd be overcome with fear when I finally came face to face with the person who's been destroying me, but I'm not. I was so close to reporting the wrong person to the police. It would have destroyed my friendship with Georgina.

'You have been making my life a living hell for the past two weeks. I've lost my business and most of my clients because of you. Noah and I might not be able to get a mortgage. I've almost lost my best friend. I was in a car accident, for crying out loud. You could have killed me!' I have so much more I want to say, but I'm running out of steam fast, barely able to inhale enough oxygen to get the last few words out.

'Oh, please,' she says with a laugh. 'It was barely a nudge with the car. If I wanted to kill you, you'd be dead, wouldn't you?'

'B-But... I still don't know *why* you've been doing this to me. We've been friends for almost a year, Sally. Why start destroying my life now? I don't understand.'

Sally smiles. 'I like how you assume it's all about *you*.'

Her words make no sense. I don't mean to come across as self-absorbed here, but who else would it be about? Sally must notice the quizzical look on my face because she chuckles, and it makes me want to lunge forwards and slap the smirk off her face. She's finding my misery amusing.

'You'll just have to do your best to put the pieces of the puzzle together, won't you? I'm not going to make this easy for you, *Mills*. But my threat still stands. If you go to the police, tell anyone else that it's me, you'll be dead. I can promise you that. I'm not finished with you yet. Not by a long shot.'

There are so many things I want to say, questions to ask, yet they all form one giant mass in my head, and I can't say any of them. The words and sentences make no sense, like a jumbled-up book with none of its pages in the right order. I sink back down to the sofa, staring blankly at her.

Sally picks up her bag and hikes the long strap onto her left shoulder. As she does, I notice something I've never noticed before about her left hand. Also – and I should have picked up on it straight away – she called me Mills. The only other person who calls me Mills is...

'Noah. This is about Noah, isn't it?' I ask.

Sally stares at me a moment. 'Took you long enough. Well, I've leave you in peace for a while... Let you mull things over. Oh, and one more thing... I really did enjoy the treatments over the past year. You're a great beauty therapist, Amelia. Take care.'

And she's gone.

She potters out the door like nothing has happened, like she hasn't dealt me a massive blow to the chest, leaving me gasping for a full breath. My head's dizzy, like I've spun around in circles the way I used to do when I was a kid.

I think back to her left hand.

She wasn't wearing a wedding ring, which is a small detail in the grand scheme of things, but it gets the cogs whirring again. Have I *ever* seen her wearing a wedding ring? Have I overlooked the fact that she talks about her husband, yet she doesn't wear a ring, and... here's the even bigger kicker.

I've never met her husband.

It's possible she doesn't have one and has been lying to me the entire year, making up a cover story.

Who the hell is she? For all I know, she isn't who she says she is.

Then, it's like a switch has flicked in my head.

If this is about Noah, then I'm going to get to the bottom of this.

And now, it's *my* time to stalk *her*.

CHAPTER THIRTY-THREE

I've made up my mind. Never been more certain about anything in my life. I'm going to get to the bottom of why Sally is targeting me and what it's got to do with Noah, and I'm going to do it myself.

No police. No Noah. No Georgina. No help from anyone.

I know what she's capable of now. If she finds out I've gone to the police, will she carry out her threat to kill me? I can't risk it. Yes, I'm scared, but more than that, I'm afraid for Noah. What if she decides to go after someone else I care about? If I can somehow get the upper hand, find a weakness, or figure out what's been driving her to come after me, then perhaps I can regain some of the control I've lost.

She's played me for a fool the whole time, lulling me into a false sense of security. I trusted her, confided in her, even listened to her own whining and moaning about her life.

Was any of it real?

One of the many questions I need answering is whether she intentionally befriended me a year ago to lead me on and mess with me. Or did something happen recently that's made her turn on me without warning, splitting apart our friendship? Because I truly did think we were friends.

I looked forward to her visits, and we shared a lot of personal truths, but now I realise she was only saying all that stuff to get me to open up so she could learn more about me, possibly use it against me somehow. She's been in my flat, searched through my laptop bag, found my book of passwords, connected to my Echo Dot, and used it as a listening device to spy on me. She's gone above and beyond what a stalker would do. Stalkers lurk in the background, watching, waiting, but she's infiltrated my life, violated my personal space in the worst possible way.

There's only one way to find the truth, and that's to turn the tables on her, so I pull up my laptop, sit at the kitchen island, and start doing some internet digging on my so-called favourite client and friend.

It doesn't take me long to run into a problem.

Sally Ringer doesn't exist.

Not the Sally Ringer I know.

There are several women who share the same name, scattered all over the world, but none who match. What do I actually know about her? She has a husband called Hank and had a stalker called Aaron from a year ago, but neither of those things has ever been confirmed or proven. I've never met Hank. She showed me a picture of him once, but it could have been a photo of anyone.

As for her stalker, it's highly likely he and the whole scenario were made up too. Perhaps to get me to trust her or feel sorry for her. She told me recently that she slept with him, and I judged her for that. It's difficult to distinguish the lies from the truths.

I give up my search for her on social media because it's a dead end.

I think hard for a moment. If Sally has been the person behind the destruction of my business, then how has she managed to get hold of all my clients' contact details? Several of them, if not all, have received messages telling them to stay away from me. She must have somehow copied my phone. I remember her mentioning once that she was very savvy with her technology, and she always had gadgets and all sorts of electronic devices in her bag. I saw them when she accidentally dropped her bag and they all fell out. She gave me a reasonable response to each one, even showing me a few of them, explaining what they did and how they worked. I'd been completely absorbed and laughed, saying she could teach me a thing or two about technology sometime.

All the pieces of the puzzle are beginning to slot together now.

I think back to when she first contacted me. She sent me a text message, like most new clients do. Hardly anyone calls me directly the first time, not until we know each other a little better.

Hi. My name's Sally Ringer. Is this Amelia from AJ Beauty? I'm looking for a beauty therapist. I live in Cambridge. Happy to come to you, or maybe some home treatments too. I've heard you're really good! Do you have a space available next week? Thanks. Sally xx

I SMILED *as I picked up my work diary. I did have a space available, as I'd only just started my business, so I texted her* back the available times, keeping it light and professional. I was tidying up the treatment room after my last client left. I had another due in thirty minutes, which gave me enough time to eat my lunch and stack the dishwasher.

I carried my phone into the kitchen after I was done tidying and set it on the side while I prepared a ham sandwich. It lit up, signalling a call. I was expecting a call from Noah, but it wasn't from Noah.

It was an unknown number.

'Hello?'

'Oh, hi! It's Sally. You've just messaged me back with the available times for next week. I thought it was easier to call rather than text back and forth.'

I brushed a stray piece of hair behind my ear, feeling a little caught off guard. 'Oh, yes, of course. Hi, Sally. Thanks for your message. Do any of those times work for you?'

'Yes. Can I book the Tuesday midday slot, please? I'd love a back massage.'

'Of course.' I thought it was a bit strange that she'd decided to call when she could have easily put that in a text, but other than that, I didn't think anything of it. 'Would you like to come to mine?'

'Um, yes... but... will there be anyone else around? Your husband, or...'

'We're not married, but no, Noah will be at work. We'll be alone. I'll text you my address. As you're a new client, I'll need the first ten minutes to go through some forms and a health questionnaire.'

'Perfect. Thanks. I guess I'll see you next week, then! Bye!'

'Bye, Sally.' I hung up and finished making lunch.

AT THE TIME, I didn't question why she had asked about someone else being in the flat. She was, after all, a woman coming into a stranger's house about to take the top half of her clothes off, so of course she wouldn't feel comfortable having a man around. I always try to book appointments at home when Noah isn't in, exactly for that reason.

But now, thinking back, it raises a red flag. How did she know I *had* anyone living with me? Did she make a general guess, or was it merely a throwaway comment? Or did she already know about Noah? I look up from my laptop.

Noah.

It keeps coming back to Noah.

Something she said earlier pops into my head.

'I like how you assume it's all about you.'

What if Aaron, her stalker, wasn't a made-up story, but a cover for Noah? Surely, Noah didn't stalk her... didn't sleep with her?

Noah's odd behaviour, the way he's also been warning me not to speak to the police, that he'll handle it. His lying about visiting his parents because his dad was ill. But Noah doesn't know Sally. He's never met her. I've been trying to get us all to meet up for a drink, but it's never happened. What if Noah *does* know Sally, just like he knows Charlotte?

He still hasn't called me.

I pick up the phone and call him again, leaving a message when it beeps straight to voicemail.

'Hi, Noah. Listen, I don't know what is going on with you, but I need you to call me back as soon as you get this.' I pause, deciding to take the plunge. 'I know you weren't at your parents' looking after them while your dad was in hospital. Your dad is fine. I need you to tell me why you've been lying to me. Please. Come home, and we'll talk. I'm not mad. I'm just...' I hang up because I don't know how to finish that sentence. I am mad. Mad as all hell, but I remember what his mum told me. I can't push him or risk him toppling over the edge completely.

He doesn't call me back.

My frantic WhatsApps remain unread all day.

The twenty-four hours he promised me pass by.

Noah's disappeared, and I don't know why.

I need to speak to him, to find out what this has to do with Sally, but he's ghosting me. Either that... or he's done something really, really bad, something I can't think about without my throat closing and tears spilling from my eyes.

Please, don't let me be too late.

CHAPTER THIRTY-FOUR

Again, I could easily be jumping to conclusions, making things fit because I want them to, but the day Noah called me to tell me his good news about his promotion, two weeks ago, was the same day – hell, almost the same *hour* – the threatening messages started.

That's it. It has to be.

Somehow, Sally is connected to Noah and his work. Perhaps she works with him, but he's never once mentioned her name. My heart sinks as I realise that after all this time convincing myself it's not an affair, the clues are all adding up, pointing in that direction.

Maybe Sally is punishing me because Noah won't leave me to be with her. Whatever the reason, it's time I face up to Noah and ask him outright. But he's still not answering my messages or calling me back.

I want to trust him. I do. But how am I supposed to do that if he refuses to share his thoughts with me? I'm his future wife. We are supposed to be moving forwards, and now, somehow, he's got himself mixed up with something that's been affecting not only him, but me and my life too. Sally is now targeting me for something Noah has done. Has he known this the whole time? Is that why he's disappeared and is refusing to look me in the eye?

I'm fed up with sitting still, waiting for him to contact me.

I grab a few things and stuff them into my shoulder bag. I hesitate at the knife block on the side, wondering if I'm scared enough of Sally to grab a weapon to defend myself. It still seems absurd that she's been behind everything. I trusted her. She told me so much about her life, secrets she swore she couldn't or wouldn't tell anyone else, and yet now I find out she's been lying this whole time. It's the ultimate betrayal.

I decide against the knife, knowing that if I was caught with it, I'd be in trouble, and that's the last thing I need right now.

I pause at my front door, remembering it's the first time I've stepped foot outside for a few days. My car is still in the garage, and they're waiting to be paid for the work that's due, which I can't afford thanks to my business imploding. I still haven't contacted the bloody insurance company. All these admin-type jobs that need doing have been pushed to the side, forgotten because of everything that's been happening.

I'll have to take the bus to Noah's work. That's where I'm heading. It's where I'll find the answers I'm looking for. I'm sure of it. If Sally does work there, then I'll find out.

The whole time I'm on the bus, I glance at the other passengers, taking note of the way they move, the way they sit and talk. Most are staring down at their phones, their necks bent at an awkward angle, while others stare blankly out of the window, refusing to make eye contact with anyone. I sit at the back with my bag on my lap, clutching it tight. From here, I can see who gets on and off, and I know for certain there is no one behind, watching me.

Sally can't have eyes everywhere. Unless she has somehow installed a tracker on me, there's no way she'll know where I'm going...

And that's the moment I search through my bag, emptying it out on the seat next to me, checking for any alien items I don't recognise.

I'm pretty sure there's no tracker, unless... I stare at my phone, thinking back to when she's been in my flat. Have I ever left her unattended with my phone? Would she have had enough time to crack the password and install a tracking app on it? Is it possible, or have I turned into a paranoid freak?

The bus jolts to a stop as I flick through my phone apps, checking and rechecking each one. I don't come across anything that looks suspicious, but that doesn't mean there isn't a tracker on it. I hold down the power button, switching it off. Better to be safe than sorry. If Noah calls, then it doesn't matter, because I'm on my way to see him anyway.

Forty-five sweaty minutes later, I arrive at Blackmore Prison. I'm not even sure if they'll let me in, especially if Noah's on shift, let alone allow me to talk to him, but I need to start somewhere.

I sign in at reception and ask to speak to Noah, informing them who I am. The officer at the desk calls the request through. I've never been here before. Noah has never wanted me to come to his place of work. He said that prisons aren't suitable for civilians to visit, and he's not wrong.

The building is void of any sort of personality or colour. Grey. Cold. Lifeless.

'I'm sorry, but it doesn't look as if Noah's on shift today,' says the officer, replacing the receiver in its cradle.

'When was he last in?' I ask.

'Um...' The officer types a few things on the keyboard, staring hard at the screen. 'He's not been on shift since last Friday.'

Before he went away to his parents', yet he told me he was going to work.

'Okay. Can I speak to Rob, please?' I ask, feeling my blood pressure rise.

The officer lets out a huff, then phones through again, speaking low so I can't hear. 'He'll be out in a few minutes.'

'Thank you.'

'Take a seat.' The officer gestures at the hard, red plastic chairs in the corner. I shuffle over to one and sit down, my knees pressed together, bouncing up and down on my toes. I'm jittery, I know that, like I've downed one too many espressos in a short space of time.

I don't have to wait long for Rob to enter the reception area. I've never met him in person before, but Noah has told me a lot about him. He's much taller than I imagined. Six-two at least. He's older too. Mid-fifties, maybe. Handsome. Rugged.

'Hi, Amelia. It's so lovely to officially meet you.' He extends his hand and I take it as I stand up, shaking it firmly.

'Hi, Rob. And you.'

'You're here to see Noah, but I'm afraid he's not here. Is there something I can help you with? You said it's an emergency.'

I keep my voice low. 'I need to know what's going on. He's hiding things from me.'

Rob's smile falters slightly as he glances behind at the reception desk. 'Maybe we should talk privately,' he says.

'I think that would be best,' I reply.

Rob nods and gestures to a nearby door. 'Right this way. Can I get you a drink? Tea? Coffee?'

'Um, maybe just a water?' My mouth is parched.

'Of course.' He lets me walk ahead of him, then shows me into a small side room. 'I won't be a minute.'

He leaves to fetch my water, so I take a seat on the grey chair in the corner. There's a table here too, but it's not set up like an interrogation room. There's no two-way mirror like in the movies. Rob enters and passes me a plastic cup of water. I take it, my hands shaking.

'Thanks.'

He sits down on the chair just across from me. 'So... You say Noah's been hiding things from you? What sort of things?' His tone is light, as if he has no idea what I'm doing here, but I reckon he does.

'I don't know exactly, but he won't talk to me about it. He told me he was coming into work, but he's not here. I'm worried about him, Rob. Something's not right. Have you noticed anything odd going on with him?' I decide to hold back on a lot of the details to start with, to test the waters about whether Rob knows more than he's letting on.

Rob inhales deeply, then nods. 'Yes, I have,' he says. 'But it's... complicated.'

'How so? Because, as his fiancée, I think I have the right to know what's going on with Noah at work. Is he being threatened? Does anyone by the name of Sally Ringer work here?'

Rob tilts his head. 'Sally Ringer? No, never heard of her.'

'She's a client of mine. I met her roughly a year ago, and

the threatening messages started the same day Noah got his good news about his promotion. They have to be connected somehow.'

Rob scratches his neck, which is slightly flushed. He looks as if he'd rather be anywhere else but sitting in front of me. There's even a sheen of sweat on his forehead. But the words he says are the last ones I expect him to utter.

'Noah didn't mention anything about you being threatened.' Rob's expression is as if he's been slapped in the face. It looks like I'm not the only one Noah has been lying to.

'What do you know about Sally?' I ask.

'I have no idea who that is, but... Noah said you were aware of what happened a few weeks ago.'

'What happened?' I can't breathe. I don't even know where to start with asking the copious amount of questions that are rumbling around my head.

He's clearly revealed something he knows he shouldn't have because he swallows hard, then sucks in a breath and holds it. He stands up, unable to look me in the eyes anymore. 'Shit,' he mutters.

'Rob... what the hell is going on? What's Noah been keeping from me? What happened a few weeks ago? I know it must be something bad because he's been acting strange since then.'

'To be honest, Amelia, it's been going on longer than that, almost as soon as he started working at Blackmore, but it all officially kicked off five weeks ago.'

The words echo around the small room. The walls close in, and I get tunnel vision staring at the man in front of me, whom I've never met before, but who holds all the answers I need to unravel this mess. It should be Noah telling me this, but he's disappeared and refuses to respond to my messages.

He's given me no other choice. I need to know how bad it is. I need to know what Noah's got himself into. What has he done that's so bad he felt the need to lie to me? Something tells me it's not just an affair. What's worse than that?

'What did Noah do, Rob?' I ask the question slowly.

Rob swallows, his Adam's apple bobbing. 'Amelia... Noah didn't *do* anything.'

'Then what...'

'It was what was *done* to him.'

All the moisture is sapped from my mouth.

'Noah was... sexually assaulted in the workplace.' Rob swallows again, his face beetroot red. 'Raped. He was... raped.'

My hands fly to my mouth, pressing hard to stop the horrible scream from erupting. My stomach clenches. I want to lurch to the side and vomit, but my body is frozen. Unable to move, not even an inch. 'B-By a prisoner?' I manage to get out.

'No.' Rob shakes his head. 'By a colleague. Her name is Tracey Jones.'

CHAPTER THIRTY-FIVE

Her. Her... name.

I don't hear the name Tracey. I hear Sally.

Tracey. Sally. They have to be the same person. No. They *are* the same person.

Hard proof isn't needed. I know it deep down in my gut, my soul. I'm not wrong about this. I may have been wrong about a lot of things lately, but this is different.

A loud ringing, like tinnitus, sounds in my ears. Dizziness washes over me. I close my eyes, but it doesn't help. It makes the room swim. In and out. In and out. Makes me feel as if I'm on a spinny teacup ride. I lean forward and put my head between my knees, the way they do in movies, and try to take a deep, cleansing breath. Nothing helps. My body won't respond the way it needs to do to stay alert and conscious.

A hand gently touches my leg, snapping me out of my trance-like state.

'Amelia, I'm sorry to tell you like this,' says Rob. 'I had no idea you didn't know. Noah assured me he'd told you. He told me you knew about him going away recently for the sexual assault victim course, and...'

I lift my head, tears overflowing. '*That's* where he was?'

'Yes. Why? What did he tell you?'

'He said his dad was in hospital, in the ICU, and he had to visit and help look after his mum.'

'Oh.'

'Tell me everything.' Anger ripples through my body, but it's not directed at Noah. Not anymore. 'What does this woman look like?' I need to be sure, even though every nerve ending, every fibre in my body is telling me I'm right.

Sally Ringer is a fake name. Tracey Jones raped my fiancé.

'About your age. Dark hair and eyes. Slim figure.'

'It's her,' I whisper, holding back a gag in my throat.

'Who?' responds Rob, frowning.

'The woman who's been stalking and threatening me. Sally Ringer.'

'But why would she–'

'Tell me more,' I say. 'How did it happen? When? How could it happen? I thought...' I don't want to sound disrespectful to Noah, but he's a big guy. Much bigger than Sally–Tracey. How would she have overpowered him? How would she have raped him? It's different for a woman to sexually assault a man. I know it happens, but it's so rare, hardly ever talked about or seen on social media or the news.

I don't understand how it happened, but I *need* to.

Rob shakes his head. 'I shouldn't be telling you this. Would you prefer if someone else – another woman – was in the room with us? Someone from HR?'

'No. I don't care about that. Just tell me. Please.'

Rob sighs, scratching the side of his neck. He's sweating

again. 'Obviously, I don't know the intricate details, but Tracey worked at Blackmore Prison for several years before Noah arrived. She was here even before I arrived a couple of years ago. Apparently, she was reported several times for sexual misconduct in the workplace against other officers as well as prisoners...'

'Why the hell wasn't she fired?' I snap.

'She's... she's an attractive woman. She played the part well. She denied everything, and no one could touch her, not without proof. The thing is, this all happened before I started working as the Custodial Manager here. It wasn't handled properly by the Custodial Manager at the time. Everything got swept under the rug. No one wanted to handle the fallout that would inevitably come from a female police officer sexually mistreating her male colleagues. She was on several warnings with me for various other things not relating to sexual misconduct, but she never put a foot out of line here with regard to her previous... digressions.

'But then... Noah started, and I guess she set her sights on him. He... and I hate to say this to you, Amelia... but he admits to kissing her, but only one time at a work function when he was drunk, and that's it. That was roughly six weeks ago. But she had what she needed. She threatened him, blackmailed him, told him she'd come after you. There was proof of the kiss. She orchestrated the whole thing, and, when he said he wouldn't sleep with her, she... Well, she took things up a notch.' Rob stops and sits down on the chair next to me again. 'Do you want me to stop?'

Tears fill my eyes. 'No. Just... tell me the rest. Quickly.'

'On the night in question, five weeks ago, Noah was on his break in the back room. It's a small room where officers can have a sit-down during their breaks, watch some TV, even take a nap if they need to. There aren't any cameras in there. Tracey entered and handed him a drink, which was spiked with Rohypnol and Viagra.'

I can't hold it in anymore. I fall to my knees and retch, but only bubbles come up. I haven't eaten a proper meal in a while.

'Amelia, I'm going to stop now. I don't think you need to know any more, but please know that as soon as I figured out what had happened, I took the correct steps to report it. Tracey immediately lost her job and is no longer allowed to work at any prison. There is, and will be, a court case against her, but it's taking time. Mainly because Noah is holding things up. He needs to write a statement explaining everything that happened, but he hasn't written it yet. He has been going through therapy for the past couple of weeks, including the course he's recently been on to help him come to terms with his assault. I don't know why he hasn't told you, but my best bet is he feels embarrassed, ashamed. I think I'd feel the same way if it happened to me. His assault has been kept as private as possible, which is why it hasn't been in the media, but word does get around the prisons. He's been given a hard time by the prisoners here who have somehow found out and are calling him a lot of derogatory names.'

I push myself off the floor and shuffle my bum back onto the chair. 'Is she under police surveillance? Why wasn't she arrested?'

'It's rather complicated. Because Noah has been putting the brakes on, she was let out on bail, but no, she's been given strict warnings to not make any contact with Noah.'

'So... she can't get to him, so she's been coming after me instead. Punishing me. She contacted me almost a year ago and we've become friends, so it's like she's been planning this for a long time. Surely, that's against her bail conditions as well?'

'Technically, yes. Have you contacted the police about the threats you've received? If they know she's been causing issues, and they know her alias name, they can put a stop to it.'

'No, I haven't. She kept threatening me, telling me things would get worse if I did.'

Rob doesn't say anything. I know what he's thinking. He's thinking I was wrong to not contact the police. Obviously, if I'd known the extent of her hold over Noah, then I would have done it in a heartbeat.

Another thought I have is if Noah had told Rob I was aware of what had happened, then why wasn't I offered some sort of therapy? I know it's not about me, and I don't mean I deserve therapy to deal with it myself, but maybe I could have been offered guidance on how to help Noah get through it. Because I am completely blindsided by this and not sure how I'm supposed to help Noah recover.

Both the prison service and I have failed him in more ways than one. They should have handled it a lot better, and I should have pushed Noah harder to tell me what was wrong. Rob admitted himself that Tracey's misconducts at the start, even before he started working at the prison, were brushed under the rug, made to seem like they weren't important because she was an attractive woman working in a male-dominated career. It's rare, I know, but not unheard of, and the fact that she's escalated her abuse against my Noah is sickening.

He's been navigating this trauma by himself for weeks.

No wonder he's never initiated sex or wanted me to

touch him, flinching every time I reach for him. I was so stupid, selfish, thinking it was because of me. It wasn't. It was because he was in pain after what she did to him.

All this time...

'Did she target Noah right from the start?' I ask.

'I don't know the early details, I'm afraid, but yes, she made it clear from the day he started here that she was interested in him, but he never reported her to HR. After they kissed, she escalated her attention to him. The fact that she befriended you so long ago makes it clear she had the intention to destroy your relationship from the start.'

'What exactly do you intend to do now?' I ask, snapping myself out of my spiralling thoughts. 'What's happening, because Noah has disappeared, and...'

'I suggest the first thing you do is contact the police and tell them everything. There's no tiptoeing around this now, Amelia. Noah will be brought in and questioned, as well as you. There's no holding it back. This will get out into the media, but... depending on how Noah handles it, I don't think it's safe for him to work in the prison system anymore.'

I hang my head. Rob's right. There's no stopping the avalanche Noah has been trying to hold back by himself. Things have escalated now that another person is involved, i.e. me. Sally – Tracey – has been targeting me because of Noah, and I'm determined to out her, to make her pay for what she's done to him.

'Fine,' I say, 'but before this gets out of hand, I need to speak to Noah first. If he's not here, I don't know where he is. He's disappeared, and he's not answering any of my calls or messages.'

'I can try him.'

I nod. 'Yes. Please. I'm going to call some of his friends and see if they've heard from him.'

'Try not to worry. We'll get her.'

'She's played her hand now. I know it's her, so she won't go back to her old tricks of trying to scare me with threatening messages. I'm not worried about her, but I don't know what her plan is next. We need to find Noah.'

'And we will.'

I nod again, but inside, I already know it may be too late.

CHAPTER THIRTY-SIX

NOAH

My phone vibrates in my pocket, signalling yet another missed call or frantic message from Mills. I switch it off. She must be going crazy, knowing I've lied and wondering where I am. She may have even called Rob at work, needing to speak to me, but I asked him to deter her for as long as possible. I'm trusting him to keep all this quiet. He has done so far, but he's been pressing me a lot lately to come forward, write the statement and get this court case officially started, but I've been stalling as much as I can, and now I'm about to take it all back and say it was me who attacked her.

I've been sat on the isolated bench by the duck pond in my favourite park for hours. I'm supposed to be writing my statement, planning how I'm going to tell my story to the police.

I look up as footsteps sound on the gravel path.

It's her.

She's found me.

Why is she here? Hasn't she done enough harm? She's not supposed to be anywhere near me. She's breaking the terms of her bail. I haven't seen her in person for several weeks.

That face. That beautiful face smiles back at me, and all at once, I'm taken back to that day in the break room.

I won't lie, but when I first met Tracey a year ago, she took my breath away. How could she not? She was the most attractive and charismatic woman I'd ever met, and she completely drew me in, like a shiny lure to a hungry fish. I was a pathetic fish, hanging on her hook, and I even kissed her after one too many drinks at a work function only a few weeks ago, and from that moment on, she reeled me in.

Closer and closer. Inch by fucking inch.

And then she dealt the fatal blow.

I was stunned by how fast she turned everything around on me, accusing me of sexual harassment, telling me I was a perv, that I'd followed her to the ladies' toilets and tried to make a move. It was all lies. It was she who did all those things to me. I told her to stop gaslighting me, otherwise I'd tell people, take it higher, but she said no one would believe me. I'm a six-foot-two man who weighs just shy of a hundred and ninety pounds. She's a petite, attractive woman who looks as if she couldn't hurt a fly.

She kept threatening to tell Mills we'd kissed. At the time, I didn't think Mills would believe it meant nothing. I'd never told her anything about my attractive colleague. I never mentioned her name. I couldn't risk Tracey telling her. I loved Mills. I still do, but now it's different. *I'm* different. I'm never going to be the same man as I was before Tracey drugged and assaulted me.

Yes, I've been away this week at a therapy group for sexual assault victims, staying at my parents' because it was being held in the nearby hospital, but it hasn't helped.

Because all it's done is confirm my initial doubts about no one believing the men who are sexually assaulted by women. A lot of the men who were there had been assaulted by other men. There was only me who had been assaulted by a woman, and it made me feel worse. It felt as if even the other men, the victims, were looking down on me, like I was weaker than them because I'd let it happen. I should have been strong enough to stop it, but I wasn't.

I didn't even try to stop her. I could have tried to hit her, subdue her somehow.

The drug made me lose all physical ability and function in my limbs and head, yet the Viagra she added ensured that... I feel sick thinking about it. I can remember most of it, especially the way she smelled, sweet and sensual, and...

'Hello, Noah,' says Tracey, giving me her usual megawatt smile. 'May I sit? I think we need to have a chat. I've just come from seeing your lovely fiancée.'

I hesitate, but then nod. I'm powerless against her. 'What did you say to Mills?' I ask as she sits next to me. She's too close. Her perfume tickles my nostrils. It's almost impossible to hold back a gag as I remember the same smell that night.

'I didn't need to tell her anything. She finally figured it out, but it took a while, didn't it? A whole year!' She laughs, sending a sickening chill through my veins.

'What do you mean?'

'Don't tell me you haven't figured it out either? I've been keeping an eye on her, on you, since I first met you, Noah. I've been in your flat. It's lovely, by the way.'

'I don't understand...'

'You never have met Amelia's favourite client, have you?'

I stop, think... and it hits me in the face like a slap.

'You're Sally?'

'Sally's my middle name, yes.'

'B-But...' I can't form words. I had no idea just how far she'd gone to infiltrate my life. Why me? Why's she so obsessed with me?

'I need you to stop, Tracey. Please. I'll do anything you ask, but please stop targeting Mills. She's got nothing to do with any of this. If I'd known you were Sally earlier, I would have–'

'You would have what, Noah? Let's face it, you wouldn't have done anything, because you're too afraid to lose her.' She laughs. 'You men really are all the same, aren't you? Weak when it comes to the opposite sex. We hold all the power because you want what's between our legs.' She spits on the ground in front of me. 'But you know what really pisses me off? Weak, pathetic men like you who blame everyone but themselves. You're the one who got yourself into this mess, Noah. You.' She pokes me with a stiff finger. 'I told you all you had to do was go along with what I wanted. All you had to do was sleep with me willingly. That's it. But you didn't. And now your precious Mills is going to pay. She has been paying, Noah. You think she'll ever look at you the same way again once this gets out? You think she'll even believe you? Of course she won't, because no one believes men like you.'

I hang my head and stare at the ground beneath my feet, focusing on a small pebble, which I roll around with my foot.

'All this time,' I say. 'All of this has been because I said no and wouldn't sleep with you?'

Tracey laughs again. 'Wow, you think very highly of yourself, don't you? It's because, whether you believe it or not, Noah, I chose you. I wanted you. I like to control men, you see, and it's not just about sex. It's about power. I still have power over you. Now, I think the best way for you to deal with this is to do everyone a favour and end it, Noah. Put yourself and everyone else out of their misery.' She rises to her feet. 'I'm fed up of playing with you now. You bore me. Just end it. Everyone will be better off. Trust me. Write the statement, hand it in, and then find some way of ending your life, and it'll all be over. I promise. Mills will be left alone.'

I look up at her, squinting against the light. 'Do you promise you'll leave Mills alone?'

'I promise.' She leans forward and lightly brushes my cheek with her hand. 'Such a pity,' she says.

Then, she walks away.

I stare after her until she disappears.

I don't know how long I stay sitting on the bench. My skin burns where she touched me. Eventually, I stand up, walk to the nearest supermarket, and buy two litre bottles of vodka.

I don't know how I'm going to end it yet, but at least if I'm wasted, I might not feel anything.

CHAPTER THIRTY-SEVEN

I leave the prison and head to the bus stop, head hanging like a heavy weight, my chin almost touching my chest. I'm so deflated, defeated, but all I can think about, all I can focus on is that I need to find Noah. His mother's words replay in my head. I know she said he wasn't at risk of suicide, but she doesn't know what he's been through, does she? Surely, he wouldn't have confided in her about this. When I spoke to her, there would have been more terror in her voice if she knew.

He could very well be at risk. All this time, it's never been about me. I've been a pawn in Tracey's game of manipulation. She's been using me to punish Noah or blackmail him into staying quiet. He may feel as if there's no other way out.

I switch my phone back on and continue to call his mobile and send messages, despite none of them getting through. His phone is off. I cry and explain that I'm sorry, I got it all wrong, I know about Tracey, and I don't blame him. I'm hoping if he does listen to the voicemails or read my messages at some point, he'll see I'm no longer angry, but concerned for his well-being and safety. I want him to come home to me, so we can sort all this out and he can get the help he needs. I'm going to be there for him no matter what, no matter what it takes or how long. I need him to know that.

As I wait for the next bus, which will take me to the police station, I call his friends, leave messages where I can. I finally get hold of Tom, a friend of his from university, who doesn't even live in Cambridge. He lives somewhere in Cornwall.

'Amelia, hi! It's been a while. How are you?' His voice is light, care-free, already telling me the likelihood of Noah being with him is low, but I have to at least ask.

'Hi, Tom. Is Noah with you? Have you seen him lately? Has he messaged you at all?'

There's a long pause on the line. 'Not for a while, no.'

'Are you sure?'

'Quite sure. What's going on?'

'It's a long story. Please, can you call me if you hear from him?'

'Yes, of course, but... should I be worried? Is he depressed again?'

My breath hitches in my throat. I should have realised that it may not only be his parents who know about his previous depression, especially as the worst of it was during his time at university.

'Um, yes, I believe so. He's been struggling lately.'

'Shit. I'm sorry to hear that. I thought he was over the whole thing. I guess I never realised how badly it affected him. I know I and a few others took the piss out of him after it happened, but we never realised how bad it was for him.'

I hold my breath, hoping he'll come out and say it. Whatever *it* is. What happened all those years ago that dragged him down into the pits of depression he's been struggling to climb out of ever since?

Tom continues. 'Did he ever get professional help with all that?' he asks me.

'Um... yes, he did, but that was before I met him... He's been having some issues at work lately, and I think it's all come back to the surface again.'

'Shit. Well, at least that bitch had the sense to back off after she got found out. We all thought it was hilarious that Noah had a chick as a stalker, but he was clearly terrified of her.'

'Right...' I grip the phone so tightly my hand starts shaking. The bus pulls up alongside me. 'Listen, Tom... what was her name again? The woman who stalked Noah at university.'

'Oh, gosh, I can't remember. It began with C, I think. Camilla. Claire...'

'Charlotte?'

'Yes! That rings a bell, but I think she went by Charlie.'

The bus driver gestures wildly with his hands, beckoning me onto the bus, but I can't seem to move my legs. My feet are glued to the tarmac.

'I... I... Thanks, Tom. Listen, please call me if you hear anything.' I hang up before he responds and jump onto the bus, feeling as if I've entered a trance-like state.

Ever since I found out about Charlotte's mental health diagnosis, I've put her to the back of my mind, knowing she wasn't a threat to me anymore, but I've been so blind. Again. Thinking it was all about me.

Charlotte didn't just know him at university. She was the cause of his depression because she stalked him. She's not completely innocent in all this, but I'm not sure if she's connected to Tracey. She can't be. Charlotte is a separate issue altogether.

I arrive at the police station a sweaty mess. I'm now running on a combination of adrenaline and shock. As soon as I'm sat down in front of an officer, I talk faster than I ever have in my life, tripping over words and repeating myself several times. I explain as much as I can, everything I can remember, but there are still several blank spaces I need to fill in. I tell the officer I don't think Charlotte and Tracey are linked, but the fact is, two women have ruined Noah's life and have been using me to get close to him.

And both have appeared at the same time, which begs the question. Why now? Tracey may have started targeting Noah a year ago, wanting to get close to him and therefore using me to do that, but there must be a reason why she's started threatening me within the past two weeks. Not to mention Charlotte messaging me around the same time.

The officer takes note of all of this. He introduces himself as DC Hunter. He says they will focus their efforts on Tracey and bring her back in because she has breached the terms of her bail agreement. I tell them as much as I can remember about where she lives, from what she's said, but it could have all been lies. She always came to me. I've never been to her house, so I'm no help with locating her, but now I know why she preferred to keep me away.

The whole time I'm in the police station, I keep glancing at my phone, hoping Noah will call, but he doesn't. I tell DC Hunter I'm worried about him, and he agrees to begin a search, especially after I provide them with the details of his mental health and I mention he may be at risk to himself.

I don't know how many hours I'm in the police station,

but when I finally emerge, I drag myself onto the nearest bus heading in the direction of home and collapse on the nearest seat.

I hope I've done enough and it's not too late, but more than that, I hope to God that me telling the police won't cause Noah any further issues, and Tracey will be found before she can get to him.

I barely register my stop, and the bus pulls away from the kerb before I realise I should have alighted, so I hop off at the next one, then walk home. It's only about five hundred yards or so, but it feels like I'm walking a marathon. My body is exhausted both mentally and physically as I practically drag myself towards my building.

I don't remember the last time I ate or drank anything substantial. It's been one of those background things that hasn't seemed necessary, but now I realise I must keep my strength up. I have to be able to fight back if need be.

I wish I knew what her overall plan is. Does she plan on killing me, or just causing the most amount of damage possible? Does she want to drive Noah and me apart, for him to break up with me? What does she expect him to do? Go running to her with open arms? She's deluded if she thinks that's going to happen.

Over my dead–

I stop as the lift doors open and I see what's on the floor ahead.

Noah is slumped in front of our door, his chin resting on his chest and both arms splayed out to the side.

Oh my God...

Is he... dead?

CHAPTER THIRTY-EIGHT

'Noah!' I rush to his side, crouch down and shake him, probably a little too hard, because his head flops side to side like a rag doll's, but then he groans and leans sideways, sinking all the way to the floor.

'Oh, thank God,' I say, quickly putting my bag down and assessing the state of him.

He's drunk. That much is obvious. I can smell the pungent fumes wafting from his skin. Vodka. It looks as if he's attempted to get in the door but hasn't been able to find his keys. He's managed to get in the front door of the building, so... where *are* his keys? Unless someone let him in... or brought him here...

'Noah. Noah, wake up. Can you hear me?'

I check him over for any injuries, but he looks clean. There's no blood. Well, he's not clean. He's filthy and sweaty, red in the face.

He groans again, blinking his eyes open. 'M-Mills?'

'Yes, it's me. Come on, I need to get you inside.'

I grab my bag, find my own set of keys, open the door, and then attempt to get him to his feet. It's hard work. He's a big guy, but I manage to keep him steady enough to shuffle through, using the wall and me for support.

I get him to the bathroom, where he sinks to the floor, groaning. 'Noah, did someone drop you off here?'

He sits up, his back against the bathtub. 'Huh?'

'Did someone bring you home and leave you at the door?'

He nods. 'Someone.'

'Who? Was it Sally – um, Tracey?'

His eyes widen, like he's seen a ghost. 'H-How…'

'Have you been getting my messages? I've been calling you all day.'

He shakes his head. 'Phone died.' He closes his eyes and takes a deep breath. 'I-I'm sorry…' Then, he breaks into a thousand pieces and sobs like a child on the bathroom floor. I sit next to him. He leans into me, burying his face into my shoulder, and weeps. I've never witnessed him crying before, and it's enough to rattle me to my core, especially now that I know the reason.

I bite my lip until it bleeds, trying to hold back my own tears. My body visibly shakes from the effort. I must be strong for him. This isn't about me. My emotions don't matter right now.

'I've got you, Noah,' I say, wrapping my arms around him. He doesn't flinch, not like he usually does. He grips me tighter and tighter, but I don't squirm or make any effort to move away, despite it being a struggle to suck in a breath.

His barriers are crashing down all around him, and the floodgates have opened. I need to be strong enough to hold back the tidal wave. For him.

Because he's mine.

He's my Noah. And he's hurting. He's falling apart, and I need to be here to pick up the pieces, no matter how many there are or how long it takes.

Someone hurt him, and I swear they're going to pay.

One way or another. They are going to pay.

AN HOUR LATER, he stops crying and descends into silence. I peel myself off the floor, leaving him where he is, and fetch a glass from the kitchen, then fill it with water. While he drinks, I run the bath behind him and fetch a clean towel from the cupboard in the hallway. I then call the police station and inform them that Noah is home with me. They tell me they haven't been able to locate Tracey, but are confident they will soon. I hang up, not sharing their confidence.

I return to Noah. He watches me, silently, taking in my every movement.

'She dropped me off,' he says.

I look at him. His face is red and his eyes are puffy, the whites streaked with red lines.

'Tracey?'

'No, it wasn't... *her*. Someone else. Someone... from my past.'

'Charlotte.'

He tilts his head. 'H-How do you know?'

I crouch in front of him. 'Noah, I know about both Charlotte and Tracey. I know who they are. I know what happened to you, but not all the fine details. Let me get you clean and dressed in some other clothes, then maybe we can talk... if you feel up for it. Or if you'd rather go to sleep, we can talk in the morning.'

Noah nods and hands me the empty glass. 'I-I never wanted you to find out.'

'I know,' I reply, reaching out and lifting his damp, sweat-stained t-shirt over his head. 'But now I do, and I'm still here. I'm not going anywhere, Noah. I promise.'

He looks me straight in the eyes, something he hasn't been able to do for a long time. 'I love you,' he says.

I squeeze his hand. 'I love you, too.'

I help him into the bath. He's still under the effects of alcohol, so his coordination is completely off. He sits and allows me to sponge his arms, chest and back. We don't say a word, but we don't need to. Not right now.

I'm just relieved he's here and he's alive.

Charlotte must have found him and brought him home. Maybe she doesn't have any ill will towards him anymore, or wants to hurt him or me, but I won't know for sure until I find out the story of what happened all those years ago between her and Noah.

I need to be patient.

After he's clean and dry, I help him into some clothes and then assist him to the bedroom, where he crawls under the covers, closes his eyes and drifts off to sleep.

I sit on the edge of the bed with him for a long time. It's strange. I've never felt protective of him before, not in this way, but right now I know I'll do whatever it takes to keep him safe and get him the help he needs.

I don't know if he'll ever be the same Noah again. I have to come to terms with the fact that my soon-to-be husband is a survivor of rape.

Every time I think of that word, a lump forms in my throat.

I can't go to sleep. I don't even want to, despite my body

fighting against me to close my eyes, only for a moment. I won't be able to sleep soundly until I know the woman who did this to Noah is locked behind bars.

Or, more appropriately, dead.

She deserves nothing less.

CHAPTER THIRTY-NINE

I do succumb to sleep at some point because, when I next open my eyes, I find myself slumped across the bed, still holding Noah's hand like a mother would while her child is sick. He's still out for the count, so I gently slide my hand out from his grasp and tiptoe out of the room to make a cup of coffee and have a wee.

I check my phone for the first time since last night and see several missed calls from the police, Rob, and several texts. Nothing else, not even from Charlotte or Tracey/Sally. I'm hesitant to send a message to Charlotte, thank her for bringing Noah home, not until I know the full story. I need to know what I'm up against. What she did to him. Why his depression started in the first place.

Light footsteps make me look up from my phone just as I'm about to call the police back for an update.

Noah's awake.

'Hey,' I say. 'Coffee?'

He nods and shuffles to the nearest kitchen stool, one that wasn't destroyed by William the dog, then leans on the countertop like it's the only thing holding him upright. He looks pretty ropey. He probably doesn't feel great either, but I think he's aware we need to talk. There's no getting around it anymore. No way to stop the inevitable conversation I'm sure he's been dreading, wanting to avoid for the past few weeks.

We listen to the kettle boil. The steam swirls around the ceiling. It clicks off, and that signals Noah to say, 'Mills, I don't even know where to start. There's so much to say, but... I don't know how to start.'

'Tracey. Start with Tracey, but I know her as Sally. She's the client I always tell you about, the woman I've been trying to get you to meet for ages.'

'Yeah, I know.'

'So you've known all this time who Sally is but never felt the inclination to tell me?' I try not to sound accusatory, angry, but the bottom line is if he'd trusted me enough to tell me the truth, then none of the past two weeks would have happened, and I wouldn't have lost all my clients and been scared half to death about having a stalker.

Noah hangs his head. 'No. I didn't know. Not till yester-day. I promise you I had no idea she'd been in our home, that you'd been hanging out with her. If I did, I would have... I would have said something. I thought I could handle it. She was... trying to control me by saying she'd come after you, but you never said anything, not until a couple of weeks ago, about anyone threatening you. I had no idea she'd fabricated a whole 'client-friend' relationship with you. Hell, she even said she was going to go to the media and say that I... ra... attacked *her*.' He gulps and turns pale. I grab him a glass of water and push it across the counter. He takes a sip. 'Thanks,' he mumbles.

'Noah, do you know why she suddenly decided to start threatening me two weeks ago? Why now? Why not straight after it happened? Or a year ago?'

'She heard about my promotion and, clearly, didn't like the fact that her career was over and mine was progressing. She wanted to make me pay.'

'And the promotion and the possible move to another prison is because of everything that's been going on?'

Noah looks up at me. 'Yes. I asked to be moved elsewhere, if possible, but I'm not sure what's going to happen now. I did go to my parents', but it wasn't to look after my mum while Dad was in hospital. My dad's fine. It was a five-day therapy course for survivors of r... sexual abuse.'

I look at the ceiling, contemplating my next words carefully. It's the million-pound question. 'Why didn't you tell me when this happened all those weeks ago? You told Rob, but not me. I'm going to be your wife, Noah. I'm hurt that you didn't trust me enough to tell me.'

He fights back tears as he speaks slowly, stumbling over almost every word. 'I'm sorry. I just couldn't tell you. I felt... emasculated. Less of a man. Weak. Stupid. I thought you might not believe me. Fuck, I even thought maybe you'd think I was lying to cover up the fact that I had an affair instead, because she had proof we kissed one time. It didn't mean anything, I swear. I don't know what the hell I was thinking. I just knew I couldn't tell you. I almost... I almost ended it with you. I wanted to break off the engagement. It's why I've been so distant, not wanting to have sex, and... I've been drinking more.' He hangs his head again. 'It's the only way I can block it out...'

This is taking a lot out of him. I can see it in his body

language. Even his breathing is laboured, like it's a monumental effort to form the words.

I love him so much, and I want to believe we'll get through this, but he needs to do his part too. He needs to tell me everything.

'I tried to keep it from everyone, but Rob noticed something wasn't right, so I had to tell him, then he took it up to HR, but I told him I wanted to keep it under wraps. I didn't want anyone to know who didn't need to know. She was fired, and then the court case started. It's been hell on earth. Rob stood by me. He's a good guy, but my colleagues, the prisoners I worked with, they all found out and made a joke of it. Rob's been watching my back, but... somehow, Tracey found out about my promotion a couple of weeks ago and decided to punish me some more. I thought it was over, but she was only getting started. She's been pushing me to write a statement saying it was me who attacked her, so her name is cleared. She wants me to call off the whole court case. I had no idea she'd go after you like this, I swear. I thought you were safe, that I'd succeeded in keeping you out of it, but I was wrong. When you started getting those threatening messages, I didn't think it was her. Not at first. At one point, I thought it was Charlie – Charlotte – but Tracey wanted to let me know she could get to you. She could hurt you if she wanted.'

I take a deep breath. I need to ask about Charlotte, but I'll come back to her later. 'What does she want from you? She's been found out. She's been fired and can no longer work in the prison industry. She's lost her reputation. Why are you holding back the court case?'

'I'm not strong enough to deal with everything. She

wants me to drop the charges and tell everyone that I ra... attacked her. It will be easier that way.'

'Easier for her, maybe, but she can't seriously expect you to do that.'

'That's what she wants.'

'You've been in contact with her?'

'Yes. She's been messaging me, but she's kept her distance physically.'

'Why didn't you report her for breaching bail?'

Noah blinks, staring at the ground. I fear I may be pushing him too hard, asking too many questions, but I can't stop now. He doesn't answer.

'We can take everything to the police,' I say. 'I've already spoken to them, and they are out there right now, searching for her, and when they find her, she'll be arrested and locked up. She won't get away with this, Noah. It's over. You're safe.' I reach out and squeeze his hand.

'It's never going to be over!' Noah yanks his hand away from me and thumps the countertop with both his fists. 'Don't you understand that? She's always going to have this power over me. Always. How many men do you know who've been... attacked by a woman? None. Because men don't talk about it. We're too ashamed. We're too... fuck!' He stands and kicks the stool over. It clatters to the floor.

His chest rises and falls, rises and falls, faster and faster. He clenches his fists at his sides, as if he's about to explode. I swallow my nerves and walk up behind him, carefully sliding my hand around the closest of his hands. His fist unfurls and then squeezes my hand tight, too tight for comfort, but I don't flinch or attempt to pull it away.

Noah turns his head and looks me in the eyes. 'I never

thought I'd be a victim of ra...' He clenches his jaw. 'R-Rape. I can't even say the damn word without wanting to puke.'

'Noah, you listen to me. You're *not* a victim. You're a survivor. And I love you. We're going to get through this together, no matter how long it takes, okay? I'm with you on this, but I need you to trust me. I need you to let me help you.'

'I do. I'm sorry I didn't before, but it was my own male pride getting in the way.'

'I understand.'

His body relaxes and he lets go of my hand, stooping down to pick up the stool he kicked over. He sets it right.

'Now, tell me about Charlotte. What's her story?' I ask.

'She contacted me several weeks ago, only a few days after... it happened. It was honestly the worst timing in the world. She appeared out of the blue and said hi, that she wanted to make amends and she was sorry, but I took it badly. I told her to leave and never contact me again. I couldn't deal with her arriving on the scene at the same time as everything else, but trust me, I had no idea she would track you down and pretend to be a client of yours as well.'

'What happened? You knew her back at university?'

'Yeah. She wasn't on my course, but I met her on a night out and we hooked up a couple of times. She was cool. I really liked her, but... I didn't see it going anywhere, and I ended it, but she took it really badly. Like... *really* badly.' He takes a breath. 'She started following me around campus, waiting for me outside of my lessons, sending me strange gifts, even camped out in the hallway outside my room at my halls of residence. She'd draw love hearts in her own blood outside my door. I reported her, in the end, to the cops, but they barely did a thing. She hadn't done anything dangerous, but then... the letters started.'

I suck in a breath and hold it for a moment. I have no idea where he's going with this. Did she attack him eventually, or do something like Tracey did? Even the thought makes me sick to my stomach, but I hold it together while listening to Noah. He's opening up a lot easier than before, the words flowing from his mouth at a steady rate, rather than stuttering and agonising over every syllable.

'She... She sounded completely bonkers, I won't lie. It scared me. It didn't sound like her, almost like she had a different personality on paper. She blamed me. She said horrible, vile things about me, about my... manhood and ability in bed. She said other stuff too, derogatory stuff, but it was enough to send my confidence plummeting. It shook me up. She took it further and posted it up on the university notice boards. Thank God social media wasn't as big as it is now, because I'm sure she would have plastered it online too.

'My mates laughed at me, even Tom. My parents realised something was wrong and got me to seek help, but I was nineteen and embarrassed to speak to a therapist about it. I couldn't tell another man that a girl had shaken me to my core with just her words, and I couldn't see a female therapist because I was afraid she'd laugh at me, think it was funny.'

Noah takes another deep breath, refilling his lungs. It's like he has to remind his body to breathe. I know the feeling.

'Charlotte kept following me, kept upping the stakes and threats, but she never physically hurt me. One night, I was really drunk, and I lashed out at her in front of a lot of people. I didn't hit her, but I threatened to do it, and a lot worse. I lost control, but I was made out to be the bad guy.

She accused me of all sorts, abusing her, and worse. After that, I sank lower and lower and, rather than attend therapy, I begged the doctor for antidepressants, because I was scared I was going to do something stupid. Charlotte dropped out of university, and I never saw or heard from her again until a few weeks ago. I eventually moved on, managed to work through some things and got on with my life, but... then Tracey... I just feel like maybe certain women think I'm weak and an easy target.'

His body language is closed again; head down, arms crossed over his chest.

'You're not weak, or an easy target,' I say firmly. 'You're Noah, and both these women thought it would be easier to tear you down than admit to themselves that they're the weak ones.'

'What has Charlotte said? I know you thought it was her sending the messages at first, but... has she done anything bad? I feel like I've stuck my head in the sand for the past two weeks, thinking it's all about me, but you've been the target of both of these women's abuse this time, and I've ignored it, thinking if I did, it would be better for everyone in the long run. I'm sorry.'

I shake my head. 'No, Charlotte hasn't technically done anything bad or dangerous, but... she has borderline personality disorder and is also bipolar.'

'What does that mean? She has a split personality?'

'No, but it does explain her erratic behaviour and mood swings. There's... something I haven't told you either, about my mum... I told you she left when I was fifteen, but that's not the whole story. She had borderline personality disorder too. It was horrible. One day, I'll tell you more about it, but... and I'm not trying to defend Charlotte here, not at all, but it does explain her behaviour towards you back then. People with the disorder have suffered through some sort of trauma in their early years, so it's highly likely something was happening to Charlotte around the time you knew her, or maybe it had already happened before you met. It doesn't change or forgive what she did, but...' I stop, unsure if I should say anything else.

How would I feel if I was in Noah's position? Would I be understanding towards Charlotte, or would I continue to blame her? It's what I did with my mum after all.

'But she was suffering too,' finishes Noah.

I nod. 'People with mental health disorders like that... It's hard to understand, I know, but after my mum left, I never wanted to know why or understand the reason she acted the way she did. I hated her, blamed her for everything, but she was spiralling and coming undone, and I never did anything to help her. I don't know why Charlotte is back here, in your life, getting to know me after you told her to leave you alone, but something tells me she's not doing it to get back at you. She wants to see how you are because perhaps you meant a lot more to her than she did to you. She said that she felt a connection to me, that we'd become friends, but it was all in her mind. She acted the complete opposite.'

Noah nods. 'Okay, but...'

And then we hear the front door open.

A few seconds later, there's an unmistakable sound of something hard dropping to the floor.

Thump.

CHAPTER FORTY

We're both stunned into silence, frozen in fear for a moment, but then reality clicks into place. Someone has opened the front door. The chain is across, so they can't enter the flat, but... what was the noise that followed the door opening?

'You can keep him, Mills! He's not fucking worth it!' comes a loud, angry voice.

It's her.

Tracey.

She's baiting me.

Noah and I lock eyes. He knows what I'm about to do without me saying a word or moving a muscle.

'No. Don't,' he says. 'It's what she wants.'

I don't care. This woman has done unimaginable things to the man I love and has been making my life a living hell. She now has the audacity to come back to my home, knowing full well that she's at risk of being caught. The police are after her.

She's here for one reason and one reason only.

For a reaction.

She's about to get one she's not expecting.

I turn and sprint down the hallway towards the front door.

I DON'T KNOW what's come over me. I want to physically hurt this woman, and it has nothing to do with what she's done to me over the past two weeks. This is pure and simple revenge for what she's done to my Noah.

Noah shouts at me to stop, yelling something about calling the police and they'll handle it, but all I see is red, and then white smoke as I barrel into it; the only barrier between me and the front door, and the building's stairway beyond.

Our whole hallway is filled with thick clouds of it, but luckily, it's not fire-related. There's no heat from anywhere, no orange flames blocking my path.

It's tear gas, and I know that because as soon as it reaches my eyes, mouth and lungs, I instantly cough and my vision blurs. It's quite possibly the scariest reaction ever because, even though I try to suck in air, there is none. My body reacts instinctively, coughing to get the gas out of my windpipe and lungs. Everything burns, as if my lungs and throat and eyes are self-combusting inside me.

I grab my loose top and cover my nose and mouth, running straight through the smoke. I wrestle to undo the chain and yank open the front door, stumbling into the hallway beyond, desperate for some relief. Oxygen. I need oxygen.

The gas follows me out, spreading further into the stairway, but I don't stop. There's laughing ahead and below. Fast footsteps.

'Tracey!' I bellow as I throw myself towards the stairs.

There's no time to wait for the lift, which is at the bottom of the building. She must have walked up the stairs, tossed the gas canister through the small gap caused by the chain, and now is in retreat.

I don't think about how she could have opened the door without a key...

My chest is tight. My throat squeezes closed as the gas takes full effect. When does it wear off? I've seen video clips on the news and in movies of people suffering the effects of tear gas, but my reaction is nothing like that. It's worse. The gas was released in a confined space, not out in the open, like riot police controlling a heaving crowd do, where it can disperse safely.

I ran straight into it and inhaled fully. My lungs still feel as if they are on fire.

I jump down two or three stairs at a time, using the banisters for momentum, but I'm almost blind because my eyes are streaming with tears. I'm gaining on her. Her footsteps get closer. She's not laughing anymore. A few more turns and I catch a blurry glimpse of the top of her head.

'Tracey! Noah's called the police! You won't get away with this!'

She stumbles below me, crashing to the floor, tripping over her own feet in her haste to escape.

I seize the opportunity and throw myself on top of her, like a woman possessed. We slam into the floor, me on top. My lungs expel what little air they have left, and I cough some more, clawing at her clothes to get a grip so she doesn't get away.

'Fucking bitch!' she shrieks. She kicks out her left foot, catching me in the ribs.

I grab a fistful of her hair and yank.

I catch a fist to the lip, instantly tasting blood, but I manage a blow to her right eye too. We're rolling around on the floor, on one of the small landings between stairs, dangerously close to the edge of the next set of steps leading down.

I somehow manage to scramble to my feet, still barely able to see anything through the tears streaming out of my eyes. Warm snot dribbles out of my nose. I don't care. I grab Tracey's top and haul her to her knees. She's breathing hard, probably shocked that I gave chase and managed to catch her. What did she expect? That I was just going to let her get away? Not a chance.

'You're going to pay for what you've done,' I seethe through gritted teeth, struggling hard to hold back a body-rattling cough.

She spits in my face.

It happens in a flash.

She falls, teetering on the edge of the stairs, but before I can react and grab her, she tumbles backwards, her body contorting into unnatural positions as she bounces down the hard staircase to the corner landing below.

She lands awkwardly, after a sickening thud. Her left leg is horribly bent at a forty-five-degree angle.

Shit.

Oh God...

What have I done?

CHAPTER FORTY-ONE

Everything happened so fast, and now I'm standing at the top of the short flight of stairs over a body lying below me. I lost control, only for a minute. No, not even a minute. A second. Less than a second. But it's all over now.

I can't take it back even if I wanted to.

Someone I love has suffered unimaginable torment at the hands of this evil person.

And now she's dead. Very dead.

From the odd angle of her neck, it probably snapped as she flipped and tumbled down the stairs. I didn't realise I'd pushed her that hard. I'd reacted out of instinct, running through the smoke like a woman possessed, then chasing her down the stairs. She'd been laughing as she ran away from me, thought it was hilarious, that she was going to get away with it.

She's not laughing now, is she?

Over the past few weeks, she's pushed me to my breaking point, and this is the fallout. A split-second decision that will change my life forever. There's no coming back from this.

It was an accident.

That's what I'll tell the police, but will they believe me after everything that's happened, after everything she's done to me and Noah? I had a motive to end her life, and they'll see that as clear as day. Yes, it may have been an accident that happened in the heat of the moment.

But there are no accidents, are there?

Not when it comes to murder.

I had no intention of killing her when I raced after her. I didn't want her to get away before the police arrived. Noah will have called them already, so they'll be here soon, and...

Oh God...

As fresh tears bubble behind my eyes, I wipe them away with the bottom of my top. I cough violently, expelling the remainder of the tear gas from my chest, which still feels as if it's in a vice. I breathe in as slowly as I can, testing my lungs' abilities. My throat burns. I need water or something to cool it down.

'Mills!' Noah's voice from far above me jolts me into reality. He coughs, clearly affected by the gas as well, but he didn't run straight through it like I did. Hopefully, he opened some windows to disperse the gas before running after me.

'Noah!' I don't attempt to get up because I'm not sure I can.

Thundering footsteps echo down the stairway until finally Noah reaches my side. 'The police are on their way. Did she...' He stops.

I don't need to look up at him to know he's seen the body. 'Shit...' he whispers as he steps past me. He walks down the stairs towards her, slowly, like he's afraid she's going to jump up and attack him. Noah bends and checks for a pulse in her neck.

I wait, holding my breath.

'She's alive,' he says, looking up at me.

The breath I was holding whooshes from my lungs. I cry as relief washes over me.

Noah stands and walks back up to me, kneeling and wrapping his long arms around my trembling body.

And there we stay until the police arrive.

'Up here!' shouts Noah, finally leaving me and standing to meet them. Voices echo from below, the thud of footsteps on the stairs, the crackle of radios, but I don't move. I don't take my eyes off Tracey, who is still lying in the same place where she fell.

Noah's voice makes me blink several times, and I see him staring straight at me. 'Mills, can you hear me?'

'She's in shock,' says a male voice I don't recognise.

A duo of paramedics assess Tracey while another crouches next to me, flashing a light in my eyes that I barely notice.

Then, a police officer steps closer, the one to whom I spoke yesterday. I can't remember his name. It all seems so long ago now.

'I tried calling you,' says the officer. 'I left messages. I tried to warn you she had slipped past us and could be a threat to you both. We had someone on the way to your flat, but she got here first. I'm glad you're both safe.'

'T-Tear gas,' I say weakly.

'Thank God it wasn't a petrol bomb,' replies Noah, looking up the stairs towards our flat. 'Is she...' I start. 'Noah checked, but...'

'She's alive,' says the paramedic next to me, who is now

dabbing my split lip with damp gauze. 'Broken leg by the looks of it, and she will have a nasty concussion when she comes to.'

'I-It was an accident.'

Noah squeezes my arm. 'It's okay. The CCTV in these hallways will prove it, but...'

'I-I ran after her. I shouldn't have, but I couldn't let her get away. She might have disappeared by the time you got here.'

'I know.'

The officer takes a deep breath. 'I'll admit, it was reckless running after her like that, but you were very brave to do so.'

I cough again, wincing as the paramedic dabs at my split lip some more. 'Brave or stupid,' I reply.

The officer looks at Noah. 'Noah, we'll need you to come to the station to provide a statement as soon as you're able.'

Noah looks up at him. 'I will. I'm not afraid anymore, now that I have the most amazing woman I've ever met standing by my side.'

'I was always standing by your side, Noah,' I say.

'I'm sorry I didn't notice when it mattered the most.'

CHAPTER FORTY-TWO

An oxygen mask is placed over my face and secured round the back of my head. It's a relief to be able to breathe properly, but my throat and eyes still sting. There are so many people in the stairway; police, paramedics, me and Noah... and Tracey, who is placed onto a stretcher and carried down the stairs and outside to the waiting ambulance.

I'm advised to go to hospital to be thoroughly checked over, but I decline. I have a split lip and a bruised rib, but otherwise appear to be unscathed. Once the gas has dispersed from the stairwell and our flat, we'll be able to go back inside. The police officer, who reminds me his name is DC Hunter, says Tracey will be placed under arrest as soon as she wakes. Noah and I are also required to provide statements at the police station, but have been told we can go later today or tomorrow morning, once we have calmed down and recovered from the initial shock.

There are a lot of things I want to say to Tracey. A lot of things I want to do to her, but there's no chance of getting close enough now, not without a police presence.

Noah clutches my arm, pulling me away from the ambulance she's lying inside. A couple of paramedics are finishing their checks before closing the back doors.

'Wait,' I say. I approach the back doors of the ambulance. 'Does anyone happen to have a paper and pen?'

The paramedics swap odd glances with each other before one of them rummages around in a nearby box and pulls out what I asked for.

'Be quick,' he says. 'We need to get her to hospital to set her leg.'

I glare at him. 'She can bloody well wait another minute.'

Noah stands nearby, watching me while I hastily scribble words on the paper. My hands shake so much that a lot of the letters are illegible, but I know she'll be able to deduce what I'm trying to say. I finish the note, fold the piece of paper in half, then half again, and hold it out for one of the paramedics.

'Here. Please put that in her pocket and be sure she gets it when she wakes up.' The medic looks at it, frowning. 'You can read it if you want,' I say.

He thinks better of it and slides it into the pocket of Tracey's jeans.

The back doors close, and the ambulance pulls away, its sirens wailing.

'What did you write?' asks Noah, walking to stand beside me. He slips his hand into mine and squeezes.

I look at him and smile. 'Just giving her a taste of her own medicine.'

IT TAKES several hours for the flat to be free of the remains of the tear gas. The police take photos and whatever evidence they need, including the now-empty gas canister. Noah fusses around me, offering to run me a bath to soak my aching body, but I'm too on edge, too hyped up on adrenaline to even take a seat.

He makes me a peppermint tea, saying caffeine is the last thing I need. He's probably right. I feel as if I could go and run a marathon, despite my sore ribs.

'She could have hurt you,' says Noah. 'You shouldn't have run after her like that.'

'I know, but...' I don't have anything left to say. I made my choice. What's done is done. I caught her before she could escape, and she would have done if I hadn't intervened.

'I'm just glad you're okay and you weren't hurt,' says Noah, pulling me in for another hug.

'I can say the same thing about you.'

We hold each other for a long time. I never want to let him go.

'I hope she rots in prison for the rest of her life,' says Noah when he eventually breaks the hug.

'She will, I promise you.'

'I... I want to do something to help other men like me,' says Noah. 'For men who have survived r-rape, be it from another man or a woman.'

I smile, squeezing his hands. 'I think that's a wonderful idea.'

CHAPTER FORTY-THREE

NOAH

I've been so wrong about everything. Mainly about Mills. How could I have doubted her? I fell in love with her for a reason, and I should have trusted myself, trusted her from the start, but Tracey stole my ability to trust anyone. She made me doubt myself and those around me whom I loved.

Mills is the most incredible woman I've ever met. I broke down in front of her, split apart into a thousand pieces, and she didn't leave my side. She listened. She asked questions, but most importantly, she believed me. She never once doubted what I was saying was true.

She ran after Tracey like a woman possessed. Didn't question it. Just ran. We were lucky Tracey didn't use anything stronger than tear gas. I think she reached a point where she knew she'd lost. What sane woman would run into a building and release a smoke bomb? She could have decided to kill us with a petrol bomb. I'm not sure Mills would have run through fire to stop her. Maybe she would have done, but the injuries she could have sustained would have been life-changing, if not life-ending.

Tracey's a smart woman. She would have known there were CCTV cameras, that the gas wouldn't kill us, just make it hard to breathe. It was her last-ditch attempt to hurt me. She must have known it was useless to fight back. Maybe she did expect to get away, but that didn't happen. The police would have caught her eventually. Now, she's in hospital with a broken leg and a severe concussion, and her left hand cuffed to the metal bed.

I meant what I told Mills after we returned to the flat. That I want to start a refuge for men like me. I don't know where to start yet, but I know Mills will be there to support me every step of the way. DC Hunter, who is in charge of the investigation, has warned me to stay away from Tracey while the case is made against her. I'm not to speak to her without supervision from my lawyer, whom I'm yet to hire. That's fine with me. I have no intention of visiting her in the hospital while she recovers, or in prison, where she'll be held once she's ready to be moved.

I never want to see or speak to her again. I'll have to face her in court, and I know there's going to be a lot of tough times to come. I'll have to face up to what happened, but I'm ready for it because I have Mills by my side, in my corner, fighting alongside me.

Last night, I had a plan to end my own life, but Mills saved me.

Before that, though, it was Charlotte who found me and brought me home. I owe her my life. I just hope she can also get the help she needs.

The road ahead of me is long and treacherous, but I'm ready for whatever the future holds.

EPILOGUE
ONE YEAR LATER

Wilma barely flinches as I yank off the last wax strip from her leg. She's the epitome of poise as she lies on the massage couch, which is propped up like a lounger. Hasn't even broken a sweat.

'You know,' she says, 'it must be so interesting being a beauty therapist. You must meet all sorts of fascinating people.'

I chuck the dirty wax strip into my disposable bag. 'Yes, I've certainly met some interesting people over the years.'

'Gosh, yes, you must have done, but you've also met some dreadful people. That awful time you went through a year ago. Honestly, it still shocks me whenever I think about it. I tell someone at least once a week. As soon as I received those random messages telling me to not use you anymore and calling you all sorts of names, I knew something dodgy was going on.'

'If only more of my clients back then thought the same thing,' I say with a sigh, beginning to tidy up the area while Wilma sits on the edge of the therapist's couch.

'And to think the person who was threatening you was one of your own clients.' She shakes her head, tutting. 'Dreadful. Honestly, some people. What happened to her in the end? Didn't she fall down the stairs or something?'

Wilma already knows all the details, inside and out, because I've told her several dozen times, but she enjoys it when I tell her the story. She laps it up like a thirsty dog. I get the feeling it's because her own life is rather dull. Those aren't my words. They're hers.

I've had to repeat the same story a lot over the past year. What I wouldn't give to bury the whole thing and ignore it, shove it under a rug, but then that's what Noah tried to do. It's what Tracey wanted all along: to get away with it, for people *not* to talk about the fact that a woman raped a man.

As difficult and painful as it is to talk about, I must keep fighting, spreading the word, and bringing people like Tracey to justice. We've tried our best to keep Noah's name out of the media, but it was leaked eventually, most likely by someone he works with. He's had interviews with journalists and newscasters, and there's even a podcast about it, highlighting the rare subject of a man being sexually assaulted by a woman.

My clients and friends are aware of what happened to Noah, but most have the courtesy to not bring it up in front of me because it's still a very sore subject, but I know they're curious.

Wilma hangs on my every word as I regale her with the story once more.

'Yes, she threw a canister of tear gas through our door after stealing a spare key that we kept in the kitchen drawer, then she ran down the stairs. I chased after her and she slipped and fell, breaking her leg. She was arrested, charged, and is currently still awaiting trial for the sexual allegations against her.'

'It's like something out of a movie,' Wilma says.

'A horror movie, perhaps,' I add.

'Yes, of course. How is Noah?'

'He's dealing with everything surprisingly well, all things considered. He's in therapy and on prescribed medication, but he's responding much better than I ever thought possible.'

And it's true. Noah has surprised me throughout every step of this journey. I've held his hand, stood by his side for the whole thing, but now he's beginning to step forward on his own, confront his inner demons, and talk about it openly with his therapist. In the end, he chose a male therapist to speak to. I left it up to him to decide. I'm so proud of how far he has come. I know he still has a long way to go, but he's shown how determined he is to not let this define who he is. He's taken control of his life and accepts that what happened wasn't his fault.

'How's the wedding planning coming? Thank you for my invite. I'll be there with bells on!' says Wilma.

I smile. Our upcoming wedding in three months' time is a much safer and enjoyable topic of discussion among my clients, so I happily tell her that everything is on track, the flowers have been ordered, as has the cake, my bridesmaids are having their fitting for their dresses next week, and my final fitting for my dress is the week after. We did have to postpone it several months due to Noah's therapy, but now we are rapidly approaching the date, and we couldn't be more excited for the next step.

'How many bridesmaids are you having? What colour are they wearing?'

'Three bridesmaids. My best friends, Georgina, Hayley, and Zoe. They are in lavender.'

'Oh, lovely. Such a pretty colour.'

While everything with Tracey was going on, I resigned myself to the fact that the wedding was going to have to be postponed. It was the last thing I wanted to think about anyway, as I was using up all my energy and focus on helping Noah, but he suggested it one evening, after he'd been on his medication for a few weeks. He said he didn't want to put off the wedding any longer. He wanted to marry me as soon as possible.

I finish packing all my items into their various bags. Wilma pays and helps me carry my stuff to the car. 'Oh,' she says as she shuts the boot. 'How did your mortgage meeting go with the bank?' Her husband is a bank manager and recommended us some decent mortgage brokers.

'Did I not tell you? We got the mortgage!'

Wilma claps her hands together. 'That's brilliant. How exciting! A wedding and a new house on the way then. You know what happens next, don't you?'

'Let's not get carried away,' I say with a laugh, even though it irritates me when people assume we'll jump straight into family planning. It's the last thing on my mind. Noah has to get better first, and I don't care if it takes another year or another ten. We won't be having children until both he and I are ready. If that means never, then so be it.

Wilma gives me a hug. 'See you soon. I'll text you.'

'Bye. Have a great day.'

I watch her walk back into her house, then get into my car, automatically checking my phone for an update from Noah. He checks in with me as often as possible throughout the day. He's still working at Blackmore Prison, but now he's the Custodian Manager, having taken over from Rob. This means he doesn't have as much contact with the prisoners as he used to, which is a blessing in disguise.

His promotion has suited him, and he's much happier in general. Rob has moved prisons to start a new job a little outside Cambridge, but still checks in from time to time. They've formed a tight friendship and often meet up for beers on a Saturday night. There was a chance of Noah never being able to work in a prison again after what happened, but we had a long talk about it, and he told me he really loved the job, so he's worked hard and is now reaping the benefits.

I read Noah's message.

> Hey, babe. All good here. Meet you outside the office at three. Love you xx

Noah has invited me to one of his therapy sessions, which is a huge step for both of us. I think I'm more nervous than he is, but I'm so honoured that he wants me there. It means he trusts me, and that's all I've ever wanted.

Another message pops onto the screen. I click it open when I see who it's from.

> Hi!

> Just checking in.

> I'm doing well here.

> Met a nice girl called Jo.

> Thank you for your letter.

I'm so glad Noah is doing well.

I'm sorry again for last year.

I wasn't quite myself.

I should have told you I knew him.

As I said when you visited me, I should have known better.

I didn't want to hurt you or him.

I just wanted to see how he was doing.

Then you turned out to be so lovely.

Thank you for your invite to your wedding.

I'll be there!

I should be able to get a day release as long as I can get someone to come with me.

Looking forward to it.

And to your visit next week.

Lots of love.

Charlotte.

xx

I smile as I type out a quick reply to her, because I know she isn't allowed to keep her phone for long periods of time.

Charlotte admitted herself into a mental health facility on the outskirts of Cambridge a year ago, only a few days after she dropped Noah off at our front door. She spotted him making his way towards the river. He was staggering all over the road, and no one was stopping to help him, so she did. I don't like to think about what could have happened had she not been there.

Noah and I visited her at the facility a few months later, once she was allowed visitors. She's back on her medication, at the right dose, and she is taking it consistently, which helps. She is also attending all her therapy and group sessions. I couldn't be happier for her. It was clear when she first got in contact with Noah and me that her mental health wasn't good, and Noah understands more about her attitude and behaviour from when they knew each other at university.

Charlotte and I have become friends. It is a bit weird being friends with an ex-girlfriend of Noah's, but she's made it clear that she didn't track him down and meet me so she could sabotage our relationship. She wanted to make amends, but when Noah lashed out and told her to leave, she took it badly, and her mental state made her react in a way that came across as very drastic. Noah is willing to forgive her and move on, so I am too.

It makes me wonder about my mother and how she's doing. Whether she's got the help she needed. I think about tracking her down from time to time, but I haven't quite taken that big step yet. Maybe one day I will, but a part of me is still apprehensive because I don't want to be disappointed again. She may not want to see me. She may not even be alive. I have no idea, and, for the moment, I'm happy with not knowing.

I still have one more client before I meet Noah later, a new client, and I'm on my way to her house now. Her name is Amy, and I'm doing her nails for a hen do she's attending tomorrow.

When I knock on her door, she opens it with a huge smile on her face, helps me in with my case and bags, offers me a drink, and makes me feel very welcome. I relax into work mode, setting up the nail bar, and we chat back and forth for a while, discussing colours. Eventually, she settles on a bright pink.

Amy approached me several days ago and, even though my books are full again, I never say no to taking on a new client. She tells me about her world travels, highlighting her favourite countries. I must say, I hang on her every word because it sounds spectacular.

Noah and I plan on going to France for our honeymoon. Nothing too extravagant, but we've both always wanted to go to Paris, so we're doing a long city break and doing the whole sightseeing, touristy bit.

Amy talks as if she's known me for years, perfectly at ease telling me quite intimate and detailed snippets of her life. It's nothing new to me. As a beauty therapist, I've heard all sorts of stories from clients. But then, when Amy changes to talking about family – more specifically, her mother – her whole demeanour shifts. Her tone of voice is lower, slower, and quite bitter.

'God, you know,' she says, shaking her head. 'Honestly, I really wish my mum would just step out in front of a bus one of these days, then I wouldn't have to put up with her nonsense anymore. You know what... maybe I'll just do it myself next time I see her. Just casually shove her in front of a bus while we're walking along the street.'

A foreboding silence stretches on for a little longer than I planned. I don't mean to not answer her, but... did she seriously say what I think she said?

Amy laughs. 'Oh God! I sound like I'm about to go out and commit murder, don't I?'

I laugh in response, then lower my gaze to her nails.

'If you could, though,' she adds in a whisper. 'Would you... you know... commit murder? If someone really, really deserved it and you knew you'd get away with it.'

I think about it for a moment and then give her my answer.

THANK YOU FOR READING

Did you enjoy reading *Pretty Little Lies*? Please consider leaving a review on Amazon. Your review will help other readers to discover the novel.

ACKNOWLEDGMENTS

Thank you, as always, to the amazing team at Inkubator Books, especially Connal, Brian, Lizzie, Alice, Ella, Claire and Stephen who work tirelessly to help me bring my books to life. I truly appreciate your hard work, attention to detail, guidance and support.

A big thank you goes to my identical twin sister, Alice, who not only is the inspiration behind this book, as she's a beauty therapist herself, but she actually gave me the idea for the book one day while we were out at a family fun park. She told me about a client of hers (no names were used) who had revealed a secret to her so big that it could destroy her own family if it got out, and Alice was like, "you should write a book around that" and I said, "have any of your clients ever admitted to killing someone?" and she replied, "not yet" ... and so, the idea for *Pretty Little Lies* was born.

Thank you to all my readers and supporters, fellow authors and friends who continue to read, review and share the love for my books. Some of you have been with me from the very start and it's very special to have you on this journey with me. I don't plan to stop writing any time soon.

ABOUT THE AUTHOR

Jessica Huntley is an author of dark and twisty psychological thrillers, which often focus on mental health topics and delve deep into the minds of her characters. She has a varied career background, having joined the Army as an Intelligence Analyst, then left to become a Personal Trainer. She is now living her life-long dream of writing from the comfort of her home, while looking after her young son and her disabled black Labrador. She enjoys keeping fit and drinking wine (not at the same time).

www.jessicahuntleyauthor.com
Sign up for her newsletter on her website and receive a free short story.

ALSO BY JESSICA HUNTLEY

Inkubator Books Titles

Don't Tell a Soul

Under Her Skin

The Good Parents

I Will Find You

Pretty Little Lies

Other Titles

THE DARKNESS SERIES

The Darkness Within Ourselves

The Darkness That Binds Us

The Darkness That Came Before

THE MY...SELF SERIES

My Bad Self: A Prequel Novella

My Dark Self

My True Self

My Real Self

STANDALONES

Jinx

How to Commit the Perfect Murder in Ten Easy Steps

Horrible Husbands

Room 21

The Murder Maze

The Hanging Tree

COLLABORATIONS

The Summoning

HorrorScope: A Zodiac Anthology – Vol 1

Bloody Hell: An Anthology of UK Indie Horror

Printed in Dunstable, United Kingdom